Forbidden Legacy

Also by Diana Cosby

The Oath Trilogy
An Oath Sworn
An Oath Broken
An Oath Taken

MacGruder Brothers Series:
His Enchantment
His Seduction
His Destiny
His Conquest
His Woman
His Captive

Forbidden Legacy

The Forbidden Series

Diana Cosby

LYRICAL PRESS
Kensington Publishing Corp.
www.kensingtonbooks.com

LYRICAL PRESS BOOKS are published by

Kensington Publishing Corp.
119 West 40th Street
New York, NY 10018

All Kensington titles, imprints, and distributed lines are available at special quantity discounts for bulk purchases for sales promotion, premiums, fund-raising, educational, or institutional use.

Special book excerpts or customized printings can also be created to fit specific needs. For details, write or phone the office of the Kensington Sales Manager: Kensington Publishing Corp., 119 West 40th Street, New York, NY 10018. Attn. Sales Department. Phone: 1-800-221-2647.

Lyrical Press and Lyrical Press logo Reg. U.S. Pat. & TM Off.

First Electronic Edition: August 2016
eISBN-13: 978-1-60183-752-3
eISBN-10: 1-60183-752-6

First Print Edition: August 2016
ISBN-13: 978-1-60183-753-0
ISBN-10: 1-60183-753-4

Printed in the United States of America

At times in life I meet the most amazing people. This book is dedicated to Donna Zazzali, an incredible woman who has been a part of so many special times and memories throughout my life. I deeply appreciate the gift of her friendship and cherish those wonderful memories at the lake, of swimming, baseball games, and the bonfires. A magical time indeed. Donna, thank you for being you, you're truly a blessing in my life. *Hugs*

ACKNOWLEDGMENTS

My sincere thanks to Cameron John Morrison, Kathryn Warner, and Jody Allen for answering numerous questions about medieval Scotland and England, and (Jack) John A Graham III for his insight into sword fighting. I would also like to thank the National Trust for Scotland, which acts as guardian of Scotland's magnificent heritage of architectural, scenic, and historic treasures. In addition, I am thankful for the immense support from my husband, parents, family, and friends. My deepest wish is that everyone is as blessed when they pursue their dreams.

My sincere thanks to my editor, Esi Sogah; my agent, Holly Root; production editor Rebecca Cremonese; copy editor Randy Ladenheim-Gil; and my critique partner, Cindy Nord for helping Stephan and Katherine's story come to life. Huge thanks to the Roving Lunatics (Mary Beth Shortt and Sandra Hughes), Nancy Bessler, and the Wild Writers for their friendship and support over the years!

A very special thanks to Sulay Hernandez for believing in me from the start.

To my readers:

Writing Forbidden Legacy *was a humbling journey. The betrayal of the Knights Templar by a king desperate for gold and hungry for power still echoes hundreds of years later. I worked hard to ensure that any mention of the Knights Templar in my story portrayed their bravery and loyalty and gave them the respect they deserved.*

Chapter One

R ed-orange flames crackled within a massive stone fireplace as sunlight poured through the arched windows of the throne room in a play of shadows and light. Golden beams spilled through the dust motes, illuminating the plum carpet leading to the dais, the intricately carved columns behind the platform, and the stone lions positioned discreetly on either side of the throne.

Seated on the ornate chair, Robert the Bruce accepted the writ. His brows furrowed, and he broke open the Grand Master's seal.

Paces away, keeping his expression void of emotion, Sir Stephan MacQuistan tamped his anger as Scotland's sovereign scanned the document. A missive he'd carried at a devil's pace to deliver; a task he damned with each breath.

The king's fingers tightened on the parchment. Face ashen, he leveled his gaze on Stephan. "Bloody damn!"

With a hard swallow, Stephan fought to relax his taut muscles. However much he craved vengeance, his orders were clear: deliver the writ, answer any questions, and await the King of Scotland's command.

With another curse, the Bruce shoved to his feet. He stormed to a side table and seized an elegant glass carafe. Dark amber liquid sloshed inside. Mouth grim, he filled a pair of metal goblets inlaid with an intricate Celtic weave, a ruby centered in between the breaks of the design.

The king crossed to Stephan and handed him a cup. He raised his own in silent salute. "For our Knights Templar brothers, may God bless each one of them. And for his atrocities ordered, may King Philip burn in Hades!" He downed the brew in one long pull.

Stephan followed, recognizing the taste of *uisge beatha*, the spirit distilled by the Border Abbey's monks, welcoming its potent slide.

Eyes hard, the Bruce lowered his goblet. "How many Knights Templar escaped with you to Urquhart Castle?"

"Twenty-seven, Your Majesty, along with five galleys and their crews."

"The rest of the Templars and their fleet are headed south?"

Stephan's fingers tightened around the cool metal. "Aye, to Portugal."

His gaze shrewd, the king eyed him for a long moment. "I take it the Grand Master disclosed that I am a Knight Templar?"

"He did, Your Grace."

"And informed you that in exchange for financial support and training of my knights, I will conceal the Templars' presence in Scotland?"

Stephan nodded.

A wry smile touched the sovereign's mouth. " 'Tis a bloody shame King Edward is dead. Longshanks went to great lengths to ensure I was excommunicated. 'Twould have put a burr under his arse if he'd known my religious exclusion, and the Scottish clergy's refusal to acknowledge my excommunication, allows me to offer all Knights Templar entry into my realm with impunity and bolsters Scotland's efforts in reclaiming its freedom." His smile faded. He glanced toward the entry. "Bernard!"

The chamber door opened. Moments later, a thin, stately man rushed in. "Sire?"

"Once Sir Stephan and I are finished speaking, ensure he and his men are well fed and given beds to rest."

The official who controlled access to the king nodded, then turned to Stephan. "I will await you in the corridor, Sir Stephan."

"I thank you," Stephan replied.

The chamberlain departed.

"While you see to the needs of your men, 'twill give me time to ponder the situation," the king said. "Once I decide how best to proceed, I will send for you."

"I thank you, Your Grace." After a solemn bow, Stephan turned, thankful Robert Bruce, a sovereign known for his strategic excellence and wit, now guided a portion of the Templars' fate.

Fate? A pathetic term against the false charges leveled upon an elite Christian force who'd displayed naught but the highest principles for nearly two centuries!

Blood pounding hot, he strode across the throne room, his steps muted beneath the crush of the woven rug. More than a sennight had passed since he and the other Templars had sailed from La Rochelle, yet each time he thought of the French king's treachery, outrage poured through him, a fury so black 'twas like soot upon his soul.

God's blade, in little more than a fortnight, the arrests of Knights Templar ignorant of King Philip's loathsome decree would begin. While he, and those who'd sailed beneath the shield of darkness from France, lived.

Bedamned!

He reached for the forged knob illuminated by flickers of firelight.

"Sir Stephan." Robert Bruce's voice echoed within the large chamber.

He swallowed hard, fought to quell the hatred coiled inside. Wanting to leave, he faced the king. "Sire?"

"I recognize you."

Stunned, Stephan stilled. "You do?"

"Aye. Your father introduced us at Avalon Castle many years ago. Do you remember my visit?"

"One doesna forget meeting you, Your Grace." From the first moment he'd met the noble, his bearing and intelligence had impressed Stephan. Though King Edward's hand ensured John Balliol was crowned king at Scone over a decade earlier, Stephan had always believed the realm belonged to the family of Bruce. "My father spoke highly of you."

"The Earl of Dunsmore was a man of great knowledge," Robert Bruce replied, his voice solemn, "a man known for his intellect and cunning."

Honored by his praise, Stephan nodded, surprised Scotland's king remembered him, let alone acknowledged his familial connection. "His recant of your skills in battle, Your Grace, were spoken with reverence." The recollection of hearthside stories his father had shared kindled childhood memories as well as his life ended too soon. And the damning fact of how Stephan had failed those he loved. "'Twas a long time ago."

"Indeed. But I dinna forget those I trust, those who sacrificed their lives to preserve Scotland's freedom, nor those who betray me." The Bruce took another sip from his goblet, motioned toward the door. "Go; ensure your men are settled."

"Aye, Your Majesty." Stephan opened the door. As he made to depart, the chamberlain rushed past.

"Your Grace." The king's man hurried forward. "Lady Katherine Calbraith has arrived and requests an audience. She states 'tis of the utmost urgency."

Calbraith? Anger ignited at memories of the man who'd slain Stephan's family, seized Avalon Castle, and claimed the title of the Earl of Dunsmore.

A birthright lost.

And now, as a Templar, a forbidden legacy.

He shoved aside thoughts of the despised lord. Many Calbraiths lived in Scotland. After the years passed, the odds of this lass being a distant relation to the bastard who'd slaughtered his family were slight.

Dismissing the servant's announcement, he entered the torchlit corridor, determined to keep his oath to the Grand Master. The secrets and legacy of the Knights Templar rested upon his shoulders; he'd give anything to ensure they were kept safe, including his life.

Her pulse racing, Lady Katherine Calbraith swept into a deep curtsy before the king, thankful to find Robert Bruce in residence. "Your Majesty, I appreciate your seeing me in such haste."

"Rise, Lady Katherine," he said, warmth filling his voice. "For my goddaughter, I can set decorum aside." As she straightened, he stood. A frown touched his brow, and he glanced at the entry. "Is the Earl of Dunsmore outside?"

At the mention of her father, Katherine fought back the swell of grief. "Nay. Sire, En-English knights have seized Avalon Castle."

The king's face paled. "And your father?"

Her shoulders began to shake. "My father and mother are dead, butchered by the English!"

"Oh God, lass!" Robert Bruce stepped from the dais and drew her into a fierce embrace.

Her body trembled, yet Katherine smothered her weakness with anger toward those who'd murdered her family. However much she longed to lean against her godfather, to accept the empathy he offered, it wouldna replace her loss. She tried to step back.

With a firm grip, her godfather kept her in place. A scowl lined his mouth. "Dinna hold back the tears, lass. To lock them within will make the suffering worse."

Dry-eyed, she held his gaze. Naught could be worse than having witnessed her family slain.

Lines dredged his brow as he led her to a small table, poured a tawny drink into a goblet. "'Twould seem the day for strong spirits."

"Your Grace?"

He handed her the cup. "Drink, and slow. 'Tis *uisge beatha.*"

Lively water? Appreciating anything that would cut through the rage, the unbearable grief, Katherine downed the potent mix. At the burn in her throat, she began to cough, waving the king away when he made to step forward.

Robert Bruce grunted. "I see your stubbornness hasna changed."

Tears gathered behind her lashes. Furious, she glanced toward the hearth. Whispers of blue flame danced into slivers of red, then orange, and as fast became lost in a curl of smoke to disappear up the chimney.

"Tell me what happened." His compassion fractured her composure. Katherine dug her nails into her palm and welcomed the pain, wished for another glass of the powerful brew to help guide her words.

The horror of the scenes too fresh, she recounted the castle's attack by the English troops. Her voice wavered as she described how her family was killed, and of being locked in the dungeon until she agreed to wed the Earl of Preswick, a command decreed to the English noble by England's new monarch.

Outrage mottled the Bruce's face. "Though the young king hasna a taste for war, he is a fool to believe a forced marriage will help win even a fragment of peace with Scotland." He shook his head. "With Avalon located on a strategic sea lane, the castle canna remain in English hands. 'Tis a necessary stronghold if I am ever to unite Scotland."

Hope whispered through her that her home wasna lost. She straightened her shoulders. "Sire, once the castle is reclaimed, I will strengthen its defenses and ensure its walls are never again breached."

"As much as I wish to grant your request," he said, his voice somber, "without a husband to oversee the rebuilding of the castle's defense as well as offering protection, 'tis too dangerous to allow you to return."

She shook her head. "But I must go back, bury my parents, and—"

"Nay! I will send knights to reclaim Avalon Castle, ensure your parents receive a proper burial, and bolster its defenses. You will remain at Urquhart Castle."

"Please, Your Grace, dinna deny me my heritage." She regretted the catch in her voice. "If your concern is my finding a husband"— she took a steadying breath, damning each word—"'tis a fate I will eventually achieve."

A dark brow raised. "Eventually?"

Heat touched her cheeks. "My father promised me I could choose the man I marry."

Robert Bruce straightened, his gaze softening to regret. "To allow you to choose the man you are to wed is a luxury. We are at war. Scotland's clans are nae united, England's warrior king is dead, and their country is now led by a man who hasna a desire for his father's aspirations of power. Despite King Edward II's claims to procure Scotland as his own, given out of sincerity or pressure, many nobles within his realm plot against him. Regardless his reason for continuing his father's fight, the young sovereign shall fail." He laid a hand upon her shoulder. "Lady Katherine, as much as I wish to grant you your entreaty, even after Avalon is retaken, 'twill be unsafe to allow you to return." He removed his hand. "After Scotland is reunited and peace has settled upon our land, then will I revisit your request."

Nay! I must go back. If I stay—

"... ensure you are safe," her godfather continued, his words a blur in her mind, "and then—"

"Your knights canna breach Avalon's defenses," she interrupted.

He scowled.

Holding his gaze, she lifted her chin. "If you send knights to seize my home," she said, selecting her words with care, "little hope exists of their reaching the castle before they are killed."

"Walls the English were able to breach."

"Aye," Katherine agreed, disgust sliding through her voice, "due to a traitor within lowering the drawbridge. Otherwise, entry into the castle is all but impossible."

"I am familiar with the towering cliffs, the treacherous currents, along with the near-impenetrable defenses." He crossed his arms over his chest. "There is naught you can say that will change my mind."

He couldna forbid her now! Screams of battle assaulted her mind, the English noble's brutality as he'd forced her to witness her parents' deaths and, after, ordered her locked within her chamber until she agreed to wed. Except, as had the English lord, her sovereign underestimated her. "Along with being aware that hidden catacombs lie beneath Avalon, I know of a secret passage into the castle."

Interest flickered in the king's eyes, as if he were weighing the truth of her declaration. "Your father informed me of the catacombs, but I wasna aware of a secret passage."

"Aye. However," she continued, mindful of her boldness, even risking his incarcerating her in the dungeon by her next words, "I willna reveal the location of the tunnel's entry unless I am allowed to return with the assaulting force."

The Bruce's eyes widened at her defiance. On a sharp hiss, he lowered his hands and stepped closer, towering over her. "You dare to make demands of your king?"

"Nay, Your Grace," Katherine breathed, "I–I only wish to help. I am skilled with a sword."

"You will remain here!"

Her heart dropped. 'Twas a risk to push him, but she was desperate. Who wouldna be after the gruesome events she'd witnessed? "I know I speak out of turn. It wasna my intention to usurp your authority." At his hesitation, she pushed on, her words spilling out. "I am loyal to you, I swear it, but Avalon Castle is my home; 'tis all I know," she rasped, her words trembling with grief. "If necessary, for my home and my country, I shall sacrifice my life."

He glared at her. "You are but a wee lass."

"Mayhap." She drew herself up to her full height. "But one who fights with the fury of a thousand warriors!"

For a long moment he studied her. Then his mouth twisted into a wry smile. "If I agree to let you return, you will comply with my wishes?"

"Aye, Your Grace, anything."

The king nodded. "At first light you will depart with a seasoned force to recapture Avalon Castle."

Relief swept through her. A smile trembled on her mouth. "Your Grace, I—"

"But," he continued, "for your protection, before you go, you must agree to wed the knight who leads the attacking force."

Chapter Two

With the details of finding resting places for the Templars settled, Stephan walked down the corridor. Exhaustion weighed heavily on his mind; he should find his bed until King Robert requested his presence. As if with the worries blackening his thoughts he could rest.

Hurried steps echoed from the turret.

Torches seated in ornate wall scones illuminated the chamberlain as he reached the top step, then hurried his way. "Sir Stephan, the king requests your presence."

In silence Stephan kept pace at his side, worried the Templars would be forced to remain at Urquhart Castle until they'd seized a coastal stronghold. With the importance of the cargo onboard, 'twas imperative to reach a secluded location without delay.

The king's man halted before the throne room's entry, moved aside. "You may go in."

"I thank you." After a deep breath, Stephan stepped across the threshold. He paused, stunned to discover a beautiful woman with hair as gold as the desert sand standing rigid at the king's side. Confused by her presence, more so at her unyielding stance, he closed the door.

At the soft thud, the lass turned and her eyes met his, then flared with anger.

Far from intimidated, Stephan held her unwelcoming gaze. His arrival displeased her. Whatever caused her upset wasna his concern. He had enough problems without adding hers.

Paces from the throne, Stephan halted and then bowed. "Your Grace."

"Sir Stephan." The king nodded toward the woman. "May I introduce my goddaughter, Lady Katherine Calbraith."

"My lady," Stephan said, smothering the wash of irritation her surname wrought. 'Twas coincidence, surely, that her family name matched that of a man he loathed.

"Lady Katherine," Robert Bruce said, "may I present Sir Stephan." Sapphire-blue eyes narrowed as she gave a slight nod. "Sir Stephan."

Her cool tone prodded Stephan. Between the Crusades and years in service to the Grand Master in France, never had he and this woman met. Yet the lass behaved as if through sheer resolve she tolerated his presence.

"'Twould indeed seem a fortuitous day," the king said into the thick silence, "as each of your requests to me will be fulfilled by the other."

Fulfilled by the other? God's blade! "Your Grace, Lady Katherine is nae what I seek." A fact the king bloody well knew!

"Nor I a knight, Your Majesty," she said, ice carving her words.

A smile touched the sovereign's mouth. "Your petitions have been made, entreaties I shall grant." He glanced at the woman. "Sir Stephan is a man of the highest caliber, a knight who has proven himself many times over on the battlefield and a warrior who will lead his knights to reclaim your home."

Her face paled. "But—"

"Nay," the king interrupted. "Earlier this day you agreed to my terms. Now you will abide by them."

Her fingers clenched the elegant folds of her travel-worn gown. "Aye, Your Grace."

Robert Bruce's gaze leveled on him. "And you seek a stronghold, one I will bestow upon you with your marriage to Lady Katherine."

Marriage? The word seared through Stephan's mind, a union at odds with his vow of celibacy upon becoming a Knight Templar. A pledge that, with the Grand Master's dissolution of the Order, was now terminated.

Throat tight, Stephan dragged his gaze to the woman. Despite the grand master's dictate allowing matrimony, he wasna interested in taking a wife.

Aye the lass was attractive. Her slender figure and comely face would appeal to any man, but he'd sworn his life to serving God's will and eradicating evil.

Frustrated, he struggled to find a reason to avoid the entanglement of an unwanted marriage. "I am a knight without a title or wealth. I dinna wish to dishonor Lady Katherine by having her marry below her station. Nor is a union necessary. I need naught but a stronghold."

Determination shrouded the king's eyes. "You will wed and your marriage will be done this night or neither request will be granted."

Fighting for calm, Stephan fisted his hands at his sides. He didna want a wife! But 'twould seem he would leave here shackled to the lass like an unruly dog chained to a post. He gave a curt nod. "Aye, Your Grace."

"Upon your vows, Sir Stephan," Robert Bruce said, "I will bestow upon you the title of Earl of Dunsmore."

Stephan stilled, noted the woman watching him with unveiled anger. "The Earl of Dunsmore? But—"

"Aye," the king cut in. "English troops have slaughtered Lady Katherine's family and seized her home. Avalon Castle must be retaken. A stronghold upon its recapture that shall be yours." A glint of satisfaction flickered in his eyes. "'Twill serve your needs well, will it nae?"

Stephan's mind stumbled at the enormity of his legacy, once lost, now being returned. Nae returned but bestowed upon him with expectations. "It will, Your Grace," Stephan forced out. Recovering his heritage fulfilled a long-lost dream, but a wife—a woman with whom convention would dictate intimacy at least to confirm their marriage—wasna an option he'd have chosen.

The tangle of elation and annoyance dissolved as the shame of his youth resurfaced, skeletons that had haunted him since that fateful day, memories he'd never forget. Neither did he wish to marry a woman whose father had murdered his family and stolen his heritage.

A fact the king knew.

A fact the king chose to ignore.

A fact the king decided wasna an issue in making his decision.

But why? Stephan unfisted his hands. As if the reason mattered. With his oath given to the Grand Master, a necessity to find a safe haven for the Templar knights, along with their treasure, the unwanted marriage was a turn of events Stephan could do naught about.

From Lady Katherine's displeasure, he wasna alone in his upset at their upcoming union. In the end, 'twas an alliance in which neither had a choice.

"Lady Katherine," Robert Bruce said, "I sent word to the bishop a short while ago to await our arrival in the chapel. Go. We will be along shortly."

"Aye, Yo-Your Grace." Face pale, she gave a shaky nod. Her steps heavy, as if being led to the gallows, she departed.

The door closed behind her, his fate as hers sealed. Or was it? Wit had aided Stephan out of many a mire and he prayed 'twould do so now.

He cleared his throat. "Your Grace, as you recognized me, I am given to believe you are aware 'twas Lady Katherine's father who laid siege to my home, murdered my family, and seized Avalon Castle. Yet," he continued, struggling to keep his words void of anger, "you insist on my marrying a lass who is my enemy."

"Your union will be the first tie in ending the bitterness between your clans. I need the MacQuistans in our fight to reclaim Scotland." His eyes narrowed. "Lady Katherine doesna know Avalon Castle and her father's title once belonged to your family, nor of her father's actions. That information is yours to share if you choose."

Nuptials far from erased the hatred of another man, but Lady Katherine's innocence of her father's atrocities complicated the situation. "'Tis wrong to take my anger out on someone who is innocent, nor will I hold the sins of her father against her."

"I would have thought you pleased to be awarded such a prestigious castle, more so one of your birthright, and one that will give the Templars the stronghold they seek."

Guilt at his selfishness swept through Stephan. The sovereign's decisions were dictated by his country's need, nae the emotional whims of a few. "Sire, you have my deepest gratitude for bestowing upon me Avalon. Once my men and I seize the fortress, we will take a portion of the dungeons and create a false entry to hide our cargo."

"'Tis unnecessary," the king said, the firelight reflecting off the circlet of gold upon his head. "Below the castle lie hidden catacombs."

He frowned. "Hidden catacombs?"

"With your having lived there, I thought you knew." He paused.

"Nay doubt your father believed you were too young and had planned to tell you upon your being knighted."

At the mention of his father Stephan stiffened, then refocused his thoughts to the news of the catacombs. A perfect place to hide the precious goods within the galleys.

"As well," the king continued, "there is a secret entry that will allow you and your men to slip inside Avalon unseen."

Stunned, Stephan nodded. "'Twould seem there is much about the castle to learn."

"Indeed, and we will discuss this more later, but now the bishop and Lady Katherine await our arrival."

Like a death knell, bells tolled the passage of another hour as Stephan struggled to accept the catastrophe of his wedded demise. Buried beneath the scent of frankincense and myrrh, he plighted his marriage troth with the same sense of dread as Lady Katherine, sealing a union neither wished.

Once the ceremony was over, he would have distance from his unwanted wife. He'd devised a strategy to delay the inevitable intimacy, one, judging by Lady Katherine's withering glare, she would welcome.

After he'd repeated his final vow, the bishop sprinkled holy water on them and recited a prayer of hope, faithfulness, and love. "God bless you both."

As if a curse, Stephan drank the spiced wine.

Robert Bruce nodded to the bishop. "You have my gratitude, Your Excellency."

"An honor, Sire." The clergyman departed, and silence permeated the chapel.

"Sir Stephan," the king said, "you will sail for Avalon Castle with the morning tide."

Relief swept over him. "My men and I will be ready."

"There is one more detail that I wish to discuss," the Bruce said.

As if the turn of events this day had brought had been anything but disastrous? From the sovereign's tone, whatever news he would impart, it wouldna be one of Stephan's liking. "Your Grace?"

"It concerns Lady Katherine."

She stiffened.

Mirth trickled through him. The Bruce believed Stephan would regret leaving her, when his sovereign's order melded with his own plans to sail and leave her behind. "Once the stronghold is secured, I will return and retrieve my wife."

A trip he'd make once rebuilding the castle was completed. If reconstruction took a year or more, mayhap longer if his forces were sent to fight for the king's cause, then who was he to argue?

"Nay," Robert Bruce stated.

Her face paled.

A chill crawled through Stephan. God in heaven, whatever the reason, the lass knew.

"When you depart," the Bruce said, each word crisp, "as your wife is the sole person who knows the entry to the secret tunnel, as well as the hidden catacombs, and due to her refusal to divulge the information of either and insistence upon her immediate return to her home, Lady Katherine will sail with you."

Chapter Three

Silence, thick and potent, filled the bridal chamber, the distance between Katherine and her husband nae far enough. Fighting for calm, through the window she scanned the trees in the distance, the barren ground exposed beneath the moonlight like a harbinger of her future. She didna want any part of this marriage, Sir Stephan, or the promise of their cold, empty life ahead.

"Wine, my lady." Her husband's deep voice etched with control sifted through the chamber.

How could he be so calm after the chaotic events of this day?

"Nay. I am . . ." She started to turn, stilled at the sight of the bed. The attack upon her at the age of fifteen summers raged through her mind. A tremor rent her body, then another, the horrific memories threatening to shatter her fragile calm. She cursed the images, nae wanting to recall the brutality of the assailant's touch.

"You are trembling. Why?"

Furious he'd witnessed her weakness, she forced the memory away, faced him. Unnerved by the intensity of her husband's gaze, his sheer physical size, she stepped back.

"You have naught to fear from me."

Pulse racing, she took in the muscles carving his every inch. Arms trained to wield a blade with deadly efficiency, or hold her until she bent to his will, regardless of her pleas. "Why should I believe you?" she asked, damning the inevitability of the next few hours but determined to hold her own. If he believed her weak, he would soon learn otherwise. Though forced to wed, she was a noble in her own right.

"Because," he said softly, "I give you my word as a knight that I will never harm you."

"And that is supposed to reassure me?"

Hazel eyes narrowed. "I dinna lie."

Katherine angled her chin, refusing to show fear. "And I dinna wish this union."

A wry smile flickered across his mouth. "A point we both share." The smile fell away. "Regardless of your or my opposition to our marriage, 'tis done."

Confused, she paused. "If you didna request this match, why would Robert Bruce mandate such?"

Silence.

A chill swept over her. She rubbed her arms, each moment looming with the unspoken threat of their impending intimacy. A personal relationship Katherine doubted she would ever welcome.

If she'd met Stephan at any other time, she would have been intrigued by his eyes, which held secrets, the hard cut of his jaw framed with the shadow of a beard, and the stance of a man confident in his abilities. Mayhap after a while they could have become friends. But naught was comforting about this moment. As her husband, he held the right to do as he wished.

Including take her to his bed.

A marriage in which she was stripped of all her rights, including her father's promise she could marry the suitor of her choice. "You willna tell me why our sovereign bade we marry?"

A muscle worked in his jaw. "The reason for this match is our king's to reveal."

"Is it?" she said, furious at this turn of events. "Being granted a formidable stronghold along with the title of earl seems an unusual boon for a knight supporting his king."

His nostrils flared as he towered over her, his reaction that of a man unused to being questioned. "I dinna expect you to understand the workings of a monarch, nor the challenges ahead in reuniting Scotland."

Anger tore through her. "How dare you accuse me of ignorance when you know naught of me!"

"Then we are even, are we nae?"

The pompous ass! She glared at him. "I have managed Avalon Castle for the last several years. I am skilled with a sword, in the arts of healing, and have a thorough understanding of strategies in battle."

"Mayhap," he said, "but weapons practice and discussions of tactics with nay threat of harm are poor teachers of the reality of war."

A fact she couldna debate.

Fatigue flickered in his gaze. "Lady Katherine, neither of us wishes this marriage, but 'tis done. For Scotland's freedom, 'tis imperative to retake Avalon Castle, a feat *I will* achieve." He stepped closer.

Angling her chin in defiance, she stepped back.

Stephan frowned. "Why do you behave as if you are afraid of me when I have assured you that you have naught to fear?"

Surprised by his sincerity, his tone truly perplexed, with a steadying breath she glanced toward the bed.

He followed her gaze. With a muttered curse, Stephan walked over, unsheathed his dagger, drew the tip across his skin, and smeared a line of blood upon the sheet.

In shock, she stared at him. "What are you doing?"

"I believe," he said, his words dry, " 'tis obvious. And now nae an issue."

"I . . ." Stumbling for words, Katherine glanced at the smear of red upon the linen and then toward him.

He arched a brow.

Since the attack, she'd dreaded her wedding night. Now this warrior—nay, an earl, a man who claimed her father's title through their marriage—had given her a true and benevolent gift . . . leaving her untouched.

But why? As his marital right, regardless of her wishes, he should expect her to yield to his demands of intimacy. Yet he chose to leave her chaste. Mary have mercy, had someone informed him of the assault? Was he repulsed at the thought of bedding a woman tarnished by another?

Humiliation swept her as she struggled beneath the shame of her unchaste state. Hand trembling, she gestured to the bed. "Why would you do this?"

Stephan paused as he wiped his blade. "Are you saying you wish to consummate the marriage?"

The coolness of his words made her cringe. "Nay! I . . . I was trying to understand your decision to leave me untouched."

His gaze unfathomable, he finished cleaning his weapon, and then sheathed the dagger. "There is little to understand. We have done naught but establish our boundaries. A fact I dinna plan to change," he stated, as if unfazed by the candlelight upon the massive bed, the fire blazing within the hearth, and the decanter of wine on a nearby table. Each detail intended to craft an air of seduction within the chamber. "This night you will sleep in the bed. I shall make a pallet beside the hearth. On the morrow, once you share the location of the secret tunnel's entry along with the location of the catacombs below the castle, my men and I will depart." He walked to a chest near the wall. "You will remain here until I decide—"

"I am going with you."

He halted and slowly faced her, his expression hard. "Reclaiming Avalon will be dangerous. I refuse to allow any unnecessary risk to your life. On the morrow you will tell me what I wish to know."

"Nay."

In three long strides he crossed the room, caught her shoulders.

Her fears of moments before reignited, Katherine opened her mouth to scream.

"God's blade!" He released her as if burned, his indignant glare pouring into hers. "You willna fear me!"

Her panic of moments before shifted to anger. "As if you can command my feelings?"

"I have given you my oath that you are safe. In regard to you traveling with me and my men, I forbid it."

"Forbid it?" The arse! "I am nae a woman you can order about."

The hard glint in his eyes sharpened. "Wars are fought by men, nae for the weak and those guided by emotions."

She angled her jaw. "I can handle a blade as well as any man."

"In mock battle. How will you respond when a sword is driven into your friend, fighting at your side, while you struggle to fend off two or more attackers? Can you keep your focus on defending yourself while hearing the screams of your friend dying, his agony-ridden pleas for mercy to end his life while his blood stains the ground?" He paused. "What of the other warriors surrounding you, who lay amongst the tangle of bodies, some dead, others damning that they still lived?"

His words crafted horrific images. From his vehemence, actions he'd taken, witnessed, or worse. "You may be a seasoned warrior, but Avalon is my birthright. Regardless of your approval, I will join in the attack when the castle is reclaimed. If you and your men tried scaling the walls without my aid, you would have little luck."

"I well know the challenges ahead."

Surprised, she frowned. "You have visited Avalon?"

"I am familiar with the stronghold."

At his brusque words, unease slid through Katherine. She recalled the faces and names of those who had visited in the past. "We have never met."

Stoic eyes held hers with quiet evaluation. "There are many who have entered Avalon's walls whose presence you are unaware of."

Mayhap, but something about his claim implied more. If her father . . . Pain sliced through her, but she smothered the hurt. "This discussion is moot, a point dictated by our king."

Her husband's mouth tightened. "He—"

"Said I will sail with you and your men to Avalon. Neither will I discuss this further." She was exhausted. Between the horrific memories haunting her and trying to cope with the debacle of this day, Katherine doubted she would find rest in the hours ahead.

On edge, she stepped past him and walked toward the bed. He'd claimed he wouldna touch her. Now she would discover the truth. Too aware of his cool stare, keeping her steps unfaltering, she moved to the opposite side of the bed, the farthest away from him and the smear of his blood upon the sheet.

Proof of her supposed innocence.

Her body trembling, she slid beneath the blankets. With a silent prayer he'd remain away, she closed her lids and forced her breaths into a steady rhythm.

The crackle of the fire filled the chamber, a warm, cheery sound at odds with the impending sense of doom.

Soft steps echoed on the aged wood. The rustle of clothing.

She peered out.

Her husband was making a pallet.

Thank God. "Where did you spend your youth?" she asked, curious about the man to whom she was now bound.

"My past is unimportant."

"As your . . ." She cleared her throat. "As your wife, do you nae think I should know?"

"Nay."

Add stubborn to his list of traits. "I detect a French accent, and another I dinna recognize. Did you live in France?"

Silence.

The man could frustrate a priest. "My godfather said you are a fair man."

Stephan's deep sigh rumbled into the silence.

"Your evading my questions will do naught but increase my curiosity."

At his silence she turned on her side and stared at the flames. A spark popped in the hearth, the glowing ember tumbling into the ashes and fading to black.

Unsettled, she glanced toward her husband.

Firelight outlined his long, muscular frame as he lay on his back, paces before the hearth. The tension of his muscles assured her that he wasna asleep. "You and your men sailed to Urquhart Castle. I find it intriguing that a knight leads a fleet of ships."

Firelight illuminated his eyes, opening, narrowing. "Lady Katherine, we share a chamber out of duty. Dinna seek more. 'Twill be a long, hard day of travel on the morrow. Go to sleep." He tugged his blanket higher and closed his eyes.

Katherine shot him her most fierce glare. 'Twas fine with her. She welcomed their distance, was thrilled by his intention to keep their marriage unconsummated, and thankful that once they'd reclaimed her home and finished rebuilding the castle, Stephan would be away serving their king.

A time she would embrace.

She shifted to a more comfortable position. Although they'd established their boundaries with the other, the feeling that he was withholding important information from her lingered.

As if whatever secret he kept mattered at this moment. She closed her eyes and tried to empty her mind.

The shout of a guard on duty echoed from outside. The somber tones of the church bell rang out the late hour. Another guard called from farther away.

Frustrated, she abandoned the pretense of trying to sleep and stared at the ceiling. Flickers of shadows cast by the flames danced overhead.

Clothing rustled.

Curious, she glanced over.

Stephan was kneeling near the hearth, a crucifix in his hands, his lips moving in a soft whisper.

What was he saying? Keeping her movements slow, Katherine edged closer.

"For thine is the kingdom, the ..." Fire popped in the hearth, smothering the softness of his words. "... ever. Amen." He crossed himself and then quietly started again.

Why was he repeating the prayer? With each repetition, she grew more intrigued, fascinated by his dedication, his stillness, his absolute calm. If she had nae just married this man, she would think Sir Stephan's actions those of one who served God. But a man of the cloth would never be allowed to wed.

And what of her husband's vehemence in leaving her untouched? She dismissed any connection. He'd explained his reason. From his prayers, 'twas obvious he was a man of deep faith.

And a knight.

His mention of battle was told with the conviction of someone who'd faced the horrors of combat many times over. His unshakable belief that he and his men would seize Avalon, that of a hardened warrior confident of the challenges ahead.

Neither would he disclose more about his past. From Stephan's curt reply when she'd asked, it was clear he intended to withhold even the smallest detail that could bind them on the most basic level.

As he started the prayer anew, she closed her eyes, focused on his steady tone, the soothing cadence. Exhaustion blurred her thoughts. Katherine embraced the haze of sleep and sank into the welcome darkness.

A church bell echoed in the distance.

Groggy, Katherine peered out. Red coals glowed in the hearth but, through the window, blackness still claimed the sky. She'd dozed.

Stifling a yawn, she glanced at Stephan's muscled form. After he'd assured her he'd nae harm her, and having watched him during his prayers, she believed him, though the peace of having a protector didna erase the grief of losing a family she loved.

The shouts, the stench of blood, and the screams of the attack on Avalon stormed her mind. With each memory, emotion built until she ached.

Needing to be alone, Katherine studied his breathing for several moments. Confident her husband was asleep, she slipped out of bed, crept to the entry. She glanced back.

He hadna moved.

Relieved, she slipped into the corridor, tugged the door shut.

The hewn wood settled into place with a soft thud.

Heart pounding, she froze, half-expecting Stephan to pull the door open and demand her return.

Torchlight from several nearby sconces flickered in the silence.

Thankful he'd remained asleep, she started down the corridor. Though the chill of fall filled the air, she would go to the wall walk and find a place where she could be alone to think. As she rounded a bend, several paces away, a large door stood ajar, a golden glow spilling from a chamber into the hallway.

The chapel.

The chamber where she'd sealed her marital fate earlier this day.

With quiet steps she walked to the door, glanced inside.

The king knelt before the cross, his head bowed in prayer.

Worried as to why he was awake at this hour, she stepped inside.

At the slight creak of the door, the king turned. With a frown, he made the sign of the cross, stowed a crucifix beneath his garb, and then stood. "Is something wrong?"

Heat stroked her cheeks. "I was thinking of my family and I . . . I couldna sleep."

"So you came to pray?"

Emptiness filled Katherine as she took in the large cross hanging on the wall. "Aye," she replied, the soothing scent of frankincense offering her a measure of comfort. "I am surprised to find you up this late, I pray all is well?"

"Aye. I have a few details to attend to before I find my bed." A frown curved her godfather's mouth. "I am surprised your husband has allowed you to leave the chamber on your wedding night."

The warmth in Katherine's cheeks grew. "In truth, he doesna know."

The Bruce arched a skeptical brow toward the door and then met her gaze.

"I waited until he fell asleep. I needed time alone, to . . ." The pain of loss overwhelmed her, and a sob escaped. She sniffed. "I am sorry. I canna stop thinking of how my family died."

With a somber nod, the Bruce stepped forward, and drew her against his chest. "'Tis understandable after all you have endured."

At his compassion, her fragile control broke. Great sobs rocked her, and for several moments she wept. When nay more tears would come, when her cries were naught but quiet shudders, he released her and stepped back. "Come, kneel beside me and pray."

With a sniff, she knelt. The polished wood cool against her knees, she made the sign of the cross. As her sovereign murmured a prayer at her side, she followed along, the familiar words, the cadence, comforting.

"Amen," she said, matching his motions as he made the sign of the cross.

He shifted back to the sturdy bench, motioned her to sit at his side.

On edge, she settled beside him, keeping her focus on the cross hanging on the wall. For a long while she remained unmoving, comforted by her godfather's presence, the scent of aged wood and a hint of frankincense. Calmer, Katherine glanced over.

Sage eyes met hers. "You heart is broken with the loss of your family, but I sense there is more on your mind."

Anxiety slid through her. "Stephan is a difficult man."

Surprise flickered on his face. "Has your husband mistreated you?"

"Nay," she whispered, unsure how best to proceed. "'Tis that he is more stubborn than a cornered badger."

The king relaxed a degree. "How so?"

She hesitated. "He is nae pleased that I am sailing with him and his men."

"Nor did I expect otherwise. He is a warrior, a knight of deep faith who sails on the morrow to engage in battle. He doesna wish a lass to distract him."

Katherine stiffened. "My father taught me to fight, a skill my husband chooses to dismiss. He doesna know me."

"Nor you him."

She met her sovereign's thoughtful gaze. "Nor will he allow me. When I asked but the simplest questions regarding his past, he refused to answer."

The Bruce gave a slow nod. "Sir Stephan is a man who needs a woman of strength and patience, and one who will support him."

"He needs a good boot to the backside."

A chuckle rumbled in the king's chest. "Said with such exaspera-tion."

"Sire, how do you reason with a man who willna talk with you?"

Her godfather leaned back. "I remember once when my men and I marched into battle. Your father and I came across a mule stuck in the mud. He was braying and causing a commotion. It took eight men to free him: five pulling from the front, two pushing from the back, and one banging a stick against his shield in hopes the noise would make the stubborn beast bolt."

The image of the men trudging into the muck, their curses as they shoved, prodded, and pulled the thankless animal had a smile curving her mouth.

"Aye, 'tis funny now," Robert Bruce said dryly. "Rest assured, at the time the blasted mule seemed more trouble than he was worth. Several grumbles of making him the night's fare were met with hearty agreement."

Her smile faded. "Did you kill him?"

Mirth twinkled in eyes like a seasoned bard's. "The thought crossed my mind when the thankless beast nipped me." He chuckled. "In the end, your father climbed upon the animal and pulled his tail. With an outraged bray, the mule kicked, lunged, and all but freed himself."

Laughter tumbled from her throat.

"Your father lasted about two bucks and then landed flat in the mud."

Tears misted her eyes as she continued to laugh, happy ones that entwined with the sad that had run down her cheeks earlier. "H-He never told me that story."

Her guardian smiled. "Nor would I expect him to. He landed on his arse and wounded his pride."

She giggled, sniffing back the tears.

"Aye, 'twas a time to remember, but I learned an important lesson that day."

"Which was?"

The king's gaze grew somber. "We needed the mule to work with us. Until he did, there was nay prying the animal out. Your father found a way that, regardless if the beast liked it or nae, had the crea-ture working with us." He paused. "An intelligent woman like you would be knowing how to look past the external, to find what matters to a person, and to nurture that into more."

She grimaced. "Mayhap you should have left the mule in the mud."

Humor erased the sadness in his eyes. "Mayhap, but if we had left him, later, when your father was injured in battle, we wouldna have had a simple means to transport him to a healer."

"His left shoulder?" she asked, remembering how he'd favored it.

The Bruce nodded. "What is important to remember is nae to give up on a challenge. In the end, with time and patience, you may find the rewards more than expected."

More than expected. With Stephan, something she doubted. Tiredness washed over her and she smothered a yawn. "I thank you for listening and for your words of wisdom."

Pride shone in the king's eyes. "I have confidence you are the woman for Stephan. Together, in addition to rebuilding Avalon, I believe you will create a strong marriage as well."

A shiver crept up her skin and she stood. "I will retire now, Your Grace."

He nodded but didna stand. "Sleep well."

In silence she left, her mind pondering the story of her father and the message within. Robert Bruce might have faith that she was the woman for Stephan, but Katherine held naught but doubt. Neither did the king's beliefs regarding her and Stephan matter. In the end, he would go off to war and she would have her home.

Another wave of fatigue swept over her. More than ready to find her bed, she opened the door, stepped into the corridor, and stilled.

Paces away, Stephan stared at her, his arms crossed over his chest, a scowl darkening his face.

Chapter Four

Lifting the edge of the crate, Stephan turned his face to avoid the blinding rays of the sunrise and shifted back. He glanced at the lean, muscled knight at his side, a man with whom he'd fought many a battle, thankful his friend sailed with him on this journey. "Thomas, move to the right."

"Aye, my lord," Thomas MacKelloch replied, his voice rich with amusement.

"You willna be laughing," Stephan said, edging to the left, "when 'tis you taking a vow to wed."

"I, my friend," Thomas said, his tone smug, "plan on avoiding such mayhem."

Stephan grimaced. "As if finding a wife was my blasted intention?"

His friend's smile faded. "Any of us would have agreed to marriage to protect the Templar treasure."

"I know." Stephan shifted farther to the left. "The stronghold's central location will allow us to travel wherever needed with ease. In addition, the catacombs hidden beneath Avalon Castle will provide the safe location the sacred goods require."

The man holding the box to his right, a dragon curled around a Celtic cross tattooed on his shoulder, nodded. "'Twill be a great relief once the cache our ships carry is hidden."

Stephan met Aiden MacConnell's gaze, thankful he, too, sailed with their fleet. Thomas's expertise as an archer, along with Aiden's, was renowned. He welcomed both men's skill in the upcoming attack on Avalon. "It will. God help us if any besides Templars learn of the prize we carry."

"Indeed," Aiden said. "Nor do I envy you the task of keeping a wife."

At the mention of Katherine, her image of last evening came to mind. How shimmers of firelight had caressed her golden hair, deepened her cheekbones, and made her appear a cross between a fairy, a siren, and a waif. Stephan grimaced. God's blade, what types of thoughts were these? He was going daft!

"Task, aye," Stephan said, irritation hardening his burr. "I dinna wish a wife, but if saddled with such a burden, I would rather the woman be an old crone who finds pleasure in mundane tasks, nae a brazen lass who meddles in the duties of a warrior."

"You have known her less than a day," Thomas said. "Once we arrive, perhaps her wish to fight alongside us will fade, and she will want to do naught but immerse herself in running the stronghold."

"Mayhap," Stephan said, "but after a few hours in her presence, I have little faith of such."

Aiden shifted a step. "A lass who knows how to handle a sword with skill is nae common."

"Neither am I convinced that she can back her claim. Words are easily given." Stephan edged back a wee bit, glanced at Aiden. "Are you clear on your side?"

"Enough so the crate will fit," his friend replied.

"Good. Set it down." Together, they lowered the large box beside another.

A scrape sounded as the bottom settled into place.

Stephan straightened, cursing his sluggish mind. Neither did he expect otherwise after he'd caught but scrapes of sleep throughout the night. Blast Katherine for slipping from their chamber in the first place.

At least he'd had the pleasure of witnessing her shock as she'd exited the chapel and the anger in her eyes when he'd instructed that such future actions wouldna be tolerated. She'd remained silent, a fact that had left him surprised. From her stubbornness, he'd expected defiance. After the long day, a confrontation he was more than ready to indulge. Instead, she'd stormed to their chamber. And, much to his chagrin, in but moments had fallen asleep.

Unlike him.

Aiden leaned against the crate. "Though your wife believes she is a skilled fighter, sparring in the safety of the bailey far from prepares a man, much less a woman, for the dangers in faced in battle."

"A fact I made clear," Stephan said. "Regardless of her wishes, she willna be allowed to fight."

"Wise." Thomas moved beside the knight, crossing his arms. "You should know that the men are nae pleased to have a woman aboard."

Stephan's chest tightened at the disclosure. "A feeling I share, but a fact I canna change. 'Tis the king's order." He shook his head. "Though the Bruce didna say why, I believe he was impressed by Katherine's stubbornness in refusing to share the entry to the secret tunnel beneath Avalon."

A smile touched Aiden's mouth. "The lass sounds like she will be a challenge."

Stephan grimaced. His wife's slipping from their bedchamber without telling him bespoke a recklessness he refused to tolerate, a fact he'd made clear. If she would adhere to his expectations was another matter.

"Speaking of which," Thomas said, his voice rich with appreciation, "I see a lass heading toward the shore. Would that be the fair Lady Katherine?"

Eyes narrowing, Stephan turned.

Dressed in a sturdy yet flattering gown of blue, her hair braided in an intricate weave and secured behind her head, Katherine strode with a regal step toward shore.

The candlelight last eve had bathed her in a tender hue, but illuminated by dawn's golden glow against the backdrop of the castle, she looked more like the warrior she claimed to be.

God's blade, why was she here? He'd instructed her to await him in the castle until he returned. Aye, the lass would be trouble and then some.

Paces from shore, her head tilted. Amenable blue eyes met his. "Good morning, my lord."

Stephan nodded, far from fooled by her soft, agreeable façade. Naught was docile about the lass. "My lady. I will be there momentarily."

The dimples on Thomas's face deepened.

Stephan shot him a glare. "Nae a word."

His friend arched a brow in mock surprise. "I have said naught."

With a muttered curse, Stephan strode toward the gangplank, nae glancing toward the other Templar, confident Aiden's expression was equally amused.

Aware the men onboard watched her approach, head held high, Katherine started up the wooden walkway extending from the pier to the ship.

The slap of water against the hull and the salty tang of the ocean ignited memories of sailing with her father. Melancholy stormed her, and she pushed the thoughts away, refusing to show any weakness before these men.

At the entry to the galley, a large man blocked her path. "Halt—"

"Sir Cailin," Stephan interrupted, "may I introduce you to my wife, Lady Katherine."

The man with a shock of red hair surveyed her with a sage eye and then bowed. "My lady, 'tis a pleasure to meet you." He stepped back, his remote manner at odds with the welcome in his voice.

"Sir Cailin," she said with a nod.

"I will leave you with your husband." After a glance toward Stephan, the knight strode away.

A shiver trickled across her skin as she caught the other men on deck studying her. By their wary expressions, they were displeased with her appearance. Neither could her presence be helped. After his warning of his expectations when it came to her last eve, if Stephan and his men sailed without her, she doubted he would ever return for her, a risk she refused to take.

Her husband's shadow engulfed her, and she faced the man she'd been sentenced to for life.

"We sail within the hour. I had planned to escort you aboard," he said, his tone crisp, his gaze direct. "A fact I made *clear* this morning before I left our bedchamber."

The arrogant toad. She leaned closer. "In case you have forgotten," she whispered, "I am nae one of your men to be ordered about."

Fire flashed in his eyes, then disappeared as quickly.

'Twould seem he wasna as composed as he wished her to believe. Pleased, she forced a smile. "Aware you are anxious to depart, I saved you the trip."

His nostrils flared. "This way." He strode toward the ladder.

The smooth, aged wood rocked below her as she followed. "'Tis a grand ship," she said, noting the artistry, the care taken in crafting the smallest fixture. This wasna a simple galley designed to haul goods but a seaworthy vessel built with purpose.

He shrugged. "It serves my men and me well."

An understatement. At her approach to the docks, she'd surveyed the other ships moored nearby preparing to sail, each as impressive. In her lifetime she'd seen many vessels but none so well built or maintained. With the time spent at sea, 'twas usual to find hints of rust or wear aboard ship. Wherever she looked, she found the wood highly polished, the knots securing the sails tightly woven, and beneath the morning rays the brass fixtures gleamed. Each item a testament to meticulous care.

"Watch your step as you descend the ladder," Stephan said. "I will await you at the bottom." He paused. "Unless you wish my assistance."

Frustration built. From his dismissal to allow her to fight to reclaim her home to his every other action, he'd labeled her a hindrance. "I can climb below without help."

When she reached the bottom, he led her to a spacious cabin. At the door he paused. "Once I finish above deck, I shall return." Stephan departed.

Beneath the glow of the lantern hanging from a sturdy hook, she noted the minimal furnishings. A bed, chests to hold clothes and goods, several of them hers. Given the craftsmanship of this vessel, she'd expected to find the furnishings of the captain's quarters lavish.

Katherine recalled Stephan's simple yet sturdy garb, the same type he'd worn when they'd first met. After their marriage, as an earl and with access to her inheritance, she'd expected him to procure higher-quality attire.

He'd chosen otherwise.

Why? Had the limited time before they sailed prohibited him from addressing the issue, or was there another reason? As if his garb was her biggest worry. With her fate sealed through marriage, she had more important concerns than how her husband dressed.

The image of Stephan praying the night before came to her mind. However much she wished to dismiss the stubborn and frustrating man from her thoughts, there was a calm about him that perplexed her. He acted more like a monk than a knight.

A bell rang from above deck.

They were preparing to depart. Having enjoyed standing along-side her father when he'd sailed toward open sea, Katherine hurried above deck, ignoring her husband's grimace when she walked past him. At the ship's bow, with the cool, salty breeze fluttering against her skin, she leaned against the rail.

With the confidence born of a man used to the ways of the sea, Stephan called out orders while his men retrieved lines, checked equipment, and secured ropes.

Though her husband hadna disclosed his having lived in France, the ease with which the men worked in unison, making their departure appear effortless, exposed that he and his crew sailed, and often.

Was he a merchant based in France? At first she'd believed him a warrior. With his quick mind, a knight feared on the battlefield. He and his men's expertise at sea hinted otherwise. Their muscled bodies attested to long, hard hours of wielding a blade, nae those of lean men who made their livelihood sailing the ocean. If asked, she would say they looked like . . .

Pirates.

The shot of panic faded to humor. As if Robert Bruce would meet with those who lived outside the law or subject her to a life with a brigand. She trusted her godfather. Whatever her husband was, he wasna a scoundrel. Stephan's skills on land and sea explained why her sovereign had chosen him and his men to reclaim Avalon Castle, but the reason gave little insight into why the king had insisted they wed.

A gust of wind filled the sails with a firm snap.

The ship lunged toward open water.

Katherine closed her eyes and tilted her face toward the sun. She savored its warmth, the briny air, and the rush of water against the bow as the galley cut through the oncoming swells.

Memories filled her. 'Twas as if at any moment her father's heavy steps would reach her. Then he'd be standing by her side.

Grief welled inside her, and she dug her fingers into the polished rail and opened her eyes.

Her parents were dead.

Murdered.

However much she loathed the thought of marriage, she would do whatever was necessary to reclaim her home.

"'Tis best if you stay below."

At her husband's terse voice, she stiffened. Katherine kept her focus on the incoming swells. "For whom?" she asked, irritated that so lost in her thoughts, she'd nae heard his approach.

Stephan stepped beside her, glanced over. "Our time together, however brief, doesna have to be one of strife."

She took in his strong face, the harsh cut of his jaw. A warrior. Indeed, a man to be reckoned with, but perhaps a reasonable man as well. "I agree."

"Then you will remain below until we arrive at Avalon?"

She laughed, his question so foolish she couldna do otherwise.

Darkness smoldered in his eyes. "It wasna a jest."

Indeed, there was naught laughable about the situation. She didna want to live out the rest of her days at odds with this man. An idea came to mind. She glanced around. Confident nay one was close enough to hear them, she met his gaze. "Neither of us wanted this marriage, but if we approach it like a business arrangement, the move can benefit us both."

His gaze grew skeptical. "How so?"

"From the way we shared last evening within the bedchamber, or rather apart," she said, ignoring the heat sweeping her cheeks, "I anticipate our future nights spent together will be as"—she cleared her throat—"uneventful."

"Go on."

Relief poured through her at his willingness to listen. "You seek a stronghold for your men," she continued as the galley cut through an oncoming swell. "A base of sorts for you and your knights while supporting campaigns for our king."

He shifted, his lithe, muscled body closer, the intensity of his gaze stealing her breath. "I seek naught." His deep voice rumbled. "Avalon Castle is mine. I willna barter for what I already possess."

The man was exasperating! "'Tis nae yours until 'tis recaptured."

A confident smile curved his mouth. "It will be." He nodded. "Say what is on your mind, lass."

Fine. Directness would make everything simpler. "I propose that we live together without intimacy."

He arched a brow.

"There is a large chamber that has a smaller room within," she explained, bolstered by the way he hadna immediately disagreed. "During the day each of us will attend to our respective tasks. At night you would sleep in the extra space. Or, with your being lord of the castle, if you wish a separate chamber, none of the servants will question your decision."

Intrigued, Stephan mulled over Katherine's offer. Their doing naught but sharing a chamber held great appeal. 'Twould allow him to fulfill the Grand Master's request, his vow to King Robert, and to exist without the interference of an unwanted wife.

More important, their sharing a bedchamber, regardless if each slept within a different part of the room, would satisfy the expectations of those inside the castle. In addition, the agreement would ease the tension between them. "I will have nay untoward discussion about our marriage by those living within Avalon."

"There will be none," she replied.

Neither would he make a mockery of the sacrament of marriage. "When we eat, lodge guests, or important events arise, our attendance together is expected, a practice we will follow."

"I would insist on the same. 'Tis important that we present a united front. I doubt anyone will find it odd that we are nae more than cordial to the other," she said, an edge of nerves in her voice. "Mayhap they will be relieved that you are nae a wicked man given to brutality."

Disgust swept him. "I would never harm an innocent. Those whom I punish have earned their fate."

She relaxed a degree.

And why would she nae? Though Stephan had assured her that he wouldna harm her, the lass knew little about him. "I will consider your request."

Temper sparked in her eyes. "'Tis my castle we journey to."

"A castle that I have nae yet seized," he drawled, "a fact you informed me of moments before."

Blue eyes narrowed. "Make light of this if you choose, but I am nae entertained by your decision to ponder a choice that clearly works for us both."

Stephan held her gaze, intrigued by the fire in her eyes, their color reminding him of the azure depths of the Mediterranean, how the colors lingered in one's mind like a spell cast. Irritated by the whimsical thought, he nodded. "Then I will agree."

Relief flickered in her eyes. "I thank you."

"Thanks are unnecessary. As you stated, the choice clearly makes sense for us both." Satisfied with the arrangement, he strode toward the stern, where several of his men worked. With his and Katherine's relationship void of emotional interaction, for the first time since their debacle of a marriage he found hope that their union would indeed suit his purposes.

Hours later, sweat coated Stephan's brow as he angled his sword and deflected Aiden's attack. "A good move, but I have seen better. Mayhap your squire needs to teach you how to handle a blade."

At his teasing, his friend's eyes brightened with challenge. "Is that what you are thinking?" Aiden shifted, drove his sword forward.

Stephan sidestepped and escaped his charge, thankful to release his frustration through sparring. Since speaking with Katherine that morning, they'd each avoided the other. Or, more accurately, she'd avoided him. Either way, he welcomed her absence.

With a grunt, Aiden rounded his sword, sidestepped, and angled his blade up.

Forged iron screamed at the knight's blow.

Caught off guard, Stephan cursed. 'Twas his penance for thinking of his stubborn wife when his entire focus should be on training.

Stephan feigned to the right, turning on his heel at the same time he swung his blade down, catching his friend's sword. Before his opponent could free his weapon, he jammed his blade up until their hilts collided. With a roar, he jerked the weapon free from Aiden's hands.

Surprise widened his friend's eyes as his sword clattered to the deck.

Several of the Knights Templar who had gathered nearby watched with appreciation.

"Aiden," Cailin called, "you know better than to let Stephan move too close."

The other knights leaning against the rail laughed.

"Aye," Thomas agreed, "dinna let Stephan distract you."

"Do you want me to fetch your sword?" Stephan teased, and several men chuckled.

"I will retrieve it," Katherine said as she stepped forward and lifted the weapon. "'Tis my turn to have a round with the victor."

Chapter Five

L aughter faded as Katherine stood gripping Aiden's fallen sword. She arched a brow at her husband.

Stephan's eyes narrowed.

Neither had she expected her challenge before his men to inspire praise.

His knuckles whitened on the sword's hilt. "What," he said with an easy calm that belied the temper simmering within his gaze, "are you doing?"

"I believe," Katherine said with forced lightness, "'tis obvious."

Water breaking against the bow rumbled through the silence.

The knights remained still; each man watched, waited for their lord's reply.

Nerves edged through her, but she held. 'Twas her husband's arrogance that'd forced her hand by dismissing her ability with a sword sight unseen. Once aware of her skill, he would welcome her to join in the attack on Avalon.

Stephan lowered his blade. "I dinna spar with women."

"Then," she said, allowing her frustration to fill her voice, "you have never met a woman determined to fight for her home."

"*Now,*" he said with quiet emphasis, "is nae the time for this discussion."

She stepped closer. "Aye, 'tis time to train, to hone each person's proficiency in preparation for the upcoming fight."

Her husband's mouth tightened.

"My sister is skilled with a blade," a man to her right said.

"Are women fighting an Irish tradition, Rónán?" Sir Thomas teased.

Laughter echoed among the men, and she caught several smiles. Katherine could have kissed Thomas. The knight's teasing had lessened the mood from dire to intense.

"Stephan, I think you should give the lass a round," Rónán called.

"What harm could it do?" Aiden agreed. "Besides, after one spar, I suspect the lass willna be coming back for another round."

Stephan's frown grew fierce. " 'Tis nae her blade."

She took the sword through a series of intricate moves, impressed that although heavier than she was used to, due to its perfect balance, she maneuvered the weapon with ease. Whoever had crafted this was a master at his trade. "I have handled more substantial swords."

His fingers flexed upon his hilt, and then her husband gave a curt nod. "Begin when you are ready."

Determined to surprise him with her proficiency, she stepped back, raised her blade.

"It could be a trap, Stephan," Aiden teased. "Mayhap the lass knows what she is about."

Several men laughed.

"Mayhap," Stephan replied, his tone dry.

With slow precision, his eyes fixed on hers, her husband stepped within a sword's length, lifted his blade, matching her guard. "Before we start," he whispered, "in deference to your station, I offer you a chance to withdraw."

The arrogant toad! Katherine swung against his weapon and straightened her arm with the point of her sword a hairbreadth from his nose. The shock on his face was worth the jarring of her blade as it clashed against his.

His nostrils flared. "So be it." Their blades locked, he pushed her back.

Though gentle, the force of his shove had her stumbling. She understood his intention. He expected to trounce her with little effort, to ensure she never dared challenge him again.

She steadied herself, deflected his next swing. Smothering her nerves, Katherine focused on her training over the years, the tricks taught to her by her father along with Avalon's master-at-arms. When Stephan started to raise his sword, she shifted to his right in a mock attack, and then jumped back.

His slashing blade met air.

As his weapon swept inches away, she swung her hilt against his, shoved, and prayed the increased momentum would throw him off-balance.

Instead, forged steel screamed as he stilled his weapon in mid-swing, his arm trembling from the sheer force of the act as he turned to face her more squarely, shoving their swords into an X between them.

At the sudden blade's stop and his return shove into the strong parry, unable to halt, she began to fall.

With a muttered curse, Stephan caught her wrist. "If 'twas a real battle, I could end your life now." His expression darkened as he twisted his sword over hers, placing the edge at her throat. "Forfeit."

Heart pounding, she held his gaze, stunned by his strength, shaken by the emotional impact of the man. Furious to notice such, she shoved aside the unwanted thoughts, clung to her anger.

"If 'twas real battle"—she flinched with her left arm, and a small blade appeared in her hand flat against his chest—"the dirk hidden in my garb would be in your heart."

Hazel eyes narrowed. "Weapons training isna done for one's amusement."

"I play nay game—" she whispered, ensuring her reply was as fierce. Hoots of laughter echoed from around them, his knights ignorant of the battle of wills unfolding before them.

"Then in this you shall lose." Her husband pushed her back and raised his blade, his expression tense.

She secured her dagger. They continued to spar, his moves relentless but nae rough. Instead of overpowering her as she'd assumed, he'd chosen to force her to continue swing after swing without reprieve, drain her of her strength with slow efficiency.

Though they'd agreed on a business arrangement of sorts, his actions revealed that he expected her to bend to his will. But he would fail.

Her arms trembling with exhaustion, Katherine lifted her sword for her next swing.

Irritation flickered in Stephan's face. "Enough."

With a speed she hadna anticipated, he slid his blade beneath hers, jerked her sword free.

The weapon slid across the deck.

Before she realized his intention, he caught her wrist, spun her, and wrapped his arm around her waist, pinning her left hand. "Cede."

Trapped, fears of her past assault ignited, and panic flooded her. Katherine fought to break free, but his hold was like iron, his muscled body firm against hers as if carved by granite. "Release me!"

"Admit defeat."

Katherine struggled to breathe, fought to work past the terror that with his strength, if he desired, he could take her against her will.

Enough!

Stephan was a good man, a knight sanctioned by their king. If he'd wanted her, he'd had every right to take her on the night they wed. Instead, he'd left her untouched.

The haze of terror ebbed. Shaken, she noticed the knights watching her, their expressions a mixture of confusion and concern.

Shame swept her. What his men must think of her. She tried to tug free. "Let me go, please."

At Katherine's whispered plea, Stephan glanced down. Stunned by the panic in her eyes, he released her.

Her breathing in ragged gasps, his wife stumbled back, her gaze darting around like a wild animal in search of escape.

"I willna harm you," he said, conscious of the blasted cause of her upset. For a moment he'd desired her, an awareness she must have noticed.

"Nay . . . I . . . ." Her movements unsteady, she took another step back, glanced toward his men, and red swept up her cheeks.

"Wait," Stephan said, keeping his voice calm, needing to repair the deteriorating situation.

Panicked blue eyes met his. "I—I must go. Please dinna follow." Before he could reply, she bolted to the ladder. A moment later, the soft tap of her steps from below deck faded.

God's blade! His reaction to her supple body was one any warm-blooded man would have had. Neither did his desire warrant her reaction.

Should he ignore her plea and try to talk with her? And if he did, with her so upset, would he make everything worse? Frustrated, Stephan glanced toward his men.

Lines of concern deepened Thomas's brow. "Is the lass well?"

"Aye," Stephan replied. He'd dealt with kings, bishops, and foreign leaders in far more difficult situations. He'd give his wife time to calm, then speak with her later. "We must finish securing the crates and move the last of the provisions below before the sun sets."

The men shot one another curious glances and then broke off, each heading toward their respective task.

A dull pounding in his temple, Stephan strode to the bow of the ship and picked up gear he'd left there earlier. With a grimace, he raised his face to the bluster of the wind, cursing the turn of events.

The rush of water churned beneath the bow's might, and clumps of seaweed floated past.

Steps sounded behind him, and then Thomas halted at his side. "Did you want me to see to the lass?"

" 'Tis best if I speak with her once she settles."

His friend nodded.

Stephan rubbed the back of his neck. "I should never have allowed her to spar."

A smile touched the knight's mouth. "With her stubbornness, you would have had to haul her away to stop her."

" 'Tis the truth of it. Never have I met a woman so obstinate. She would give a cornered bear a solid run."

Thomas laughed. " 'Twill make your marriage far from dull."

Stephan grunted. "Katherine is determined to join in the attack to seize Avalon. I am confident her challenging me today was to prove she was up to the task."

"I was impressed by her ability."

"She held her own, more than I expected," Stephan admitted. "Still, her skill changes naught. When we lay siege to the castle, 'twill be with men seasoned in war. My wife will remain aboard ship."

The cry of gulls echoed in the distance as Thomas studied him. " 'Twas brave of the lass to spar with you."

Stephan grunted. "Foolish."

"Few women would have dared."

"God's blade, her reasons matter little."

"They matter to her. Though, 'twas odd how she bolted, more so after having dared draw her hidden dagger."

Stephan grimaced, irritated by the reminder, that he'd nae anticipated she'd have concealed a secondary weapon. A sage tactic; one he, too, utilized.

"Initially," Thomas continued, "I believed she was embarrassed to have lost the match, which made little sense as she fought against a highly trained knight. But from the intensity of her reaction, there was something more. What exactly that was I am unsure."

But he knew. The exact moment Stephan had held her against him was etched in his mind like a chisel to stone. Heat still seared him where they'd touched. He hadna anticipated his body's response.

Or her reaction.

Resigned to his fate, Stephan scowled toward the ladder. "I should talk to her sooner rather than later."

"Aye," his friend agreed, "but with that fierce look, you will scare the lass further."

"'Tis frustration."

"Indeed." His friend's face grew somber. "I once had a sister."

Surprised by the revelation, and curious why Thomas had chosen now to disclose the fact, Stephan waited for his friend to explain. Though they'd battled alongside each other for years, never had the knight mentioned his family. Until this moment, he'd believed him an orphan.

"My sister would be talking about someone who had made her laugh. A moment later she'd have tears in her eyes and explain that she'd found a bird dead in the woods on one of her walks. Women are difficult to understand. My advice, dinna try. That is"—Thomas stared at the ocean for a long moment, then a touch of humor flickered on his mouth—"if you want to retain your sanity."

"I wish to protect my wife, naught more."

"Mayhap, but 'tis obvious she doesna want your protection." He paused. "'Tis her pride that drives her."

He shrugged. "Lady Katherine's motives matter little. Avalon must be reclaimed. I refuse to allow my wife to interfere."

"'Tis the Templar way to protect the defenseless and weak. Except," Thomas said, "the lass is neither. Consider allowing Lady Katherine to continue sparring. Honing her skills will improve her ability to protect herself and be of value to the castle's defenses in the years ahead."

Years ahead, bloody damn! He didna want to ponder a lifetime with her. "She sails with us. 'Tis enough."

"Is it? I think you are creating unnecessary strife."

He glared at Thomas. "Leave it."

"I would if your reasoning made sense. You behave as if this is personal, as if . . ." Disbelief flickered in the knight's eyes, and then they crinkled with mirth. "God in heaven, you are fond of your wife."

He scowled. "I am as fond of her as curdled milk in a cesspit."

"A strong statement for a man who doesna care."

Stephan shot him a hard look. "I dinna hate her."

"So the lass is on your mind, is she?"

"Blast it," Stephan ground out, "I dinna have time for this foolery."

"What if your wife would like to continue training with us, would you allow her?"

Stephan eyed him, weighing his question. 'Twas a reasonable request. "If after I speak with Katherine she wishes to train further, I will allow it. When we head into battle, regardless of her skills, she remains onboard."

Thomas nodded. "Fair enough."

Frustrated by the woman who'd invaded his life like a well-planned assault, Stephan headed toward the ladder. As he strode down the narrow passageway, the door to his cabin stood closed.

With a muttered curse, he halted before the entry, gave a sharp rap. "Katherine."

Clipped steps sounded on the opposite side. Metal scraped. The door jerked open. His wife's cool gaze held his. "What do you want?"

With her hair tossed by the wind, her face flushed with outrage, the flare of awareness that had caught him off guard before returned. Furious she had the power to make him want her, the carefully chosen explanation he'd crafted to ease the tension between them lay smothered beneath the whip of anger.

"You said we could have a business arrangement," Stephan growled. "If in your skewed mind that equates to your challenging me before my men as you did above deck, then our bargain is off."

She angled her jaw. "Challenging you before your men?"

Bloody blasted hell, the woman would ignite ire in a spew-brained hen! He leaned toward her. "Aye."

"I sought naught more than to prove to your addled mind that I am sufficient with a sword."

"An issue," he said between clenched teeth, "that is settled."

"In your mind," she replied, fury coating her words. "When the time comes to reclaim Avalon Castle, I will be ready to fight."

He glared at her, irritated that her nearness lured him to look at her curves. "You may train," he said, his voice hard. "Dinna push me for more or I swear that when my men and I attack, nae only will you remain onboard but under guard."

Outrage burned in her eyes.

She opened her mouth to speak, but Stephan turned on his heel and strode away. He cursed this day, her stubbornness, and the fact that as he'd watched her speak, he'd been tempted to draw her close and give her a kiss.

Hours later, composed after her earlier confrontation with her husband, Katherine sat near the stern of the ship and began to clean her sword. Thankfully, except for a few subtle glances and polite greetings, the men had left her alone.

The soft pad of footsteps grew near.

She looked up.

A tall, lean knight with sandy brown hair approached, a man Stephan had introduced to her earlier that day. The man who'd broken the tension on deck by making the others laugh after she'd challenged Stephan to spar. Nerves fluttering in her stomach, she lay the weapon on a soft cloth. "Sir Thomas."

He gave a half bow. "Lady Katherine."

"I hadna expected company."

The knight glanced toward the sea and then faced her with a smile. "With the wind to our backs, the sky clear of clouds, and the sun setting soon, 'tis a fine time to be standing at the rail."

"It is," she replied. "Though I doubt you came to speak of the weather."

Humor touched his gaze. "I didna." He nodded to the sturdy bench to her right. "Do you mind if I sit?"

"If you wish."

With inherent grace, he drew up a small box and sat, as if he'd lived the life of a noble. A foolish thought. He was a knight who bore his arms for her husband's cause. "And you are here because . . . ?"

"To aid in your request."

Intrigued, she lifted a brow. "My request?"

"You wish to hone your skills with a sword, am I right?"

Astonished by the knight's words after her and Stephan's confrontation, she nodded. "I do, but I admit being surprised that my husband has ceded in this and sent you to help me train."

Thomas cleared his throat. "My lady, he doesna know I am here, or of my offer."

Chapter Six

Suspicion filled Katherine at Sir Thomas's offer to help improve her proficiency with a sword. "Why would you risk upsetting your lord?"

"Your desire to hone your skills with a weapon is reasonable. Neither," he continued, his voice sincere, "will your husband be angry. Before I approached you, I spoke with Stephan regarding my intention."

"And he agreed?"

A twinkle sparked in the warrior's eyes. "More or less."

"More or less?"

"Aye, my lady. Your husband explained that the decision to join in while the men sparred was yours."

How her earlier discussion with Stephan had eroded into his issuing ultimatums sifted through her mind. In fairness, this debacle wasna her husband's fault. He was unaware of her past assault, and that the violence haunted her still. But that didna excuse the brain-addled manner in how he dealt with her, nor would she be ordered about.

Katherine nodded. "Indeed, the decision was mine."

"There you are." His smile exposed a hint of dimples. "If you are still interested in training, then, my lady, I am at your service."

She didna want to bring further discord to her marriage. As if from the cool manner Stephan had responded to her simple query their union could ever be one of them working together in peace.

His being awarded Avalon Castle hurt. 'Twas her heritage. By the king's whim, a castle he'd bestowed upon a mere knight. "I appreciate your offer, Sir Thomas, but I dinna wish your helping me to cause strife in your friendship."

"Nor will it. Despite Stephan and my many disagreements, the difficulties of battle we have weathered over the years have bonded us like brothers."

However reluctant to prod an unstable marital foundation, the opportunity to spend time with Thomas could prove advantageous. Until this moment, owing to her husband's remote manner, little hope existed for her to learn of his past. Did she want to know? Could understanding the circumstances that had carved Stephan into the man he was today make any difference?

She hesitated. What right did she have to pry into his early years when she didna plan on sharing her own? Still, any insight gained would aid her in future dealings with the stranger she'd wed.

Confident of her decision, Katherine smiled. "Then I will accept your offer."

"Excellent," he replied.

"When do we begin?"

Thomas gave a nod. "Now."

Sweat streaking Stephan's brow, he hammered the last nail into the damaged crate below deck and stepped back. The steady rumble of water against the bow echoed against the hull as he studied his work. Pleased with the repair, he glanced to the knight beside him. "This should hold now."

A hammer in his hand, Cailin wiped his brow with his elbow. "Aye."

The scrape of blades rang out from above deck as Rónán climbed down the ladder.

With a frown, Stephan glanced toward his friend. "'Tis late for anyone to be practicing."

Rónán shrugged.

Unease settled in Stephan's gut. "What?"

"Naught of great import," Rónán replied.

Aiden and several knights who'd recently come below and worked nearby glanced at him.

Irritation slid through Stephan. Whatever was going on, his men knew, and . . . Was it Katherine sparring? Blast it, after their confrontation earlier this day, with her realizing she wasna joining them on the attack on Avalon, he'd believed his wife had set aside the foolish notion of honing her ability.

Stephan scowled at the opening above and then glanced toward his men. "I will be back."

Aiden stepped between him and the ladder. "Dinna be upset at the lass."

"Let him go," Rónán said. "Lady Katherine's decision has been made. If asked, one I support."

Irritated, Stephan noted pride in his knights' eyes at his wife's daring. 'Twould seem in her brazen act she'd earned his men's favor. With a muttered curse, he walked to the ladder, shoved his foot on the first rung, and began to climb. With each step, the clang of blades increased. When he reached the top, he glanced out.

Near the bow, beneath the rays of afternoon sun, Thomas sparred with Katherine.

At his approach, his friend looked up. Humor flickered in his eyes, and then Thomas focused on his next swing.

Stephan clenched his teeth. Mayhap Katherine was determined to increase her skills with a weapon, but now he understood what, or better yet who, had prodded her to begin so soon.

Though he conceded her deftness with a blade aided their cause, Thomas was wrong to believe Stephan's interest in the lass went beyond obligation. As with every duty assigned, he took responsibility, paid attention to detail, and finished the task. Except with their marriage there was naught to finish, simply to endure.

Several paces away, Stephan leaned against the rail, crossed his arms over his chest, and watched.

With her back to him, ignorant of his presence, Katherine continued the practice.

"You are doing well." Thomas angled his sword to block her swing. "Next time before you raise your weapon, ensure your feet are braced. If you are off-balance when you strike, your blow will be weakened. An opportunity your opponent will seize upon."

With a nod, Katherine positioned herself as he'd explained. She lifted her sword.

"Good," he encouraged. "Ensuring you are in a proper stance will slow you at first, but with practice the move will become natural. During battle 'twill give you an edge. Let us run through another bout. Remember what I said."

"I will," she replied.

With practiced ease, the knight stepped forward, shifted to the left, swung.

She braced her feet, raised her blade to meet his. Steel scraped.

Pride shone in Thomas's eyes. He nodded, pushed her back. "Well done. This time, when you see my body brace and my arm begin to move, strike. The attack will eliminate my ability to plan a swing."

She nodded.

His friend started to lift his weapon.

Expression fierce, Kathryn angled her sword, charged, forcing Thomas to block the blow.

Against the churn of water pummeling the bow, honed steel screamed.

Thomas shoved her back, following with a brutal drive.

Katherine met his every swing, each scrape of their weapons swept away by the rush of salt-stung air.

Impressed, Stephan grimaced. Though she wasna a warrior, her technique showed promise.

As she prepared for her next attack, Katherine shifted her body to keep control; her eyes met Stephan's.

She hesitated.

With her grip relaxed, her sword lowered a degree.

Thomas having started to swing, cursed and lifted his weapon; steel skimmed the tip of her blade with a fierce clatter.

The sword wobbled in her hands. Red slid up her cheeks and her fingers tightened on the hilt.

"Lady Katherine," Thomas said. "When engaged in close-quarter fighting," the knight explained with firmness, "regardless the distraction, to lose focus on your opponent, even for a moment, could mean your death."

"A point well taken," she replied, her voice unsteady.

His wife was upset. Was the reason that she'd erred in his view, or due to her irritation at him seeing her spar?

As if either explanation mattered. 'Twas his ship and his responsibility to ensure all onboard were properly trained. 'Twould seem regardless of his wishes that included her. Nor could he ignore the impropriety of allowing another man to teach his wife.

Resigned to his fate, he pushed away from the rail. Given Katherine's penchant for creating mayhem, assisting in honing her skills would allow him to keep a close eye on her during the remainder of the journey. Once they'd seized Avalon, the time required in running the castle would keep her out of his way.

As they sparred, Katherine focused on Thomas, but with each turn toward the aft, she caught sight of Stephan. Neither did she care if he watched. Although when she'd first spotted him leaning against the rail, his arms folded across his muscled chest, and a scowl marring his handsome face, she'd realized a part of her wanted to earn his respect.

Furious at the realization, she angled her weapon, drove her sword forward. She didna need Stephan's praise!

Thomas locked his blade with hers. "Hold."

Arm trembling, she lowered her sword. "Was I doing something wrong?"

Humor touched the knight's eyes. "Nay, lass. Me thinks," he said, his words quiet, "that you have done everything right."

"You are nae making sense. I—"

The firm tap of steps sounded behind her. "I will take over," her husband stated.

Thomas shot her a wink and then turned to her husband. "But earlier you said—"

"I have changed my mind," Stephan cut in, his burr rough with irritation.

"With five ships beneath your charge along with preparations for the upcoming attack," his friend said, "you have more than enough weighing on your mind. 'Tis an honor to assist Lady Katherine."

Mary have mercy, Thomas didna understand that neither she nor her husband wished to be in close proximity with the other. "Your offer is unnecessary. I find Sir Thomas an expert in his instruction."

Stephan scowled at his friend. "You are needed below."

"My lady," the knight said, a smile flickering on his mouth, "'twould seem I have other more pressing duties."

More pressing duties. That she sincerely doubted. 'Twas her husband's interference. "I thank you, Sir Thomas. Your time and advice were greatly appreciated."

The knight bowed. "If you ever need me, my lady, I am at your service."

"She willna," Stephan stated.

With a light step, Thomas strode to the ladder.

"I find it odd that you wish to be involved in helping me spar," Katherine said, her voice dry, "training you made clear hours before that you disagree with."

Cool eyes shifted to her. "At times our decisions are made for the greater good."

"And I am the greater good?"

"Nay, a burden."

Hurt, furious that he could make her feel such, she narrowed her gaze. "As are you."

"Then we are even, are we nae?"

"Even?"

"Listen—"

"Nay," she interrupted. "'Twas the chance to wed a man who I love that has been taken away, my father's title that you have been granted, and my home we recapture. You have lost naught but your status as an unmarried man. Considering everything, I doubt we will ever reach a point where we are *even*."

The irritation in his eyes tumbled to frustration. "We are nae at war."

"Nay, we are wed; 'tis worse. In war one side achieves victory; the battle ends. In marriage, the only escape is death."

"Blast it, 'tis nae my desire to remain at odds with you. Upon your request to become more proficient with a blade, I should have agreed to train you from the start."

The utter sincerity of his reply left her stunned. In a sense he was apologizing, or as close as his thick-skinned brain would allow him to admit. Neither did his admission change things between them, but 'twas a reminder that Stephan was a fair man. "What did you mean by the greater good?"

Grief darkened his eyes as he stared at the sea. "For my brothers to be safe. A wish that however much I want it, willna come true."

Confused by the somberness of his voice, she frowned. "Your brothers? Where is your family?"

"Far away."

Though discord lay between them, she wouldna place their differences upon his family. "Once we have reclaimed Avalon, as 'tis spacious, they could—"

His gaze was riveted on her, the intensity as strong as if he'd struck her with a blade. "They canna."

"Stephan," she said, her words rough with compassion, "if they are your family, our home will always be open to them."

His mouth tightened.

The man was stubborn. If she were to be honest, it was a trait she harbored as well, and his mulishness wouldna stop her from acquiring her answers. "What did you mean by the 'greater good'?"

Face taut, he unsheathed his weapon. "Do you want to spar or talk?"

"I can choose?" she asked, pleased when his nostrils flared.

He raised his sword. "Nay, we spar." Stephan swung.

With ease, she deflected his blow.

"Next time," he said, the glint in his eyes sharpening to a warrior's keenness, "ensure you have a firmer grip on the hilt. Use your body as leverage to place power behind your swing."

Katherine nodded, listening to each bit of advice while they continued her training; many techniques she'd heard before, but several were unfamiliar.

After she deflected his next swing, he stepped back. Steel hissed against leather as he sheathed his weapon. "Enough for today."

Moisture clinging to her brow, she secured her sword. Working to catch her breath, her sense of accomplishment smothered the fatigue. Though they'd practiced a long while, naught but a shimmer of sweat touched his brow. "You have fought in numerous battles?"

"A few."

More than a few. He moved with an ease she'd witnessed with but a handful of knights who'd sparred in her father's bailey. "As you have traveled, you must have seen many other countries?"

"Your muscles will be sore on the morrow. I suggest you rub them with a damp cloth before you go to bed. I will have one of the men bring you some seawater to use after we sup." He started toward the ladder.

"Stephan."

Her husband glanced back, his gaze cool, the pungent ocean breeze ruffling his hair.

"I didna miss that you evaded my questions."

"Nor did I expect you to." He climbed below deck.

"And he thinks I am stubborn!"

"You are."

At Thomas's voice, she whirled.

The knight stood several paces away, his eyes thoughtful. "How long have you been standing there?"

He sauntered over. "But moments. I came to see how much you had improved."

"Did you, now? I thought you returned to see how your plan to goad Stephan into taking over my training faired."

Thomas shrugged. "Mayhap that as well. You held your own."

"I should have handled my weapon better. I have trained with a sword for several years. And before you ask, I admit that Stephan is a good teacher."

A smile touched his mouth. "Indeed, he is a master with the blade."

"A master?" she asked, her curiosity growing.

"Aye, his skill is renowned, his expertise sought out by many."

Mayhap that was the reason the king had insisted on her wedding Stephan. Deft with the sword, once they'd seized Avalon, her husband was a trustworthy man whom her guardian could depend on to keep the fortress secure. Still, other questions lay unanswered. "Why will Stephan nae speak of his family?"

The knight's smile faded. "There are some questions best left unasked."

A reply that invited more questions. Frustrated, she shifted to a different topic. "Stephan mentioned that he wanted his brothers to be safe, then refused to say more."

The slap of waves against the ship's bow filled the air.

Her frustration grew. "Have you met any of his family?"

Silence.

"Mary have mercy, you are as hard as Stephan to pry answers from."

"Lady Katherine, heed me well. Your husband is a complicated man; a good, decent warrior who has endured much and suffered more than you could possibly understand. I caution you on prying into his life."

She twisted her brow into a frown. "How dare you advise me of what I can understand when you tell me naught?"

"'Tis nae mine to tell."

"Then," she said, keeping her gaze leveled on him, "I will find a way to convince Stephan to trust me with his past."

"Your efforts will change naught," Thomas said. "Regardless of what you learn, 'tis too late to change anything."

"You are nae making sense," Katherine said, frustrated that his every comment did naught but raise more questions. "Please, tell me what is going on."

The knight shook his head. "If Stephan wishes to broach the subject, 'tis his decision." With a nod, he departed.

Fine, let him go. Neither did she care. Sir Thomas and her husband could immerse themselves in preparations for the battle. In the end, 'twas her castle they claimed, one she would keep.

Chapter Seven

Moonlight shimmered upon the ocean's surface, wisps of silver glinting off each swell. Grief built in Katherine's chest as she took in the spectacular ode to the night, the familiar tang of the sea far from helping to soothe her nerves.

"You should be abed."

At her husband's voice she stiffened.

"I couldna sleep." She glanced his way, far from wanting company. "Neither, 'twould seem, could you."

Illuminated by the spill of silvery light, his face remained a solemn mask. "I heard you leave the cabin."

"Between the ship's creaking, the rumble of water, and the snoring, I find that hard to believe."

His mouth tightened. "I dinna lie."

Exhaustion washed through her, memories of the nightmare poking her mind like sharp sticks. She rubbed her temple. "If you came here to argue, go away. I have little patience for a dispute this night."

For a long moment he studied her. "Why did you leave your berthing?"

She stared at Stephan, a stranger whose presence made her feel protected, a husband in whose company she felt like a stranger. Katherine leaned against the rail, lifted her face against the cool night breeze. "I-I awoke from a nightmare."

The quiet pad of steps sounded, paused at her side.

Though a hand's width away, the crisp, clean scent of his masculinity surrounded her. She swallowed hard, nae wanting to breathe this man any deeper into her life. Alone and in the quiet, she could have mulled over the horrific dream, worked past the pain, if only for a while.

"Of your family's murder?"

Her chest squeezed against the unbearable loss. "A-aye." Her rough whisper melded with the echo of wood severing sea. "I loved them so much. 'Tis difficult for me to accept that . . ." She drew in a steadying breath, exhaled. "To accept that those I loved are gone."

"I am sorry for your loss."

The sincerity of his words had her glancing over. Moonlight outlined his face, the square of his jaw, and his unwavering gaze. "I thank you. 'Tis difficult."

With a sad sigh he rested against the rail. "Losing those you love is never easy."

"It isna." She faced the roll of the sea, assuring herself that the slide of water on her face was the spray of the ocean, nae tears.

"Do you have nightmares often?"

She wiped the salty drops from her cheeks. "Since the attack, they come every night."

"And will continue," he said, his words somber. "After some months, however, if you are fortunate, instead of horrific dreams you will have peaceful sleep. After several more have passed you will have days when your grief doesna stain every waking moment. After years, memories of the tragedy will linger, but doesna haunt your every thought."

He paused, scanning the silver wash of sea and night.

"Regardless of the passage of time, you will see something that makes you remember," he said, his voice growing rough. "Then the hurt, the despair, will rush over you, bringing you to your knees."

The pain of his words made her ache. Whatever loss he'd suffered haunted him still. A grief she understood, a heartache she struggled daily to accept. As a knight he would encounter strife, suffering, along with witnessing death many times over. Wouldna at some point his defenses shield him from further hurt, when he'd grow numb to the taking of a life?

Shame filled her. In her misery, had she become so shallow that instead of empathy for his suffering, she'd dismissed his hurt as less worthy than her own? "How do you move past the tragedy?"

"One nightmare at a time."

From his earlier remarks, she'd expected words of wisdom, nae cynicism. "As simple as that?"

"Aye," he replied, his voice devoid of the emotion of moments before, as if he'd tucked away his feelings with efficient practice. "You focus on the next task, begin. Life doesna allow us time to flounder on misery's shore. Those of wisdom learn to forget, to care for naught except duty."

Anger stirred within her. "I think 'twould be a great dishonor against those important in our lives to try to erase their existence."

"Holding on to the memories does naught but breed bitterness."

"Is that what they have done to you?" she demanded. "Made you bitter?"

"Nay. I refuse to let them."

Empty words. From the fury edging his voice, the recollections still burned hot. Compassion filled her. Although she grieved for her family, she believed one day she would move beyond just existing, of trying to cope with the pain, and find happiness. A conviction in stark contrast to Stephan's, who was filled with naught but despair.

Her godfather knew of her optimistic nature. In addition to sending Stephan and his men to reclaim Avalon, was he aware of her husband's personal struggles? Was that another reason the king had paired her with the knight in hopes that she would help him move past his personal strife?

Thomas's caution that Stephan was a warrior who had endured much whispered through her mind. Was his friend preparing her for the challenge if she tried to work past her husband's barriers? If so, then, like the Bruce, did Thomas believe if she offered advice Stephan would listen?

As if her husband would ever listen to anything she said.

The whip of salty air slid past.

Go back to your cabin, her mind urged. *Little can be done to repair a man so broken.* To remain, to try to help him would be met with naught but frustration. However wise it would be to leave Stephan with the hurt he clung to like a blade, her thoughts returned to the fact that one day she would become strong enough to move past her grief. Her husband didna even have that.

Far from confident in the belief Robert Bruce or Thomas held in her ability, she'd try. "Happiness still exists, if only you seek it."

"Happiness?" Stephan scoffed. "How can you preach hope when your family was slaughtered?"

The ingrate! "How dare you attack me when 'tis you who fear taking a chance to care!"

"We," he said between clenched teeth, "are nae talking about me."

"You are right," Katherine said, sarcasm drenching her every word. "Talking about me is easy; then you can keep your distance. Tell me, do you have any more sage advice to offer? Mayhap counsel that will guide me on the morrow? I bow to your wisdom as 'twould seem you have mastered the—"

He caught her wrist. "Stop it."

"Why?" she challenged, nae giving a damn about his anger, far from intimidated by his firm grip. Had her husband meant to harm her, he would have done so by now. "I am nae one of your men to be ordered about, nor a squire who looks up to you with a glaze of ignorance in his eyes but an unwanted wife."

On a curse, he released her, stalked toward the ladder.

"Go," she called after him, the wind tangling her hair in her face. "Leaving is what you are good at. Another battle to fight? A war to be waged? Bury your head deep within the brutality of combat; then you dinna have to think or remember!"

He whirled. Like a caged animal, Stephan stormed back. "You dare much!"

"You, my lord, dare naught. At least I live, feel sorrow, struggle, and go on. Unlike you, a man who acts as if he has deep faith but refuses to face the potential of pain. Leave me. Hide behind your blade. I dinna care."

"Having faith doesna erase the horrors of life," he stated with rough violence, "the brutality of people, nor their destructive greed."

"It doesna," she agreed, "but faith is a continual hope that burns inside, a belief that however horrific the event, with *His* grace, happiness will arise in the future, joy we can embrace—if we so choose."

Her husband rubbed the back of his neck. "If only 'twas that simple."

Saddened that he'd grown so jaded, the anger of moments before evaporated until naught but weariness remained. "Why does choosing to be happy have to be difficult?"

"Naught in life is easy." For a long moment he stared at the roll of waves, and then he glanced over. "Your words are honorable but a belief culled from the experiences of your sheltered life."

"Sheltered?" Any lingering sympathy faded. "I traveled often with my father, met with kings, dignitaries, as well as dealt with those living with meager means. Well I know the challenges people face and overcome."

Stephan glared at his tigress of a wife, unsure whether he was more furious at her verbal attack or that she'd dared. Nay warrior had ever confronted him and lived! God's teeth, if he had half a brain he'd . . . Sanity drizzled through the blur of anger.

She wasna a warrior but his wife, a woman who grieved her family's brutal murder. He muttered a curse, furious that Katherine had driven him to this point. Worse, that she could. She should have remained at Urquhart Castle while he seized Avalon with his men, as was his right.

Instead, she'd tossed out ultimatums to a king, a bloody king! He knew she'd be trouble, a nuisance at every turn. Challenge him? Aye, the lass would try a saint!

"You have been exposed to a good deal of life," he said. To his mind, a fine concession.

"And that should what, appease me? As if your agreeing that I have been exposed to life somehow holds deep insight?" She arched her brow. "Who do you think you are? Oh, I know," she said, her sarcasm thick. "You are a knight who earned a king's favor. Your status of nobility naught of blood, but by the grant of a king. So dinna try to placate me with the toss of a few understanding words, as if hay for cattle. I am nae a fool."

Nay, she was far from that. If anything, with her insight, his wife saw too much about him, more than he himself had dared to face. Blast her! Neither would this discussion continue. "I shouldna have made light of your experience."

The tension within her body faded. Her eyes watching his filled with starlight and that damnable hope, an emotion far too dangerous to believe in or accept. Awareness stirred. Shocked by the slide of need, Stephan willed the sensation away.

"What is wrong?" she asked.

At her soft entreaty, he caught himself noticing the light shimmering on her mouth, the fullness of her lips, and the soft, sweet curve that lured him to taste. Bedamned! How could a warrior who'd served God most of his life have such strong feelings for a woman he barely knew?

More confusing, in all of his years of travel during the Crusades, never had he met a woman who intrigued him, drew him, made him think about her with more than a passing thought.

Except Katherine.

His wife.

A woman who, if he chose, he could bed.

A breeze whispered across his skin, the coolness making him realize his pulse had begun to race.

God's blade!

"What is wrong?" she asked.

"Naught." Angry at himself for wanting her, for giving her a degree of hope that he was a man who could care for her in the way she'd expect, Stephan stepped back. In her grief, Katherine sought refuge. With her defenses down, 'twas easy for her to confuse gratitude for something more, feelings he could never have.

"Know that I will protect you, always," he said, finding comfort in the familiar role of a protector. "You gave your trust to your guardian; as your husband, I demand the same."

Anger flickered in her eyes. "You demand? Our marriage was a bond made to achieve a strategic goal. Naught more. Neither do I know you enough to give you my absolute trust. If ever that time should come, you will have earned it."

He fisted his hands. "*I* am trying to offer you comfort," he said, his pulse jumping at her anger. That emotion he understood, could handle with minimal effort. "Yet you insist on challenging me on every front."

"You make rules and deem them comfort?" she asked with disgust. "I see them as naught more than you trying to make me conform to the role you think I should play."

Frustrated, Stephan paused. As if he blasted knew how to deal with women! In his world, he understood his duty, loyalty, and followed the commands of those senior to him without question.

Marriage had decimated his established routine. Now he was cast into a foreign existence where he was saddled with a woman holding the temper of a shrew, and expected to cleave to the lass along with wielding a blade!

"Enough," she stated, hurt edging her voice.

Curse this night to Hades! He'd heard her crying, had sought to offer her succor. Instead, their argument had added to her upset.

His wife started to walk past him.

Stephan caught her arm. "Katherine, wait."

"Release me!"

He held.

Wariness darkened her gaze, but he caught the hint of vulnerability as well.

"I fight," he explained, "'tis what I do. When nae in battle, I prepare for the next confrontation."

"Mayhap that is why in the brief times I have seen you, you have chosen to wage war on me instead of learning who I am."

"I have duties that demand my attention."

"Given that we are on a ship," she said, her voice dry, "which makes it difficult for you to keep from my sight, I am impressed at how often I canna find you."

Warily, he studied her. "Why would you seek me out?"

"I am a stranger here."

Stranger, mayhap, but with the little time since they'd sailed, she'd earned the respect of his men, several of whom had stood behind her decision to join in with their sparring. Even Thomas, his closest friend, had dared to intervene.

Nor would his friend's plot to push him and his wife closer succeed. Too much stood between them for a true marriage ever to exist. "It seems you have made a friend in Sir Thomas."

"The knight was kind enough to agree to help me train. An offer driven by gallantry."

Stephan grunted. Gallantry was far from the reason behind Thomas's offer. "A duty from which he has been dismissed."

She again tried to pull free. Wind slid between them, lifting a length of her hair, sweeping it across her cheek as if it were a wish.

Furious that he'd noticed, he released her. He leaned against the rail, stared at the swells, at how the sweep of moonlight spilled across them like a soft caress. "I prefer being out to sea. Many dislike the solitude, the endless days when you see naught but water. For me the vast aloneness brings peace."

After a moment, she positioned herself beside him, faced the roll of water. "As it does to me."

Surprised, he glanced at her. "I have never met a woman who enjoys sailing."

Her expression softened. "My father took me with him on many of his journeys. 'Twas at sea where I came to know the warrior, and the man who gave his life saving those he lov . . . Oh God." Her breath caught, and she started to tremble.

"Katherine—"

"Nay!"

She tried to step back, but he caught her.

Her body began to shake.

Blast it. Against his mind's every warning, Stephan drew his wife into his arms, the softness of her body foreign against his, but he held on, allowed her tears to fall, to dampen his shirt, to linger upon his skin.

As the swells rolled past, he held her until her trembling faded and she stood quiet against him. A completeness filled him, a link he'd nae expected.

"I didna mean to cry," she rasped, her voice thick with tears.

"'Tis all right, lass." Unsure what he should do, he remained still, shaken to find comfort in the way she lay against him with such trust. Neither would she would call it that. Nor would he ask.

He knew well how to lead men, to foster the camaraderie that grew between warriors with each battle faced. He paused. In a way, his marriage with Katherine was a skirmish. As with the knights he led, with each conflict faced and overcome, a bond would grow between them.

Pleased to have found a way to view their relationship that he could accept, Stephan relaxed to a degree. Like his solidarity with his men, this was a connection he could nurture. Exactly how was the question. Though the lass sought to hone her skills with a sword, he doubted talk of battle, caring for the horses, and other war-related issues would pique her interest.

The stories his father had told him came to mind, of how his mother's eyes would shine when she heard a tale that fascinated her. Neither was he a bard. But he could share a touch of his past, show his wife that he understood the difficulties from the loss she struggled with.

"When I was young," he started, finding the long-stowed remembrances difficult to share, "I, too, witnessed my family murdered."

With a gasp she looked up, the shimmer of tears lingering in her eyes. "I am sorry."

"'Twas a long time ago," he said, smothering the emotions the memories wrought.

"But you miss them."

"I do. Nor will I ever forget them." He shrugged. "But I have moved on."

A weak smile touched her mouth. "Said like a warrior."

"Emotions have little place in battle. You fight to achieve a goal. If your opposition canna be convinced to surrender, then they must be conquered."

"'Tis a brutal world."

"'Tis the life of a knight who fights for what he believes in."

"And what of the man?" she asked. "Once you lower your sword and the battle is over, what then? You canna wage war forever."

"With my life at risk with each confrontation," he replied with ease, "'tis foolish to dwell upon the possibility of tomorrow."

"As lord of Avalon, along with the people and the castle's defenses, you must consider a time beyond that of war."

Unbidden, the image of his wife at his side in the future came to mind, of her looking at him with laughter, but also with need. His gaze lowered to her mouth. Another shot of heat slid through him, and his body hardened to a painful ache.

Katherine's eyes widened with distress and she stepped back.

Confused, he moved toward her.

"Dinna come closer," she ordered, a quaver in her voice.

"What is wrong?"

She closed her eyes for a moment, then opened them. "There is something I didna tell you."

God help him, what now? Stephan nodded.

"I can care for a castle and lead men, but never can I accept intimacy. Ever."

What in bloody hell was she talking about? "Katherine, I—"

"'Tis nae you," she rushed on. "It is . . . Mary have mercy, I . . ."

Regret darkening her eyes, she bolted.

Chapter Eight

Steps from the ladder, Stephan caught up to his wife, the fear in her eyes something he'd witnessed many times in the past. Overwhelmed by the brutality of combat, the wash of blood staining the battleground, and the moans of the dying, inexperienced warriors floundered.

But she had never engaged in warfare; whatever incited her panic was personal. "Katherine—"

"Release me!"

"If I let you go, promise you willna run."

Beneath the moonlight wary eyes held his. After a long moment, she nodded.

Irritated at her hesitation, he withdrew his hand. He preferred men who understood rules, obeyed orders, and gave him their unwavering trust.

Did she nae realize his standards had been cultivated by lessons learned, by the passage of time, honed by decisions resulting in the most effective outcomes? Nay, she understood naught but her own choices based on moods, passions, neither acceptable options in times of war.

"Why are you afraid of me?" he asked, keeping his words soft, shielding his fury at the depraved reasons she might be terrified of a man's touch. Whatever the issue, at this moment 'twas imperative she learned that he was a man she could trust.

Her gaze lowered. "'Tis nae you that I fear."

Which he suspected. "Look at me."

His wife breathed sporadic gulps, fisted her hands, and turned away.

Keeping his movements slow, Stephan placed his thumb beneath her jaw, turned her toward him. Face pale in the moonlight, Katherine tried to pull free, but he shook his head, kept his hold gentle but firm. "I will never harm you, ever."

When she remained quiet, he pushed on, understanding that whatever had instilled such fear wouldna be solved this night. "I would give my life to protect you. That I swear."

A tear collected at the end of her eyelash. With a tremble, the tear plopped to her cheek, slid down to linger at the curve of her jaw. "Dinna," she rasped.

Confused, he frowned. "Dinna what? Care? Or want to know who hurt you?"

"Let me go," she whispered, "please."

Anger smoldered. "So you can run?"

"I need to be by myself for a while."

Alone, afraid, 'twas easy to succumb to your fears. "Nae dealing with the pain will do naught but nurture its existence."

Hurt eyes narrowed. "You dinna know how I feel."

"Then tell me."

Silence.

Blast it! "Who hurt you?"

The lass flinched as if struck.

"Did the Earl of Dunsmore beat you?" he asked, his temper rising at the thought of anyone laying a hand on her, the depth of his protectiveness surprising even himself.

"N-nay," she rushed out, "my father was naught but gentle."

Memories of Dunsmore impaling his father belied her claim. But now wasna the time to discuss the life-changing event, nor would such a moment ever arrive. Stephan refused to punish her for the sins of her father. "Then who?"

She released an unsteady breath. "'Twas a long time ago."

"Mayhap, but the memory haunts you still."

The flutter of the salty breeze slid through the silence.

Bedamned! "Why are you protecting him?"

Her mouth tightened.

The lass wasna going to tell him, but he would learn the scoundrel's name. God help the bastard then. "Never again will anyone touch you in brutality. If they do, I will kill them."

Moved by the vehemence of Stephan's vow to protect her, another tear slid down Katherine's cheek.

Her husband's eyes searched hers, the anger easy to read, along with the concern. After the brutal attack when she was but fifteen summers, for years she'd dreaded thoughts of marriage, but the horrors of the assault far from negated her responsibilities as the daughter of a powerful noble.

She would marry.

She would go to her husband's bed.

She would endure his touch until she bore him an heir.

Stoic, she'd moved forward, readied herself for a loveless life, prayed somehow to tolerate the physical act, and that her husband would have a kind heart.

But she'd been unprepared for a man like Stephan. A warrior who would choose his blade over having a family. A man who, as she, hadna sought marriage.

If she had met this intriguing knight before the assault, she would have wished to know him better. In truth, even now she wasna immune.

Moments before at the rail, overwhelmed by the rush of horrific memories, she'd panicked.

After the harrowing event, months had passed before the whispers had faded from those within the castle, but she knew from an errant look that people still remembered.

If Stephan learned of her having been brutally compromised, she couldna bear the shame. Never did Katherine wish to suffer his pity. Neither should she have released her guilt and frustration at her husband for another man's ignominy.

Despite her heart's quandary, a bewildering need pulled her to explain. "You are an honorable man . . ." Her whisper trailed off in the moonlight.

The glint in his eyes sharpened. "But . . . ?"

"My past is exactly that."

"Nae when it haunts you still."

"Naught you say can change what happened. Nor will I entertain further questions. And however poorly I fumbled the saying earlier, know this: A marriage of our working together, and one without intimacy, is one I can accept."

The galley rode the next swell. Another gust rich with the scent of the sea rushed past.

Calmer, feeling as though they'd reached an understanding,

Katherine shifted to a question that left her puzzled. "What is in the crates below?"

The tenderness in his expression faded to caution. " 'Tis naught of importance."

Irritation trampled her lingering frustration. "Naught of importance? We are sailing to my home; anything that affects the castle is important to me."

"Necessary cargo."

"Cargo? A vague reply that answers naught."

He crossed his arms over his chest. "Is there a reason for your inquisition?"

"I asked what any wife would want to know."

"*Most* wives," he drawled, "wouldna seek to know more than was beyond their daily duties as mistress of the castle."

The arrogant toad. "I am nae like most."

A dry smile touched his mouth as he unfolded his arms. "An understatement."

"You—"

"Neither will I entertain further questions on the topic." He pushed back. " 'Tis late and we both need a good night's rest. On the morrow, after we have broken our fast, several knights and I will be meeting to plan our attack on Avalon. As you know where the entry is to the secret tunnel, you will join us." He paused. "Unless you have decided to share that information?"

"Why would you think I have changed my mind?"

He grunted. "I didna; you are too stubborn to consider the dangers. Had I any say in the matter, you would have been forced to draw a map and remained at Urquhart Castle."

"A point," she said, her voice crisp, "you have made very clear."

Stephan watched her for a moment, as if to say more, then nodded. "I bid you good night." He headed below deck.

The man was frustrating! What did they carry within the crates? Though Thomas had helped her with sword practice, she suspected the tentative friendship they'd forged would far from sway him to reveal their cargo.

Katherine frowned as she studied the four ships sailing in their wake. How had the king found the coin to raise such a force? From the discussions she'd overheard between her father and his council, the king's coffers contained little gold. Over the past few months Robert

Bruce had struggled to support the men who'd joined him to unite Scotland.

Neither had she heard a whisper of such a fleet's existence. Nor did his supporters hold great wealth. Mayhap tired of King Edward's tyranny, the Irish nobility had sent gold to aid in the effort to drive the English from their land. It made sense and at this moment was the only logical explanation.

Exhausted, she started toward the ladder, praying that if she found sleep, 'twould be void of horrific dreams.

Sweat coated Katherine's face as she opened her eyes. Her breaths coming fast and her pulse racing, she looked around. She lay curled in a ball in the center of the bed. The golden spill of lantern light illuminated the blanket she'd covered herself with hours earlier, now shoved in the corner and tangled in a heap.

Vivid images of her nightmare rolled through her, and she scrambled from the bed. Struggling for calm, she focused on the small cabin, the steady rocking of the ship, the errant creaks of wood.

The terrible images lingered.

Oh, God. She had to get out of here! Katherine hurried to the door, paused. Last night Stephan had heard her leave. Needing to be alone, she must be quiet.

With care, she crept into the passageway.

The soft tap of boots upon wood echoed from above, near the bow. A guard on duty.

Relieved most of the men slept, Katherine glanced through the entry at the top of the ladder.

Streaks of gold sliced through the wash of purple smearing the sky.

She started up. A reflection from down the passageway had her pausing.

Aware how often the men polished the brass and other metal fixtures, she thought 'twas probably an errant reflection of the sun's first morning rays. She reached for the next rung.

A weak shimmer came from near the cargo hold.

Curious, she climbed down.

Paces from the entry, in the dim light, wedged against the corner, lay a silver round.

'Twas currency.

Unsure if she was more confused or surprised, she walked over and lifted the crafted metal. Unable to identify the denomination in the murky glow, she pocketed the coin and hurried above.

Shafts of sunlight had cut through the heavens by the time she reached the deck, the night losing its battle to the dawn.

The knight on guard nodded to her as she passed.

Near the bow, after a covert glance to ensure the knight making rounds wasna looking in her direction, she lifted the smithed silver.

Illuminated in the newborn rays, a winged creature; half horse, half serpent filled the bottom; the image of a boat covered the upper half. She turned the coin over. Scars lined an image of one beast attacking another, the remainder of the scene was too distressed to make out. She'd seen this coin before.

But where?

Of course: France. When her father had been an emissary for Scotland, she'd sailed with him to meet with King Philip. During a tour of the sovereign's castle, several coins like these lay piled inside a chamber filled with valuables from around the world. Intrigued by the design, Katherine had questioned their origin.

King Philip had explained they were from the Phoenicians.

She frowned. Why would currency from an ancient Mediterranean kingdom be onboard her husband's ship? Irishman wouldna have such coinage, so where had it come from?

"You are up early," Stephan said.

With a start, she pressed the worn silver against her palm. "I didna sleep well," she said, debating the wisdom of showing him her find. "I came above deck in hopes the fresh air would clear my head."

"Did it help?" he asked, the quiet concern in his voice feeding her guilt.

"A little."

He glanced toward her hand. "What were you looking at?"

Curious about his reaction, she opened her palm. "I found this below."

Her husband's gaze landed on the coin. Wary eyes lifted to hers.

Frustrated at his silence, she frowned. "'Tis Phoenician."

He shrugged. "'Tis currency. Common enough."

"This coin is anything but common."

"'Tis spoils of war."

Which explained why the coin was onboard, but from his evasiveness, there was something he was withholding. "Why could you nae tell me last night that your ships carried foreign currency?"

His mouth tightened. "Stay away from the goods stored in the hold."

"Why?" she pressed, aware she'd hit on a matter of some relevance. Whatever was behind his intention to keep her ignorant of the ship's cargo, it held great significance. Katherine's thoughts circled back to Robert Bruce.

"You are here to lead us to the hidden catacombs, nay more. Come," he said. "'Tis time to break our fast."

She ignored the twinge of guilt that she'd misled the king about knowing the location of the catacombs and followed. "What else is in the crates?"

Her husband rounded on her, his face hard, but beneath it, she caught a look of grief. "I refuse to discuss this further."

Oh, nay, she wasna giving up so quickly. "Why do you have Phoenician currency onboard? The other ships carry more as well as other important cargo, do they nae?"

With a muttered curse, he swiped the silver from her hand.

Furious, Katherine tried to pry it from his fingers.

He raised his hand out of reach.

"Give it back."

"'Tis time to eat." Stephan strode away.

She ran after him. "I dinna know what you are hiding, but by God, 'tis my home, and I have a right to know!"

He whirled, his eyes dangerous. "You are here out of necessity. Dinna press issues of which you have nay understanding."

"Then tell me. Keeping me ignorant willna strengthen our marital bond."

A wry smile touched his mouth. "My lady wife, I sincerely doubt either of us wishes to strengthen our marriage."

Blast it, he was right.

Chapter Nine

Seated at the table beside his wife, Stephan met the gazes of the four Templars who'd joined them, each warrior chosen for his specific skills. "Lady Katherine is the only one who knows the location of the secret entrance. Once we reach shore, she will lead us inside."

Thomas raised a brow. "That answers why the lass sails with us."

"I would think my being mistress of Avalon Castle would be reason enough," Katherine said, her words clipped.

Stephan opened his mouth to reply; Thomas held up his hand. Stephan nodded.

"My lady," Thomas explained, "'tis nae in Stephan's character to allow a woman, regardless of her station, to enter into a dangerous situation."

Red crept up her cheeks and she faced her husband. "You didna share my reason for being here?"

"Nay," he replied, unapologetic. Any discomfort his wife suffered was roused by her insistence on sailing to Avalon, something he'd made clear was unwanted. "'Twas unnecessary."

Confusion darkened her eyes. "Why?"

"My men trust my decisions without question," Stephan said.

"Aye," Aiden said. "In battle to hesitate in following an order could mean your life, or the lives of others."

Their expressions firm with resolve, the knights seated around the table nodded.

Katherine's blush deepened. "Forgive me; I should have considered such."

"You are nae a warrior, but my wife," Stephan said, pleased by her admission. "Your strength lies in the running of a household."

"Mayhap," she agreed, "but it doesna prohibit me from being knowledgeable elsewhere."

Silence echoed within the cabin.

"You have sailed before, my lady?" Aiden asked, cutting through the tension.

Surprise flickered on her face. "How did you know?"

A wry smile touched the knight's mouth. "From the way you walk."

"The way I walk?"

"Your steps take into account the rise and fall of the ship," Aiden explained. "'Tis a characteristic of those familiar with time at sea."

Stephan grimaced. Regardless of whether she'd told him she'd sailed with her father, he should have noticed the seafaring trait. Instead, frustrated at having her onboard, compounded by his upset at her finding a coin that had somehow slipped from a crate during loading, he'd overlooked the sign of her experience. God's blade, what else had he missed? "And your point, Aiden?" he said impatiently.

"Lady Katherine's experience at sea is fortuitous," the Templar replied. "With knowledge of the coastline and tides surrounding Avalon, she can offer insight on navigating the local currents."

"An excellent point," Stephan grudgingly agreed. Too many years had passed for him to recall details of the local currents. "Except for where the cliffs hide the castle guard's view, they can spot ships on the wall walk from a great distance."

Surprise widened Katherine's eyes. "You have been to Avalon?"

He didna explain he'd lived there as a child. Neither would he unearth a fact that would raise questions. The lass was like a dog with a bone when her interest was raised.

Nor were his recollections relevant. Memories of the castle and the surrounding waters were those of his youth. With erosion, flooding, and sand on the bottom often shifting during storms, the underwater landscape would have changed. But for the whirlpool located south of the island Avalon sat upon, which they would avoid.

Parchment crinkled as Stephan spread out the map of the area. "Where is the entrance to the tunnel?"

Katherine pointed to a notation warning of dangerous waters. "Here."

Concern darkened Thomas's eyes. "'Tis located near the whirlpool?"

"Aye," she replied. "The entrance is near the inlet where we must moor the ships to keep hidden."

God's blade! Stephan's plans to give the treacherous waters wide berth faded. He scowled. "You are confident our ships can safely navigate to the tunnel's entrance?"

Another swath of red swept her cheeks.

Blast it, what now? "What is it?" Stephan pressed, aware from her reaction that he wouldna like the answer.

"'Tis that . . ." She scraped her lower lip with her teeth. "'Tis that I have traveled through the secret entry but once."

A dull ache pounded in Stephan's head, threatening to worsen. "You have nay experience sailing near the whirlpool?"

Blue eyes narrowed. "Never did I claim to have sailed there."

"A detail," he stated, his voice crisp, "you omitted to mention to Robert Bruce; more, you allowed our sovereign to believe otherwise."

Thomas glanced from Stephan to Katherine. "What has Scotland's king to do with this?"

In regard to his marriage and his wife being aboard his ship, every blasted thing. "'Tis nae important," Stephan said, his voice tight, refusing to drag their fiasco of a wedding before his men. "With the near impenetrable defenses of the stronghold, and without a massive force, the secret passage is the only way to seize Avalon."

Katherine exhaled a shaky breath, exposing her nervousness.

Stephan gave his bold wife credit for her control.

"I believe," she said, meeting every man's gaze, "that we can keep a safe distance from the whirlpool's pull as we navigate to shore."

"Believe?" Stephan demanded, ready to throttle the lass. "We must create a plan of attack on mere beliefs?" Still, this wasna the first time he and his men had faced the unknown. A churn of water hardly represented the threat of an attacking force. "Tell us what you know."

In brief, she informed them of how the strong ocean currents interacted with the narrow channel near the secret tunnel's entry. "Due to the irregular depth of the bottom," she explained, "the tide merges with the current, increasing the overall speed, which widens the area impacted by the strong flow."

Rónán studied the map, lifted his gaze to hers. "In essence, during high tide there is a limited time to sail in or out before the waterway becomes too dangerous to navigate?"

"Correct. If we are near shore when the churn of water strengthens, we will be trapped until the tide begins to ebb and the water recedes to the point where the current willna drag us into the whirlpool." Katherine eyed each man. "Between the sheer cliffs and the hazardous currents, anyone plotting a siege on Avalon would believe this an impossible route, the reason the entry was made in this location."

Rónán sat back. "Wise planning."

"Indeed. And another caution," Katherine continued. "During a strong spring tide, waves can build to the height of many a ship's bow."

Unsettled murmurs rumbled around the room.

"So the best plan of action," Thomas said, "is to sail near the entry during low tide."

"Aye," she replied.

"How many hours do we have before the current grows too dangerous with the onset of high tide?" Stephan asked.

"A handful at most."

Stephan tapped his thumb against the hilt of his dagger as he mulled the possibilities. "To allow maximum time for the assault, we must anchor out and row to shore before low tide occurs. If for any reason we are forced to withdraw, we will have time to escape before the waters have grown too dangerous to navigate and leave us trapped and an easy target for the English."

Cailin glanced toward Stephan. "Before we make final plans, we must learn the local tide."

"I agree," Stephan said. " 'Twill delay us a day, mayhap two, but 'tis imperative to our success."

Thomas grunted. "If the English suspect our presence, the blasted Sassenach will barricade the inner entry."

"Nay," Katherine said. "They willna."

"How can you be sure?" Stephan asked.

Pride shone in her eyes. "Because they dinna know a secret tunnel or concealed chamber exists below Avalon."

"An advantage." Stephan leaned back in his chair. "When was the last time you used the tunnel?"

"A fortnight ago. 'Tis how I escaped."

"Escaped?" Cailin asked as the other men's brows rose in silent question.

A tremble rippled across her skin. "Aye," she whispered, her voice unsteady, "we are sailing to my home." Face pale, she stood. "I believe 'tis all the information I have that you will find useful at this time. If you will excuse me." With hurried steps she left. A soft thud echoed in the cabin as she closed the door in her wake.

The men's eyes focused on him.

"Avalon Castle is Lady Katherine's home?" Thomas asked with surprise.

With a muttered curse, Stephan stared at the door, torn between going after her and staying. God's blade, as if he didna understand the demons she faced, a torment he'd struggled against at the age of seven. Alone and without the Knights Templar taking him in, he would have ended up a beggar on the streets.

Or died.

But she'd had the good fortune of a king as her godparent. However much Robert Bruce cared for Katherine, his sympathy didna erase the horrors she'd witnessed. They had shared similar tragedies; mayhap his presence could offer her solace. Disgust swept through Stephan. As if she would ever accept comfort from him.

Neither could he forget his vow. Duty came first. The dissolution of the Knights Templar may have ended a cohesive union of warriors of God, but it far from erased his oath.

Guilt slid through him. He glanced toward the door. Bedamned! Stephan faced his men. "The English murdered her family. They forced her to witness both of her parents slain."

"God's sword," Aiden hissed.

"The bastards," Rónán spat, his Irish brogue ripe with fury.

"'Tis nae what anyone should witness, more so a lass," Thomas said through clenched teeth. "'Tis surprising the Sassenach allowed her to live."

"In other circumstances I believe they would have killed her," Stephan said, his voice hard. "Young King Edward ordered the Earl of Preswick to seize the castle but spare the Earl of Dunsmore's daughter. In an effort to begin building a Scottish and English relationship, Preswick was then to press her into marriage."

Thomas grunted. "King Edward II is a fool to believe Scotland could be quelled into submission simply by forcing his nobles to marry their enemies."

"Aye," Stephan agreed. "He isna the warrior his father was, nor, from what I have heard, is Edward of Caernarfon's heart in the claiming of Scotland, which bodes well for King Robert."

"How was Lady Katherine able to escape her captors?" Cailin asked.

"She refused to wed the earl. Furious, Preswick ordered her locked within her chamber until she agreed. Once alone, she used a hidden passage from her chamber that led to the secret tunnel."

Smiles touched the lips of his men.

"And explains why the lass is determined to hone her skills with a blade." The approval in Thomas's eyes faded. "Whatever her reasons, Lady Katherine willna fight alongside us when we retake the castle."

Surprise registered in Rónán's eyes. "But Lady Katherine believes she will-"

"My wife," Stephan cut in, his tone firm, "will accompany us ashore, reveal the hidden entry, and then lead us through the tunnel to the hidden door beneath the castle. After she has explained how we may gain access, she will be escorted to the ship."

Cailin blew out a rough breath. "The lass will be furious."

"Mayhap," Stephan said, "but 'tis a situation of her own making. Prior to our departure, I requested she draw us a map. She refused." His gut churning, he glanced toward the door.

"What about the catacombs below the castle?" Thomas asked.

Stephan frowned. "What about them?"

"With the lass furious at nae being allowed to fight, I doubt she will reveal their location."

"An issue I will deal with," Stephan said, "if it arises."

"Mayhap there is a map documenting the location of the catacombs within the castle," Aiden said, "and we willna need her help."

Stephan nodded. "I believe there is, as does the king. Mayhap hidden within an old ledger or Bible, but we canna count on such luck."

Rónán frowned. "And if there is none?"

"I am familiar with the catacombs beneath King Solomon's temple," Stephan explained. "Having reviewed notes of the various methods used to gain entry into the secret passageways, I am confident that, over time and with persistence, I can discover any hidden chambers beneath Avalon."

"If there is a delay, where will we keep our cargo?" Aiden asked.

"If the tunnel isna large enough," Stephan replied, "we will find a temporary location within the castle."

Thomas thrummed his fingers on the table. "Where did you see the maps of Solomon's catacombs?"

"The Grand Master allowed me to examine those in his vault before I departed France." Stephan glanced toward the door. He should see to Katherine, though God knew why, when she would do naught but ignore him. "We will continue on the morrow."

"Aye," his men replied in unison.

His mind turning to Katherine, his chair scraped as Stephan stood.

Thomas stepped before him as the others departed; the door closed, leaving them alone. "The lass still grieves."

Hand on the smoothed top of his chair, Stephan nodded. "Naught about her returning to her home will be easy. However hard Katherine finds it, after a month or two has passed, 'twill be more difficult. She willna have restoring order to the castle to keep her mind occupied. Then she will have time to think, to remember, to relive the horrors."

His friend lay his hand on Stephan's shoulder. "Your wife is fortunate to have you as her protector, but at this moment, she also needs a friend."

Blast it! "Do you nae think I understand what my wife needs?"

Eyes troubled, Thomas dropped his hand. "There is a difference between understanding and the ability to offer compassion. After your own youth, years passed before you let anyone close. Are you willing to risk being Lady Katherine's friend?"

"God's blade, I married her!"

"A marriage to procure Avalon Castle for the Templars, and in exchange we train the king's knights, give monetary aid, and support the sovereign in battle," Thomas said. "Each reason offering little cause to build a foundation of friendship."

A muscle worked in Stephan's jaw. "You are a warrior; you understand sacrifice," Thomas continued, "but the lass ... As well as compassion, she needs friendship, which you can give her." He departed.

Haunted by Thomas's words, Stephan strode above deck. Had anyone else given him such advice, they could have gone to Hades. But Thomas had endured horrific tragedy as well, understood the cost of daring to offer friendship, of placing himself in a position where if he risked sharing his past with another he could open himself up to be hurt.

Sunlight blinded him as he reached the deck. Stephan shielded his eyes.

Across the deck, Katherine stood looking out from the bow, hair fluttering across her cheek.

Thomas's words of friendship echoed in his mind. He grimaced. The situation wasna so simple.

A gust blew the hair from her face, exposed her chalky pallor.

God's blade! He wasna offering friendship but, as her husband, his concern. If the lass decided to speak to him, 'twould be her choice. Discussion wasna a bond but duty. Stephan strode over.

Her body tensed at his approach.

Stephan remained quiet, understanding her silent battle, the difficulty of dealing with emotions tearing you apart, the brutal hurt that could leave you an empty shell, fighting to breathe.

Katherine's vision blurred against the rush of wind, the tang of the sea strong and the call of birds echoing in the distance.

Her husband remained.

Irritated, she focused on the wisps of seaweed sliding past. Why had he come?

With an easy grace, Stephan rested against the rail, scanned the roll of water, his every movement relaxed, as if he had all the time in the world.

Behind them, came the pad of steps, calls from men to one another, assuring her the crew went about their daily chores.

Shame washed through Katherine as she recalled the way she'd fled their meeting. The flood of emotions when she'd mentioned Avalon Castle had caught her off guard. "I had to leave," she whispered.

"I know."

Unsure of how he'd reply, kindness wasna one of her expectations. From the corner of her eye, she peered over.

His gaze remained riveted on the sea.

Unsure what else to say, she remained silent. Again, 'twould seem she'd misjudged him. When she'd first met Stephan, she'd believed him a knight, a man whose life was dedicated to war. But she'd nae expected his understanding or care, more so after being forced into an unwanted marriage.

A swell rolled past. Sunlight filtered through sprays of white as the bow cut through the water, igniting shimmers of rainbows that were gone as quickly.

Gathering her courage, she exhaled. "I dinna want the men to think I am weak."

"None will judge you for your upset. Anger for which you have every right."

"Anger aids naught."

Stephan turned, his expression solemn. "Anger makes us human, a reminder that however much we hurt, however empty we feel, however alone we are in our lives, we still hold the ability to care."

Hot tears burned her throat. "After losing those you love," she rasped, "how is it possible to ever risk caring for someone again?"

Pain streaked through him, and for a moment he closed his eyes.

A wave slammed against the hull, then another.

He lifted his lids. Eyes dark with turmoil met hers. "I am unsure."

Confused, she turned toward him. "But you agreed to marriage?"

"Marriage doesna invite caring, but responsibility. Our union was an act of duty."

"For the *greater good*?" she said, remembering his earlier claim, unsure if she was hurt by his words or relieved.

A faraway look touched his eyes and his expression hardened. "Aye."

Baffled that she found solace in his presence, she looked away. Were her reasons for agreeing to their marriage so different than his? Still, foolishly, she'd nurtured the possibility that they would find common ground. If fortunate, over time build a friendship, mayhap more.

That he had stolen any hope of the latter left her empty. Her grip on the rail tightened. "Why are you here?"

"You were distraught."

"And you wanted to ensure what? As you said, I am naught but a duty. Why did you nae send another man to see to me?"

"You are being irrational."

"Am I?" Temper slid into Katherine's voice. "Because I was foolish enough to believe that you came to me because you were concerned for my welfare? Dinna worry; you have made your feelings toward me clear. I willna make such an error again."

Frustration flashed in his eyes, but he remained silent.

Well, 'twould seem he wasna as immune to her as he would like. "Why did you come here?"

Hazel eyes grew guarded and he glanced toward the aft of the ship.

"Go on," she said, finding she wanted him to remain, unsure if 'twas wise. "'Tis safest that way."

Face taut, he glared at her. "I didna imagine a woman like you in my life."

She arched a brow.

He shoved away from the rail. "Blast it, you are nae what I expected!"

Stunned by his vehemence, aware this moment was a turning point between them, she watched him, needing to see his reaction. "And what did you expect?"

With a muttered curse, he glanced toward the stern. His throat worked, and then he gave an exasperated sigh. "A wife in name only."

Which explained to a degree his leaving her untouched on their wedding night. "But . . . ?"

Eyes narrowed, Stephan met her gaze. "I didna expect a strong woman, a lass who intrigues me, a wife who is braver than many men. How can I nae admire you, or . . ." He muttered a curse.

Chapter Ten

Katherine stared at her husband, unsure if she was more stunned that Stephan admired her or at his unfinished comment suggesting more.

A surge of need caught her off guard. Mary have mercy, she desired him. After the brutal assault years before, she'd never expected to find herself drawn to a man. Uncertain how to proceed, to respond to the emotions he inspired, she focused on his admission. There would be time to mull the other thoughts later.

She sensed her husband was afraid of allowing himself to care for another, yet he'd risked that by his confession. More humbling, however much he didna approve of his growing feelings toward her, aware she struggled with the loss of her family, he'd set aside his own disquiet to be with her.

Moved by his thoughtfulness, she lay her hand over his, forced herself to smile. "You are nae what I expected to find either."

A muscle worked in his jaw, but he remained silent.

Katherine removed her hand. "I misjudged you," she continued, uncertain what to say but needing to try to explain. "When I first met you, I saw a knight bound by honor and duty, one who I was doubtful I could like." His eyes narrowed and comfort swept through her. For the first time she found herself on equal footing with him. "Now I see a man, one who, if I were asked, intrigues me as well."

"Dinna," he whispered.

She arched a brow, far from deterred by his warning. Since they'd met his considerate actions had assured her that he wasna a man given to abuse. Her husband's intention to keep her at a distance made her feel safe and, something she'd nae expected in his company, confident.

More astonishing, since the assault, she'd never completely relaxed around a man who was nae family or a close friend, or felt at ease. With Stephan she was experiencing both.

Perplexed by this startling turn of events, however much her husband wanted to keep them at a distance, she wished to become friends. From his manner, that would be a challenge, but for a man with whom she'd spend the rest of her life, 'twould be time well spent.

"I appreciate your coming to see me," Katherine said, her words sincere.

His body relaxed a degree.

With a slow glide, she rubbed her fingers along the weathered wood. "Most men wouldna have cared."

Silence.

"But then," she continued, determined to find a way to break through his cool façade, "you are my husband."

A wry smile touched his lips. "A vow of marriage offers little assurance that a man will care for his wife."

"Indeed." A point he'd made more than clear. Neither would she be lured by the bait he'd subtly cast. "Though ours isna a match of love, the king chose wisely. I shouldna have expected otherwise from my godfather."

Shrewd hazel eyes studied hers as the galley rocked upon the roll of water. "You and your godfather are close?"

"Aye," she replied, memories of his and her father's laughter leaving her melancholy. "During my youth Robert Bruce visited Avalon Castle often."

"Which by your loyalty to our sovereign," he said quietly, "would make you an enemy of England's king."

"It would," Katherine agreed. "After my refusing to wed Edward of Caernarfon's choice and escaping the Earl of Preswick's capture and leaving him embarrassed by a wee lass, even more so."

With ease, Stephan leaned against the rail at her side. "Your having made such a formidable enemy doesna worry you?"

Anger moved through her. "I refuse to be cowed by a man consumed with building power, uncaring how many innocent people he slaughters. With his father's passing, I pray for a wiser man as England's king." She shrugged. "I hope that mayhap the new king's ordering Avalon seized and me forced to wed his noble wasna driven by his own desire, but prodded by those who hold the king's ear."

"I believe 'tis the latter," Stephan agreed. "After his father's death, instead of pushing his troops deeper into Scotland, he returned to England to deal with his new duties concerning matters of the crown, as well as his impending marriage. The Earl of Pembroke, whom he left in charge at Cumnock, is far from a man driven. With Scotland in a state of civil war and his interests elsewhere, 'tis doubtful Edward of Caernarfon will be returning any time soon."

Katherine nodded, finding wisdom in her husband's belief. "I pray he is nae a cold, heartless ruler like his father."

"I pray so as well." Her husband shook his head. "Many rulers never learn that to subdue people by threats doesna breed loyalty but fear, and more often rebellion."

Emotions raw, she scanned the soft roll of the swells, unsettled by thoughts of their country's future. Katherine glanced over. "Though Robert Bruce is an excellent strategist, I worry that our king's ambitions to claim Scotland will be hindered by his lack of gold, as well as training and arms for his knights."

For a long moment Stephan studied her, his gaze intense, as if weighing his words.

Intrigued by his reaction, she shifted, aligning her body with his. "What causes such deep contemplation?"

"Have faith in our king. As you said, he is an excellent strategist, and a man whom I believe has more assets than many understand."

"Such as?"

"The source is the Bruce's to share."

But he knew. Were he and his knights' arrival at Urquhart Castle a planned event to support Robert Bruce to reunite Scotland? 'Twas logical, but it didna explain the need for her and Stephan to marry. Or had their arrival to meet with Robert Bruce been a coincidence, one that for whatever his reason, the king had determined should end in her and Stephan's marriage?

Her husband took a step back. "You seem calmer now."

"I am, I thank you."

He began to turn.

"Stephan."

Muscles tense, he met her gaze.

"I believe," she said with a smile, "that we have reached a tentative friendship."

Illuminated by the dimming light as clouds moved in from the west to shield the sun, he watched her, his expression unreadable. "Far from it, and however much either of us wishes, I doubt we ever will." Boots tapped on the deck as he strode toward his men without looking back.

In the distance, lightning cut through the night, brilliant flashes that illuminated the heavens. Stephan frowned, the clear skies to the west fading as a layer of clouds moved eastward, smothering the few remaining stars.

"A storm is moving in," Thomas said, pausing at his side.

The slap of rough seas echoed against the hull as the ship cut through the building swells. "Indeed," Stephan agreed. "I pray the bad weather blows through quickly."

"As do I." Thomas glanced toward the ladder. "How fares Lady Katherine?"

"Better."

"Better?" his friend asked, a tinge of humor in his voice. The smile on his face faded. "In a way you are fortunate."

Curious, Stephan glanced at him. "How so?"

"By assenting to King Robert's offer of marriage to Katherine, you didna have to deal with the strife of moving past the vows of chastity that, regardless of the Grand Master's dissolution, Templars cleave to."

"And that makes me fortunate?" He grunted. "Sentenced is more like it."

His friend gave a soft chuckle. "There could be worse punishments than being married to a beautiful woman."

"She is that," Stephan grudgingly agreed.

"And intelligent."

"Aye."

"And thoughtful."

"God's blade, Thomas, well I know Lady Katherine's attributes. Had we nae been forced to wed, I . . ."

Thomas arched a brow. "Would have what?"

On a sigh, Stephan rubbed the back of his neck. "I would have noticed her."

"And done nay more."

Frustrated with the entire situation, he shot his friend an accusatory look. "Neither would you." As if he wanted a blasted wife?

Regardless of the Grand Master's dissolving the Templar vows and his entreaty to marry, or the awareness that rippled through him whenever he saw his wife, Stephan didna want marriage.

"Aye," his friend agreed. "None of the Templars wished this exile from the duty we loved, a life we'd sworn to uphold until our death."

With a muttered curse, Stephan inhaled, the tang of the sea strong, the air potent with the unspent energy of the approaching storm. He debated telling his friend of Katherine's desire to build a bond between them. Unsure if he should discuss the matter, he glanced skyward.

"Something is on your mind."

Blast it. He faced Thomas. "The lass wishes to be my friend."

"'Twill make your life easier."

"Nay," Stephan said before his friend could say more. "I refused."

Surprise flickered on the Templar's face. "Why?" Thomas asked with surprise. "Friendship between you and your wife would be wise. Once the castle is secured and after we have trained King Robert's troops, nay doubt we will be heading into battle. Leaving Avalon in the hands of a trusted friend is preferable to the safekeeping of a woman scorned."

"Do you think I dinna know that?" Stephan said, all of the reasons why he should agree to a bond of friendship weighing upon him like boulders. "But I canna."

Somber eyes held his. "I understand your hesitation, but there may be another reason you havena contemplated."

Doubtful such an explanation existed, Stephan arched a brow. "And that would be?"

"That God has crossed your path with Lady Katherine's for a reason."

He grunted. "Think you a spiritual connection would make the situation better?"

"Why does it bother you to think mayhap 'tis His intervention?" his friend asked.

He remained silent, nae wanting to discuss the matter further.

"I will tell you," Thomas continued. "Because then your marriage would be something you could accept."

'Twas foolish. Insane. And made sense. He shrugged. "Mayhap."

"My advice—"

"I didna ask for it."

"In regard to Lady Katherine's offer of friendship," Thomas continued, as if Stephan hadna spoken, "let time and circumstance dictate your path. If you find your friendship growing into something more, then you will know 'tis His blessing you have received."

Stephan scowled.

"At times in our lives we are given situations we dinna understand," Thomas continued. "But later, when we look back, we see the wisdom gleaned in the challenges faced, the lessons learned that will serve us in our lives ahead."

With Katherine, it was advice he doubted. "And she is my challenge?"

"Mayhap," his friend said, "the challenge is yourself."

Blast it, the problem wasna himself, 'twas . . .

Recollections rolled through Stephan: how, upon witnessing his parents' death, he'd vowed never again to allow anyone close. Throat tight, against his every wish, he conceded the truth. 'Twas nae friendship with the lass that left him on edge. With her intelligence, beauty, and the need she inspired when they were close, his greatest fear was that he wanted more.

A rain-laden gust whipped past. Thunder boomed in the distance.

On a hard swallow, he hauled his mind from unwanted thoughts of his wife, from the damning reality he struggled to accept. "The clouds are closing fast. I will make one last round before the storm arrives. Tell the others to ensure all the cargo is secure."

"Aye." Thomas held his gaze. "Whatever decision you make, I have confidence 'twill be the right one for you both." He strode off.

God's blade, he didna need anyone! However much Stephan wanted to ignore his friend's words, they held wisdom. More important, if he agreed to his wife's offer of friendship, 'twas a bond by a few simple words undone.

Thunder boomed.

He scanned the clouds churning overhead, refusing to ponder whether their fate was indeed guided by a higher power.

Furious at the chaos Katherine had tossed into his disciplined life, Stephan muttered a curse and started to ensure the knots on the cargo, paces away, were secure.

* * *

Against the backdrop of the slate-gray sunrise, another wave slammed the hull.

Wood crunched against rocks.

The ship listed toward starboard.

Stephan shouted to hold on as he clung to the rail, prayed the galley hadna sustained major damage.

On a groan, the vessel shuddered, began shifting upright.

Determined to see the extent of the damage to the ship, Stephan pushed through the buffeting wind to the ladder. Rain lashed his body as he scrambled below.

Down the passageway, cast in the shadows of a hanging lantern swinging to and fro, Katherine stood braced at the entry of her cabin.

Worry shot through him. "Are you hurt?"

Eyes dark with concern held his. "Nay. What of the ship?"

"I am on my way to find out," he replied, his voice gruff.

"Stephan!" Aiden called from the stern.

"Coming!" He shot her a warning look. "Unless I tell you otherwise, remain here." Pressing his hand against the bulkhead to keep his balance, he started back.

Another wave rocked the ship.

The hull crunched against stone, and a high-pitched scrape ripped through the air.

On a curse, paces away, Thomas caught hold of a nearby timber, held tight.

Stephan caught a nearby beam, pulled himself forward. As he made to take another step, the crash of another swell echoed through the ship.

Wood snapped.

A stream of water gushed through the break.

Shouts for tinder, blankets, or anything to fill the gash rang out as his men ran toward the spewing torrent.

Stephan reached the damage, grabbed oiled rags from a large pile, and shoved the cloth inside.

"Move back!" a knight called. Once clear, he thrust a plank into the cloths, bracing the other end against a beam.

The rush of water slowed.

"We need another board to the right side," Stephan ordered.

Thomas wedged a wooden plank against the last.

The stream of water slowed to a dribble.

"We must have hit the reef," Thomas shouted over the roar of wind.

"Aye." Stephan glanced at Aiden as he hurried toward them, water sloshing with his every step. "How far are we from shore?"

"Close. We have kept the rudder tight, but the wind and waves have been tossing us shoreward all night." Aiden grimaced. "The last swell shoved us too near."

"We are taking on too much water," Stephan yelled. "We must beach the ship before we sink. Aiden, tell Rónán to order the sails dropped immediately, find a break in the reef and have the oarsmen row to the beach. After daybreak, we can make any repairs during low tide."

"Aye." Aiden climbed over debris and he made his way toward the ladder.

Wind howled from above.

The vessel groaned.

Another swell slammed against the hull.

"There is water on my cabin floor . . ." Katherine halted at the entry to the hold. Illuminated in the lantern light, her face paled. "We are sinking!"

Bedamned! He didna need a panicking female. "Stay there!" Stephan ordered.

Cailin nodded to Stephan. "Take your wife above. The largest damage has been taken care of. I will help Thomas and the others finish up securing the brace."

Stephan nodded. "I will have someone call down right before we impact." Furious she'd nae remained in her cabin, where he could find her if necessary, he strode to her, caught her arm, and started toward the bow.

Katherine tried to pull free. "What are you doing?"

"We," he growled, "are going up the ladder."

Her eyes wide with fear, she stared at the smashed wood where water continued to stream into the hull. "What about the men? 'Tis too dangerous for them to remain here. Thomas and Cailin are—"

"Experienced sailors," Stephan interrupted, tugging her with him. "Plans dinna always go as we hope. We will be ashore soon."

"Ashore?" She stared at him as if he had gone mad. "How?"

"We are beaching the ship." He set her on the ladder. "Go. There isna time to explain."

As he stepped above deck in her wake, a gust, laced with the whip of water, blew past.

Off-balance, Katherine screamed as she started to fall.

Stephan hauled her to him and headed toward the port side.

"Stephan—"

God's blade, he didna have time for her questions! "Hold on to the rail!"

Knuckles white, her fingers curled over the wood. "I thought you were knights, not sailors."

"We are what we need to be." Another wave crashed against the hull. White water spilled over the bow, crashed onto the deck, rolled toward them in a violent swirl.

Stephan caged her body against his, clenched the rail, and braced his feet. "Hold on!"

Storm-black water raced across the sodden planks, streaming around boxes, spilling into the hull, and rushing toward them.

On a groan, the ship angled up.

The wall of water shifted, poured off the deck and into the angry churn below.

Relieved, he faced Katherine. "Are you hurt?"

Heart pounding, her hair drenched, and each breath laden with a salty brine, Katherine nodded, more terrified than ever before. In the numerous times she'd sailed with her father, never had she experienced such a ferocious storm. "I am fine."

The bow slammed through an oncoming breaker.

Stephan took the brunt of the water surging over the edge.

More of her reserve toward her husband eroded. Though he'd assured her that he didna want her friendship, he never hesitated to protect her.

She should be thankful her godfather knew a warrior of such quality, that Stephan was a man she could respect and more.

The ship cut through another huge wave.

Her husband's gaze met hers with a fierce warning. "Dinna let loose of this railing, understand?"

On a hard swallow, she nodded.

Stephan rejoined his men and began calling out orders. As one, he, Aiden, Rónán, and several other knights pushed on the rudder.

The ship groaned, cut to the right.

A large scraping ripped through the storm-fed air.

The galley lunged forward.

The men cheered.

"Ready for a hard turn to port," Stephan called, then waved to the man near the ladder. "Warn all below deck to prepare for impact."

"Aye." The knight slid down the ladder shouting for everyone to brace themselves.

Terrified as the ship dove into the next trough, Katherine barely caught her breath before they were again thrown up.

From below, oars dipped into the water, pulled back in unison.

The horizon bobbed into view, the shore a blur of spray, sand, and rocks.

"Turn hard to port, now!" Ronan's voice boomed above the scream of wind.

Men's faces taut with determination, they pushed.

Water slammed onto the deck, slid over the side as the vessel angled down into the next trough.

Wood grated against sand. The ship shuddered, jolted to the left.

The next wave threw the craft sideways.

Through the slash of rain, Stephan met her gaze. "Hold tight!"

Heart pounding, she nodded, the salty spray whipping her face. "What are you going to do?"

"Help the men lower the sails before the vessel is cast onto the rocks." Rain-filled wind slashed Stephan as he fought his way to help several men working on the mast. In moments they'd lowered the sails. Another wave caught the ship, but with the oarsmen working in unison with the incoming wave, the craft surged forward and wedged in the sand.

His body angled against the wind, Stephan used the rail to make his way back. "How do you fare?"

Shaken. Terrified. "I-I am fine."

Another wave battered the galley. The ship rolled several degrees.

Katherine started to slide.

With a curse, Stephan wrapped his arm around her waist, pulling her snug.

Body trembling, she glanced up, the weave of danger heightening her senses, as did her awareness of him. "I thank you," she said, her words unsteady. "I would like to think I would have caught myself."

Mouth grim, his eyes held hers. "I willna take any chances."

The steel in his voice moved her. Regardless of what he wished, of his earlier words meant to push her away, he cared.

A large wave struck the hull. The vessel scraped farther up the beach.

His hold tightened. "God's blade!"

Heart pounding, she scanned the swath of rain-pounded sand and rocks, the craft parallel with the shore. "What is wrong?"

"Look at how far the waves are rolling up the shore."

Confused, she scanned the coast. "The breakers are reaching the base of the trees."

"Which tells me 'tis high tide."

Worry edged through her. "Is that bad?"

"Aye. Had we run aground during low tide, once we completed repairs, the incoming flow would have aided us in moving to open water. If the ship is too high on the sand, even with other vessels helping to drag us seaward, there is a risk that we canna wedge ourselves free." He grimaced. "If the storm continues much longer and we sustain further damage, a point that may be irrelevant."

"What if the destruction is nae reparable?" she asked, voicing her worst fear.

Eyes hard, Stephan gazed toward open water, where the remainder of the galleys battled the storm's fury. "Once we transfer the cargo, we will have to abandon the ship until we can return."

"What if while we are away, another storm pulls the ship out to sea, or another crew commandeers it?"

Mouth tight, he shrugged. "'Tis a risk we have to take."

"I am sorry."

"Lass, you have done naught to be sorry about."

"Have I nae?" she said, her voice rough with frustration. "'Tis because of me that we sail to Avalon Castle."

Hazel eyes glinted with anger. "We sail because of the English bastard's greed. Nae you. The Sassenach will rue the day they dared take what isna theirs."

His use of the Scottish name for the English matched her anger toward them. He was right. The English had tossed her into this nightmare, from which, since her escape, she doubted she would ever recover.

Until she'd met Stephan.

Since that fateful day, her husband had never promised anything he hadna achieved. Though she hadna seen him in battle, with his skill shown during sword practice, his confidence when making decisions and giving orders without hesitation, she was convinced he and his knights were warriors to be feared.

As important, now she didna feel so alone. Though he would deny the bond, Katherine believed they'd established a friendship.

Another wave crashed into the side.

Water thundered up, shattered in large drops around them, swept across the deck with a loud whoosh.

His hold on her remained firm.

Comforted in her husband's arms, Katherine leaned against him. That Stephan had erased her fears of being held by a man left her stunned. Because of his kindness and compassion, he'd allowed her to lower her shield of distrust.

Another large wave struck the hull.

"We must disembark. We will use the rope ladder. When you reach the bottom, the water will be rough but shallow." Stephan wrapped his fingers around hers and led her toward the bow.

Without hesitation, touched by a sense of destiny, Katherine followed.

Chapter Eleven

Streaks of red filled the cloud-scarred sky as the sun lingered on the edge of the horizon. The waves gliding up the beach were at odds with the towering swells that had ravaged the land hours before.

Flutters of wind caressing her face, Katherine studied the galley. Lodged in the sand at an awkward tilt, with low tide upon them, most of the hull stood exposed. The beating the ship had taken as they'd worked their way shoreward had destroyed the storm-weakened boards. The carnage of broken planks lay spewed along the shoreline.

Weariness lining Stephan's face, he sloshed through the incoming wave toward her.

The hours he and his men had worked to secure the ship to prevent the rough seas from tossing it against the outcrop of rocks had left them exhausted. "Can the ship be repaired?"

He shot the vessel a look of disgust and shook his head. "The damage is far worse than I expected. We were fortunate to have made it ashore."

Broken boards bobbed in the surf with innocent abandon, each wave shoving them farther down the coast.

She frowned. "What are we going to do?"

"After sunset my men and I will begin moving our cargo to the other vessels."

A wave rolled past the time-worn rocks poking from the sand along the shore. "And our ship?"

"Once we seize Avalon, I will return with several men to make the necessary repairs, then sail her home."

His plans made sense, but nae the timeliness of the transfer of cargo. Lengthening shadows encased the men as they rowed in from the four other ships anchored offshore, their hulls rocking against the smooth roll of the swells. "'Twill be safer to move the goods before dark."

His expression grew unreadable. "The cargo's transfer will be done this night."

"Why? And before you dinna answer," she pressed, tired of his continual evasion of her questions, the mystery that seemed to surround him and his crew at every turn, "as lady of Avalon Castle, 'tis my place to know."

A wry smile touched his lips, faded as fast. "I have nae yet decided your place."

The donkey's arse! "Though I was coerced into this marriage, Avalon Castle is *my* home. You bear the title of Earl of Dunsmore through a king's grant, nae blood." At his narrowing eyes, she stepped forward. "Nor," she continued, her words crisp, "have you answered my question."

Silence.

"Is your cargo so precious that 'tis necessary to keep the contents secret from your wife?" His hesitation prodded her curiosity. Why was he so determined to shield her from what they carried? It wasna as if the hulls were packed with gold.

Unease trickled through her. Had she stumbled upon the truth? Were he and his men involved with notorious dealings? "Have you and your men stolen something?"

He stared at her as if a rock had dropped on her head, leaving her senseless. "What?"

"The reason you avoid explaining what is in the crates. Are the goods stolen from the English?"

"Nay."

"But 'tis of great importance?" she pressed.

Mouth taut, Stephan crossed his arms over his chest. "I would think a lass would have more to ponder than wooden crates."

If 'twas nae stolen, what cargo could warrant such secrecy? "Does King Robert know what you transport?"

Stephan nodded.

The tension in her shoulders relaxed. If her godfather knew, then whatever they carried must play a part in the reuniting of Scotland. But however logical, she sensed she'd missed an integral detail. Having to pry out the few snippets of information she'd garnered, she doubted Stephan would explain further.

Neither would she be kept away. "I will remain ashore until all of the goods are transferred."

A muscle worked in his jaw. "'Tis safest if you are rowed to one of the ships before sunset. I will join you there once we are through."

"Safest?" Anxiety prickling her skin, she scoured the thick stand of trees bordering the coast. "Throughout the day you and your men have searched the area several times. This late, I would think anyone about would have made camp for the night."

Stephan shrugged, thankful Katherine's questions had moved away from the cargo. Though wed, their union hardly allowed him to share Templar secrets. "Edward of Caernarfon has returned to England, but many of his troops remain. Though nae continuing to push north, until his knights withdraw from Scotland, we must remain on guard."

The slosh of steps sounded through the shallow water.

Stephan glanced up.

Droplets rolled off Thomas's boots as he strode through the frothy tips of the oncoming wave. Paces away, he halted, nodded to Katherine, and then Stephan. "Once the sun has set, the men will be ready to begin."

"Excellent. Lady Katherine needs to be taken to Colban's ship." He made a slow sweep of the nearby forest. The growing shadows made an excellent place for anyone to hide. "Before nightfall, I will search the area to ensure we have nay unwanted visitors."

"I will send Cailin with you," Thomas said.

Stephan nodded. "I—"

A rustle of leaves sounded from the woods to their left.

God's blade! Stephan shoved Katherine behind him. The slide of steel against leather sounded as he and Thomas withdrew their swords. "Step forward and show yourself!"

At his demand, the Templars working nearby ran over, unsheathing their own weapons.

A muttered curse sounded from the dense foliage, then an elderly man stepped from it. His wizened face cast in suspicion, the stranger walked toward them. At the rim where grass gave way to sand, he halted.

Though the man's dagger remained sheathed, Stephan refused to lower his guard. He'd witnessed similar strategies: a lone man sent out while warriors remained hidden in the surrounding trees and waited until their foes secured their weapons. "State your name and loyalty."

The elder glanced toward the ship. Surprise flickered in his eyes; then his shrewd gaze shifted to Stephan. "Feradac MacLairish," his deep voice rumbled. "My home is Scotland, and my fealty is to our new king, Robert Bruce. And what of yours?"

"I support King Robert as well," Stephan replied. He nodded toward the beached ship. "During last night's storm our galley was run against the rocks. We beached her aground before she sank. What brings you here?"

Aged eyes again glanced toward the anchored vessels. "'Tis fine ships that sail with you."

Stephan stilled. Upon departing La Rochelle, they'd removed their Templar flags and any other indicators of their being of the Brotherhood. There was naught in sight to reveal their identity. "You havena answered my question."

"I havena." The gruff look on the man's face faded to a weary smile. "I fish these waters and was searching for my small boat, which broke free last night. You have nae seen it, have you?"

Stephan lowered his blade a degree. A fisherman would notice the fine craftsmanship of the vessels. And he would be familiar with the local currents, tides, and mayhap the waters surrounding Avalon Castle. "I have seen naught. Where do you live? If we see your boat, we will return it to you."

The elder gestured to the north. "A village up the shore. 'Tis growing too dark to continue my search and I was about to head back when I heard the sound of men." He grimaced at the large puncture in the side of their ship, stranded on the sand. "A nasty piece of luck."

"Indeed." Stephan sheathed his blade; the muffled slide of steel on leather echoed behind him as his men followed suit. "I am Stephan MacQuistan." He took Katherine's hand, drawing her from behind him to his side. "This is—"

The man's eyes widened with shock, and then a smile touched his lips. "Lady Katherine?"

"You know me?" she asked, the surprise in her voice matching Stephan's.

"I almost dinna recognize you, my lady," the man admitted,

a sheepish expression on his face. "Several years have passed since I saw you last. I had traveled to Avalon Castle to speak with your fath . . ." Grief crumbled Feradac's face. "God, I am sorry for your loss. A fine, kind man was your father. As I do, my clan still grieves. 'Twas a black day indeed, and the basta . . ." He paused, clearing his throat. " 'Twas a murderous act by the English." Shrewd eyes slanted an assessing look at Stephan.

"He is my husband," she stated.

The pride in Katherine's voice caught Stephan off guard, but he kept his expression unchanged, nae wanting the elder to be suspicious of their union, or think it was anything unusual. Neither could he dismiss the warmth her words brought.

Until this moment, though they'd forged a peaceable existence between them, he hadna believed she would ever look upon their marriage as more. With ease he could imagine her eyes darkening as they rested on him, how her mouth would taste, the soft, silken slide of her lips against his skin.

Or had she given her pride-filled words to the elder to suppress any questions? Hesitant at finding a way to handle the possibility of their growing closeness, Stephan smothered his musings. 'Twas safer than the unwanted thoughts inspired by believing she wanted their relationship to strengthen. Pulse unsteady, Stephan focused on Feradac. Loyal to her family and the Bruce, he would be a man they could trust, and one who would give them sound information.

"I didna hear you were betrothed, my lady," the elder said. "When did you marry?"

Red touched her cheeks. "But days ago. My husband's men travel to reclaim my home."

A smug expression settled upon Feradac's face. " 'Tis a fine lesson you will be teaching the blasted English." He shot Stephan a cool look. "But I dinna agree with bringing the lass."

" 'Twas upon my insistence," Katherine stated.

The man eyed Stephan a moment longer, then his expression moved to Katherine. A smile tugged at his lips. "Your father said you were stubborn."

"I am," she agreed, laughter in her voice, "much to my husband's chagrin."

"Nay doubt he will come to appreciate the trait, one you shared with your father." The fisherman nodded to Stephan. "If you need anything, let me know. If I canna help, I will pass word to those in the village. From herbs to swords, we will lift our arms with you."

"I thank you for your offer," Stephan replied, humbled by the man's generosity.

Movement seaward had him glancing back. Against the darkening sky, his men were rowing several boats shoreward. Though Feradac's allegiance lay with her father's clan, neither would he risk exposing to him that he and his men were Templars, or raise interest in their cargo. October thirteenth, the day King Philip would denounce the brotherhood as outlaws, would come soon enough. "If you would share the local currents, tides, and waterways surrounding Avalon Castle, 'twould greatly aid us in planning our attack."

Wrinkled eyes filled with pride. " 'Twould be an honor. I am sure other fishermen in the village will be anxious to provide what they have learned while fishing in Avalon's waters as well." He glanced skyward. " 'Tis growing late. I would be remiss if I didna invite you and Lady Katherine to my humble abode while your men finish up here."

Along with the ship's damage, several crates had broken open within the hull. With Feradac's offer, in addition to removing the risk of Katherine seeing any of the Templar treasure, the tides and other information the fishermen in the village would give was a valuable asset to their quest. He met the elder's gaze. "We thank you for your offer, and we accept."

A smile touched his weathered face.

Stephan glanced at Thomas. "Katherine and I should return by midmorning."

His friend nodded.

"Follow me." The elder headed down the shoreline, the sunlight streaming through the fading wisps of purple and black.

As they followed several paces behind the fisherman, Katherine met her husband's gaze. "I thought you wanted to leave at first light?"

"Feradac and the villagers' knowledge of the local waterways will save us much needed time," he said, his words quiet. "And they can share insight on how best to approach the secret entry."

Her face paled. "You canna tell him about the hidden passage."

Stephan glanced forward to ensure the elder continued and then halted. "I would never do anything so foolish. You question me at every turn, as if I am a smith more familiar with crafting weapons than wielding them. I am a man seasoned in war. Dinna question my tactics further."

" 'Tis worry that causes my foolish questions."

He was far from appeased, but 'twas a start. "Never would I do anything to endanger you."

Somber eyes held his. "I know."

The pride in her voice as she'd told the fisherman of their wedded state stumbled to his mind. Unbidden, warmth touched him.

The last rays of the sun embraced her face like a shimmering caress as her blue eyes lowered to his mouth.

Desire rippled through him. Throat dry, Stephan cupped her chin. "Kath-"

" 'Twill be night soon," the elder called back. "Stay close. Around the bend the shore becomes rocky. If you dinna know the way, 'tis dangerous."

A rueful smile touched Stephan's lips and he brushed an errant strand from her cheek. "However gently said, 'twould seem we have been chastised."

Mirth twinkled in her eyes. "Indeed, my husband, 'twould seems we have."

The soft richness of her voice lured his gaze to her mouth and his smile faltered. God's blade, he wanted to kiss her! Though the Grand Master had instructed the Knights Templar to marry, never had Stephan believed he would find a woman who would make him want her.

But against all reason, and despite the way she challenged him with senseless disregard, Katherine had changed everything.

Regardless of how she made him feel, his desire was a yearning simple enough to control.

Confident he had the matter well in hand, he tugged her with him as he headed toward the waiting fisherman.

With night having long since fallen, Katherine glanced around as she settled next to Stephan, thankful to be inside the fisherman's home. Besides the table and a bench seat on either side, a sprinkle of pots and pans, and two chests topped with folded blankets, hanging herbs completed the furnishings. A loft held the pallets for sleeping.

"Here you are," Feradac's wife said as she placed a bowl of stew before each of them

"I thank you, Mary. This smells wonderful." Katherine dipped her spoon into the simple fare, the fire blazing in the hearth along with the sincerity and warmth of Feradac and his family calming her nerves further. She hadna felt so relaxed since she'd escaped the English.

Images of her family flickered through her mind as she took a bite. Chest tightening, Katherine forced herself to swallow. Would there ever come a time when she could move past her grief?

"Another drink, my lady?" Feradac's wife offered.

Steadying herself, Katherine set her bowl aside. "I thank you, but I am nae as hungry as I believed."

A frown deepened Mary's brow. Sadness touched the woman's gaze, and then understanding. With a nod, she turned and joined in with the men's conversation.

Aching inside, needing a moment alone to compose herself, Katherine pushed away from the table.

Stephan stood, his gaze shrewd. "Are you ill?"

"I need some fresh air," she replied, forcing her voice to remain light.

"Though we have nay seen any sign of the English about," Feradac said, " 'tis nae safe for a lass to go about unaccompanied."

"She willna be," Stephan said. "I shall escort her."

Frustrated, wanting to be by herself, she shook her head. " 'Tis unnecessary."

"It is too dangerous to be alone. Besides," her husband continued, "I would like to stretch my legs as well."

She hesitated, confused by the unresolved need he stirred within her. 'Twas unfair to weigh the feelings he inspired against the brigand who'd assaulted her, a man who didna deserve to breathe. Stephan was a good man, a leader she respected.

The gentle way he'd held her onboard the ship came to mind. In his arms she'd felt secure, wanted. Shame washed through her. Mayhap her husband's decision to escort her outside was for the reason he'd stated. The desire she had seen in his eyes earlier might have been only her imagination.

Mary have mercy, look at her mulling over being alone with a man she was attracted to. And a kiss, if that was what he wished, was far from wanting her in his bed.

Stephan opened the door, gestured for her go first.

"Take this wrap, my lady." Mary hurried over to a length of wool hanging from a nearby peg. " 'Twill keep away the chill."

" 'Tis kind of you," she said as the woman helped her don the woven cloth. With a confidence she didna feel, Katherine stepped into the night.

Stephan followed, closing the door in their wake.

Alone.

On edge, she walked toward the water, the gurgle of waves surging ashore lending a softness to the night.

"The skies are clear," her husband said, keeping a leisurely pace at her side.

A smile touched her lips as she gazed at the stars embracing the waxing moon. "Aye, preferable to the overcast skies of the storm."

" 'Tis." Pebbles crunched beneath his boots as he walked. "The information Feradac and his clansmen shared will be of immense help in our planning for the attack."

"Indeed." Upon their arrival at the fishing village, while the men had talked, she'd sat beside Stephan and listened. With the insight the clansmen had shared about the currents, the way the water flowed and shifted with the tides, as well as the places to avoid when they neared Avalon's shore, they should reach the secret entrance with little risk.

Air rich with the scent of the sea filled each breath as she meandered along the time-worn rocks to the edge of the shore. At the rim of smoothed stone Katherine paused, noting the small islands on the horizon and, a touch farther, the distant shoreline.

The moon hung low in the sky, reflected across the water in a silvery wash. 'Twas as if all within its path was touched by magic. Over the years, she'd found solace in such a night, a time when the world grew still, a moment to believe in dreams. Now, with her family torn from her and her struggle to accept the loss, those peaceful times, like her innocence, were lost.

Pebbles crunched as Stephan paused at her side.

The rumble of waves filled the silence.

"Will having lost one ship cause problems for the attack?"

"Nay. Our initial assault will be by land. But we didna come to speak of war."

At his serious tone, she glanced up. Secluded from prying eyes and within the cast of the moonlight, she met his all-too-seeing gaze. "What upset you inside the hut?"

She remained silent.

"Did you think I wouldna notice?"

Foolishly, she had. Katherine scanned the water, finding a part of her wished to share the reason for her grief. It was reckless to consider such, but the night seemed to call for truth. "Listening to Feradac and Mary telling their tales of the past reminded me of times with my own family. 'Twas why I . . ." Against the grief, she forced herself to go on. "Why I needed to be alone."

Far away, the howl of a wolf echoed into the night. Unsure of his reaction, she glanced over. Within the sheen of light, his eyes watched her with a mixture of sadness and grief.

"You are a woman of great bravery."

At his praise, the flutters of need he ignited in her were foreign and terrifying. "When I was to wed a knight loyal to our king," she said before she didna dare, "I was furious, believing you saw my father's title and castle as a prize to be won."

"And now?"

"Though King Robert chose you for your skills of war and to be my protector, I believe his decision took into account your compassion as well."

A frown tightened his mouth. "I live by my sword. Dinna paint me as a man with a tender heart; 'twill lead you to naught but disappointment."

"Will it?" she asked, intrigued that he'd portray himself as a man of coldness when moments before he'd been naught but gentle. Or, to his warrior's mind, had his tenderness been a necessary choice in dealing with a difficult situation? And what of earlier this day, when she'd caught him looking at her with interest? Did he find her appealing, or was that thought nurtured only in her mind? A part of her hesitated to ask, but she needed to know. "Though I never would have considered it possible," she said, "I believe my godfather understood what I needed more than I."

"And what was that?" he asked, his voice quiet.

"A man strong enough to listen, one with a kind heart to care, and one who wouldna judge me by my past."

" 'Tis naught to judge. Though nae a warrior, you are trustworthy, of strong intellect, and know how to handle a sword." He eyed her. "I couldna tolerate a weak-willed lass given to the vapors."

She laughed, nae wanting to be charmed by his gruff laud. "I am too stubborn for such a weakness."

"You are."

"Which pleases you immensely?"

Beneath the moon's glow, his gaze locked on hers, and the wisp of humor faded.

The moment shifted, grew intense, the slide of light and shadows embracing them like a wish.

Face taut, Stephan's breathing grew unsteady as he watched her, and the need within her built.

On a soft hiss, his hand gently lifted the curve of her jaw, his eyes holding hers. "Know this: you are nae what I want."

Heart pounding, she held his gaze, refusing to back down from this insanity. "I said my guardian was wise, nae that I wanted you," she said. "With your overbearing, arrogant manner, I would rather kiss a boar."

"I am confident, nae overbearing."

She scoffed. "If confidence was stone, you could build a fortress."

Despite his fierce frown, a smile flickered on his mouth. "You are naught but trouble."

Blast it, she could have dealt with his anger, a curse, his raging like a madman at the moon, but his humor weakened her every defense. "I am, at that, one I doubt you will ever be able to handle."

"A challenge?"

"The truth. Though with your bravado," she pushed, enjoying throwing him off balance, doubtful many dared to try, "being a warrior who has overcome numerous challenges, faced death many times over, I canna see you shaken by anything, much less a mere woman whose strength lies in the running of a castle."

Laughter crinkled at the corners of his eyes, along with admiration. He skimmed his thumb across the curve of her jaw, his eyes darkening to an awareness that had her blood sizzling. "Had I a brain in my head, I would toss you in the sea, swear you drowned of your own foolishness, and be done with you."

Unbidden, she laughed.

"Bedamned your making me want you!" His eyes scorching, he hauled her against him, covered her mouth with his own.

Chapter Twelve

Cool night air swirled around them as Katherine trembled from the intensity of Stephan's kiss.

With an oath, her husband released her, his breath coming fast, his eyes hot. "Bedamned!" He stepped back.

Stunned to find herself calm, she realized the truth. She'd wanted his kiss, driven him to the point of giving in to his need. Pleasure swept over her that she had such power, but a kiss wasna making love.

More important, if he asked, *could* she give him intimacy? Had she opened a door she didna wish to enter?

The spill of waves echoed in the potent silence.

She started to step toward him.

"Stay, do you hear me?"

"What?"

"Dinna move." Stephan stalked down the shoreline, kicked a rock, whirled, stared at her for a long moment, and then trudged back. "Do you know what you have done?"

Mary have mercy, her husband was angry because he wanted her. A smile threatened to surface; she suppressed the urge. Of all the reactions possible, his outrage at his own desire for her wasna one she'd considered. And should have. He was a knight, believed his life given to war, and able to conform his emotions as every part of his life to his own needs.

Except with her.

Giddy at the thought, she angled her chin. "I did naught; 'twas you that kissed me."

His eye narrowed in silent warning.

Far from intimidated, Katherine stepped closer, thrilled when his entire body tensed. "And a fine kiss it was."

" 'Twas harsh, unforgivable," he rasped, "despicable treatment of a man's wife."

"Are you saying you would like to make amends?" she asked innocently.

"I . . ."

Emboldened, she placed her hands on his shoulders. "I think you should try again."

Frustration, anger, and need racing through his eyes, he pulled her against him, his mouth a breath above hers. "God help me." With infinite tenderness, he brushed his mouth over hers, skimmed his lips along her jaw, the soft curve of her neck.

With his every touch, taste, a slow ache grew within her. *Need.* A feeling she had never believed she could experience, until Stephan. Humbled that he would be the man who could move her beyond her fears, Katherine laced her fingers behind his neck, his tongue moving across her flesh in a wondrous slide.

"Kiss me, Stephan," she whispered. "I canna wait any longer."

Shimmers of moonlight whispered over his face as his eyes locked on hers. His nostrils flared. "Say you want me."

Pulse racing, the anticipation driving her mad, she lifted her face closer. "I want you."

On a groan, his mouth took hers, gentle but demanding.

Captured by the whip of passion, trembling as his lips roamed hers, she sank into the kiss. At his taste, the heat of man and need, desire swirled within her at a restless pace until all thought blurred.

On a growl, he angled her head, took the kiss deeper.

Lost to sensation, needing more, she pressed her body flush against his, met his every kiss and demanded more.

"I want you," Stephan rasped as he backed her against a nearby boulder while his lips continued to destroy her will. His body trembling, he pressed intimately against her.

Memories of the attack screamed in her mind. The crude laughter. The tearing of cloth as the assailant had ripped her dress. Panicking, Katherine shoved. "Stop! Let me go!"

Eyes wide with confusion, he released her. "Wh-what is wrong?"

Shame filled Katherine as she gasped for air. Wanting Stephan's kiss, she'd believed herself strong enough to move past her fears. "I am sorry."

"I shouldna have touched you."

Mary have mercy, he'd done naught except what she'd asked, had yearned for. "I . . ."

" 'Tis late and we must rest," he said, his voice remote. "There is much to do on the morrow."

'Twas their first kiss, a moment to remember. But she'd panicked and transformed what should have been special into a disaster. None of this was his fault.

Emotion swamping her, Katherine struggled for calm, fighting the urge to flee, the hurt tormenting her mind. He was confused; how could he nae be? He needed to understand. " 'Tis nae you."

Shadows and moonlight shimmered across Katherine's face as she stared at him, but Stephan caught the distress in her eyes, an anguish that tore him apart. All because he'd bloody kissed her.

Kissed her?

A pale term for how he'd touched her. He'd meant for the kiss to be uncomplicated. Confident one taste of her would extinguish his feelings for her—feelings that grew stronger with each passing day—he'd given in to need.

But as the softness of her lips pressed against his, the straightforward task had crumbled beneath need, and he'd taken with mindless disregard.

Blast it! If Katherine despised him for treating her with such boldness, 'twas her right. He was a Knight Templar, nae a man who could sate his desires with a woman, regardless if she was his wife. Though the Brotherhood had been dissolved, he and his men remained loyal to their sworn oath.

Foolish, even for a moment, to think otherwise, more so to allow himself to weaken around her. However well intended, steps toward darkness didna offer a path back.

He scowled at the moon's silvery rays, the shimmers in league with the quiet rush of waves to craft a seductive setting. With his desire for his wife building, he'd allowed himself to be tempted.

"Stephan," Katherine whispered, anxiety sliding through her voice.

He smothered his yearnings beneath duty. "We must return. As

Feradac said, 'tis dangerous to linger." Neither would he remain when he still wanted her.

She stepped before him. "I wanted your kiss."

"As your husband, I am your protector," he stated, furious that regardless of what he willed, his body ached for her. Too easily he could envision laying her upon the water-slicked sand, her body naked against his own.

"Aye," she replied, her words firm, "but a marriage is more than defending one's family."

In her world perhaps. He lived by a rigid set of rules.

Eyes wide with worry and frustration watched him, but torn by his own emotions and wanting her too much, he refused to linger on the reason. "I should nae have kissed you. Nor will we speak of this further."

"You are nae to blame," she rushed out. " 'Tis I. I am nae a woman who can come to your bed. Please dinna despise me."

Confused by her words, he frowned. "I could never despise you."

Relief swept her face but worry remained. "I am a difficult woman to live with."

"An understatement," he replied, his words rough.

Embraced by the soft whispers of wind, her eyes softened. "Mayhap, but I dinna think you would find interest in a lass with a milder nature. Nor do I swoon."

Damning her ability to break down his shields, he glared at her, irritated at how the shimmers of moonlight caressed her face, lingered on her mouth. On a muttered curse, he caught her hand, led her up the rocky incline.

"Where are we going?"

"Back to the hut," he said between clenched teeth, where they should have blasted remained. A valuable lesson. Though he must produce a son to bear the title of the Earl of Dunsmore, it wouldna be this night. In a year, two, with several battles behind him, mayhap the way they looked upon the other would change.

Unless she learned her father had murdered his family. The upheaval of this night would be a pittance to what the truth would do.

Several days later, flickers of torchlight scraped the damp walls as Stephan followed Katherine through the catacombs, the air rich with the tang of the sea. Since their return from the fisherman's village and having boarded another ship, shaken by all she had made him feel, he'd keep his distance.

Once he'd regained control of his unwanted desire for her, however much he hesitated to allow himself and Katherine to grow closer, Thomas was right: 'Twas wise to nurture their friendship. When he sailed to battle, he would leave the castle in the hands of a capable woman he could trust.

The demands of discussing the currents and tides surrounding Avalon with his men along with preparing for the attack had usurped most of his time.

When he'd found her at the bow the night before, staring at the sky and looking so lost and forlorn, he'd gone to her, an act of duty, nay more. A poor husband he would be to abandon her when she struggled against the loss of her family.

Nae that she'd wanted him near. His wife's icy request to leave when he came near ran though his mind. God's blade, how had a simple kiss caused such disarray?

Simple?

He grimaced. There was naught simple about the kiss or the lass. The way she looked at him—part waif, part siren—twisted him in two. How was a man to be logical when with each passing moment he wanted her more?

However much he wished otherwise, he yearned for her, in his arms, in his bed, in his life. Stephan swallowed hard as he accepted a fate he'd rather deny.

He wanted his wife.

An acknowledgment that changed naught. Too much lay between them for a real marriage to exist.

King Robert had given him the choice to tell Katherine of her father's horrendous act. If he told her, the fragile bond between them would be destroyed. With her caring nature, how could he nae believe she wouldna be horrified by the truth, believe that he could never accept her in his life, much less fall in love with her?

Love?

With a curse, Stephan discarded the thought. At most their union would grow into a strong friendship. And even if the possibility existed, he refused to allow their relationship to become more.

Memories assailed him of Katherine's father's attack on Avalon. Of how at seven summers, terrified as troops stormed the castle,

Stephan had hidden, nae lifted a blade to try to save his family. Instead, with the blood of those he loved staining the ground, he'd waited until late in the night and slipped away.

A coward.

A man undeserving of love.

A shameful act, one, if King Robert had known of it, would have severed any chance of Stephan regaining his legacy.

Neither would seizing Avalon erase his wife's distress. However much Katherine wished it, never could she reclaim her former life or find in him a husband who could give her the comfort she desired.

Torchlight flickered on the walls of the tunnel. "How much farther?" Stephan asked, the soft pad of his men's steps echoing behind him.

" 'Tis but a short way," Katherine replied.

Ahead, the waver of torchlight outlined a large boulder, ending the tunnel.

She halted. "We are here."

With a frown, Stephan scoured the indentations where the massive rock pressed against others. "I dinna see an entry."

Pride gleaming in her eyes, she nodded toward the boulder. " 'Tis but a shell. The inside has been carved away to allow the stone to move with ease. In the event anyone ever discovered the secret entrance to the tunnel, my father had it crafted to provide another layer of protection."

Disquiet trickled through him. The hewn rock was a façade the Templars used. More disturbing, the talent necessary to carve rock with such precision prohibited the practice by most stonemasons. "Wise."

"My father was that and so much more. A man respected by many." She crossed to several smaller stones on the right. At the rough depression, she slid her fingers until they caught, then removed the flat rock and set it on the ground.

An iron ring lay beneath.

Wrapping her fingers around the crafted metal, Katherine pulled.

Steel grated against stone.

With ease, she withdrew the loop connected to a long rod.

Dull clacks like small stones echoed from within, a thud as each rock settled. The faint gurgle of water. With a soft scrape, the large stone swung inward.

Stunned by the complexity of the entry, the ramifications of what this intricate design meant, Stephan glanced toward Thomas.

His friend's brow furrowed. " 'Tis clever," he said, his voice dry.

"Aye," Stephan agreed. 'Twas more than clever, but a complex device only a limited number of stonemasons could create—all of them Knights Templar.

And what of the catacombs woven within the surrounding rock? He'd owed their existence to keeping food stores and other goods for the castle, supplies that would defray the need to travel to restock essential goods often. Now, he suspected otherwise.

Was it chance Robert Bruce, a Templar knight, had sent him and his men to Avalon Castle? Or had this stronghold been created as a precaution in case a dire situation ever prompted an evacuation of the Templars from France? If the Brotherhood had dug these tunnels, it explained why King Robert would have sent the Templar ships here.

A slow pounding began in his head. It couldna be. If Avalon was a Templar refuge, then Katherine's father had been a supporter of the Brotherhood. However much Stephan wished otherwise, many nobles, for their own reasons, backed the Order.

Appalled to consider that the man he loathed with his every breath might well be a savior of their cause, Stephan's thoughts shifted to the Grand Master. Nay doubt Jacques de Molay had known of the catacomb's existence. Regardless of how much Stephan didna like Katherine's father's involvement, the rationale made sense, supporting the reason why the Grand Master had sent him and his men to Scotland and, more specifically, to King Robert.

Outrage poured through him. For years he'd served Jacques de Molay. If true, why hadna the Grand Master informed him of these important facts before he'd sailed?

As quickly, Stephan's frustration fled. Busy making preparations for the entire Templar fleet to slip from the port of La Rochelle prior to the eve of Friday the thirteenth, the Grand Master didna have time to explain every detail of his plans.

God's blade, how many other castles existed with a maze of tunnels below built to store Templar goods? With the imminent arrest of the Brotherhood, nay doubt Jacques de Molay had sent any remaining documentation of Templar strongholds with the other knights who had fled, or tossed them into the flames. God forbid if any of the Brotherhood's records fell into King Philip's hands.

Shaken at the dire possibility, Stephan glanced toward his wife, despising the question but needing to ask it. "Lady Katherine, did your father ever fight in a Crusade?"

She frowned. "Why do you ask?"

"Did he?" Stephan repeated, damning his impatience.

"Several years ago he sailed to Armenia, something to do with La Roche-Guillaume. I was never told more."

La Roche-Guillaume, the last Templar stronghold within the holy land. A precarious foothold lost to the Muslims at the time of her father's visit. Stephan shot a knowing glance at Thomas and several other knights within hearing; his men's eyes were dark with questions, ones he wished answered as well. "Are there records of your father's travels?"

"Aye, he kept detailed notes of his every voyage. They are stored in a separate ledger alongside a book with all the family records. Unless," she whispered with dread, "the English have discovered these documents."

God forbid. Stephan's hand trembled as he lifted the torch. The halved and culled stone entry was a fine example of Templar ingenuity. Aside from the reminders of her family's slaughter, neither did it bode well that all indications pointed to her father being a supporter of the Knights Templar. The last thing he wanted was to discover any admirable trait about a man who'd butchered his family.

Irritated, Stephan surveyed the large opening. "I see but the one tunnel. Onboard you said there were three, entries we'd planned to use for a coordinated attack."

"Once inside, a short way ahead this tunnel seems to end. Behind another false wall, the one passage splits into three. Only those who know where they are will find them. The one on the left leads to the walls behind the bedchambers, the middle ends at the dungeon. They are smaller than the main shaft, which will take you to the chapel."

"The chapel?" Stephan asked, finding the destination curious yet appropriate.

"Aye. If ever Avalon came under siege, whoever rang the church bell to sound the alert could slip inside the tunnel to help the others escape. Except," Katherine said, her words unraveling to a whisper, "on the night of the attack."

"What happened?" Stephan asked, nae wanting to unearth memories of her witnessing her parents' deaths. But every bit of information offered insight, facts that could be useful during the upcoming assault.

Her lower lip trembled. "Unbeknownst to my father, a traitor lived within the castle. On the night of the attack, he killed the men on guard. Then he lowered the drawbridge and allowed the English knights entry. Near midnight, the English murdered many of our brave knights while they slept and seized the stronghold with minimal resistance."

Sickened by the man's treachery, by all that Katherine had been forced to endure, Stephan lay his hand atop hers. "Once we seize Avalon, identify the betrayer."

She swallowed hard. "He is dead, killed by the English during the attack."

A fitting punishment. Another worry slid through his mind. "You are confident that the English didna see you escape?"

"Aye. I crept behind the guard outside my door, knocked him on the head, and then left my door ajar before slipping into the tunnel. When the English discovered I was missing, I wanted them to assume I had had help."

Pride touched Stephan. "Impressive."

A blush swept her face. "My actions were those any member of my family would have taken if they had lived."

A rueful smile touched Stephan's lips. Even if the English had suspected there were secret tunnels, without knowledge of the ways the Templars used to disguise hidden doors, they never would have found them.

He glanced toward a nearby knight. "Return to the galley. Inform each captain that we are ready to attack. Warn those remaining onboard to keep a close watch on the surrounding rocks and waterways for any indication of the enemy. Though we searched for signs of English troops during our approach, I willna take any chance that archers are positioned for an ambush."

"Aye," the man replied.

"Once the castle is seized and 'tis safe," Stephan continued, "we will signal with three rings of the bell. If the ship's crew hears five or more, 'tis a warning that our plans have gone awry and they must prepare for our return and a quick escape."

With a nod, the knight headed back.

Stephan faced Katherine. "The catacombs you mentioned to the king: how many are there?"

Within the torchlight, red swept up her cheeks. "I am aware they ex-exist but . . ."

Irritation swept over him as he remembered her earlier ignorance of the local currents. Nay, she had to know. Unless . . . He exhaled a rough sigh. "But nae more?"

Her blush deepened.

Temper slid through him. An important detail she'd kept from Robert Bruce to ensure she sailed to Avalon. With or without a map, he would find all hidden entries beneath the stronghold.

"Then," Stephan said, his voice cool, "lead us to where the tunnel separates."

Dirt crunched beneath Katherine's slippers as she started along the torchlit path.

Stephan followed. The musty odor, owing to the cavern's infrequent use, assured him the Englishmen remained ignorant of these routes.

After a short distance, the passageway began to widen. At the next turn, the tunnel ended.

She opened the entry. Anxiety in her eyes, Katherine gestured to a well-crafted wooden ladder that disappeared into a darkened chute. "At the end is a trapdoor."

Stephan nodded. "Is the hatch locked?"

"Aye," she replied. "From underneath. I barred it when I left, slid a stone to the side beneath into place. Usually 'tis left unsecured, but I refused to take a chance of anyone discovering the tunnel."

His mouth tightened. "Where does the door open in the chapel?"

"Behind a large statue in the back," she replied. " 'Twill allow you to enter unseen. With night upon us, the knights should be abed, their locations within the castle as I explained onboard. The moon being almost full should give us an advantage as we move about."

Large boulders sat on either side of the ladder. With a grimace, Stephan gestured to each. "The hidden entries to the other tunnels?"

She nodded.

"Where are the levers to open them?"

"On the side of each large stone you will notice two smaller rocks, appearing as if set haphazard on the floor. Each bears a small

X with a hook on the top of one of the lines," she explained. "Behind them is a stone slab like the ones I removed before. As with the others, a ring connected to a forged rod lies within. Once withdrawn, the door will open."

"Is there anything more we should know?" Stephan asked. The *X* with a hook was a Templar mark.

Her brow furrowed. "Nay."

Stephan nodded to Cailin. "Take Lady Katherine back to the ship."

Chapter Thirteen

Katherine's eyes narrowed. "I *will* stay and fight to reclaim my home!"

Stephan expected his wife's anger. Once her temper abated, she would see the wisdom of his decision. "You will return to the ship. It has been decided."

"Decided?" she repeated, her voice deadly calm.

"A woman's place isna in battle. You will return with Cailin of your own accord or be carried."

With a look of disgust, she glanced toward her escort.

Cailin remained motionless, his expression unreadable.

Her blue eyes leveled on Stephan. "I trained aboard ship to fight."

"You did." Stephan crossed his arms. "A few days of sparring hardly prepares anyone for the harsh realities of battle."

"I have been taught to wield a blade since my youth."

Stephan remained silent. Her skill with a weapon, though passable, wouldna keep her alive against those who lived by the sword.

"All along, as I trained," she seethed, "you allowed me to believe that when we attacked I would fight."

"Never did I say you would join us. That you crafted in your mind." He paused. "Neither should you forget that your presence onboard was allowed due to your deception to our king."

Guilt flickered in her gaze. "Mayhap, but in my place you would have done the same."

"Dinna toss the blame for your ruse elsewhere. You will go. Neither I nor my men need your presence to distract us. Choose how you will return to the ship."

Fury blazed in her eyes, outrage that, if it could have touched the earth, would have scorched the ground. Katherine stepped back. "I will return to the ship. On my own."

The lass was desperate to exact revenge, the extremes she'd used to return to Avalon proof of it. "Once the battle ends you will be allowed inside the castle."

Katherine strode toward the exit of the tunnel, the crash of waves battering the rocks growing louder ahead. The angry flicker of torchlight along the scarred walls matched her own.

Dinna toss the blame for your ruse elsewhere.

The arrogant, pompous . . .

Was her husband right? Had she shifted her anger at those who'd murdered her family to Stephan, whose goal from the first was to achieve the task given to him by their king? From the unwanted marriage to being forced to take her with him when they'd sailed, his life had been tossed upside down. Like hers.

Still, he didna comprehend the importance of her being part of Avalon's recapture. 'Twas more than a castle lost in war to England. After the Earl of Preswick had seized her home, he'd forced her to witness her family murdered. By his own hand, the English noble had made this her vendetta.

Distant shouts erupted behind them.

Her heart pounding, she stared down the blackened shaft. "They have begun the attack!"

Cailin muttered a curse. " 'Tis too early. There must have been Englishmen in the chapel who saw them as they entered."

Mary have mercy! "They will need every man to fight."

"I was charged with escorting you to the ship, my lady. A task I will accomplish."

"Sir Cailin, go. I am safe in the tunnel."

Beneath the torchlight, red brows wedged into a frown. The knight hesitated, and then he shot her a cool look. "Dinna move."

Katherine remained silent.

Worry clouding his eyes, the warrior lifted the torch, and then bolted toward the clash of blades.

She waited a moment, then another. Katherine started after him. Hesitated. She had a right to join the men. Shoving aside her doubts, she ran back down the tunnel.

Familiar with the passage, guided by the flickers of distant torchlight, she pushed on. A short distance ahead, light from overhead brightened the gloom. She reached the bottom of the ladder leading to the
chapel.

Overhead, the scrape of steel rang out, melded with screams and
rough-hewn curses.

Images of the Englishmen slaughtering her father's knights filled
her mind. Katherine stayed the urge to retch. Furious at her weakness, she placed her foot on the step. Every sword was needed. She
began to climb.

The wing tip of an angel painted on the chapel ceiling came into
view.

She hurried up. Near the top of the ladder, scrapes of steel, grunts
of men, and the slam of metal against wood echoed with ferocious
intent.

Through the opening, a blade swept past. Brutal shadows blackened the images of faith upon the ceiling, depicting the struggle of
life against death playing out within the sanctity of the chapel.

Stephan's warning that her presence would distract him and his
men had Katherine hesitating. Never did she wish to cost any man
his life for her pride.

Pride.

She swallowed hard, the battle above a gruesome backdrop to
the truth. 'Twas more than the English noble's making it her vendetta but pride that had her daring to offer ultimatums to a king, and
pride that had convinced her to marry a stranger. If she were honest, her every action had been driven by her need to avenge her
family's murder.

Reason blurred her mind until it tumbled to the truth. Lost to her
need for vengeance, she'd nae considered the lives that could be lost.

Because of her.

Shaken, she moved down a rung. Her husband's instructions to
keep away from the battle were nae because he didna care but because he did. Humbled, she moved her foot to the next step.

"Stephan, behind you!" Thomas yelled from above.

Pulse racing, she climbed to the top, peered out.

Sword raised, Thomas cursed, bolted from view.

Was Stephan hurt? Terrified for his life, she climbed two steps.

The opening remained empty.

What was she doing? She should return to the ship. Katherine started to go down.

Her husband's pain-filled curse rang out.

A thud.

She had to know if he was alive! Trembling, Katherine climbed to the rim, peered out.

Across the room, Stephan rolled to a halt on the floor. Blood streaming from his shoulder, his face a mask of anger and pain, he pushed to his knees.

Framed by a figure of Mary hanging on the wall behind him, an English knight lunged toward her husband.

Stephan lifted his blade, fended off the blow. He struggled to his feet. Swayed.

Terrified for his life, Katherine scanned the chapel. Every one of his knights fought off attackers, some battling two men or more. Without help, weakened from his loss of blood, Stephan would die!

Lost to every thought but saving him, ensuring she kept out of sight, Katherine crawled behind the statue and then stood. Trembling, she withdrew her sword.

Another man charged Stephan from his left.

Her husband whirled, used his blade to shove the man back.

The Englishman to his right swung.

A line of blood cut across Stephan's side. He stumbled back, steadied himself. Barely.

The knight charged.

Her husband drove his sword into the attacker, plunged his dagger in the other man.

With a shout, another Englishman stepped over his dead comrades, attacked.

Steel screamed as Stephan deflected his blade, swung his sword in a tight circle, jerked free, and drove his weapon into the man's heart.

Shock and pain etched the Englishman's face.

Muscles bunched, Stephan withdrew his sword, whirled to meet the next aggressor.

Two men charged.

* * *

Ignoring the pain, the stickiness at his side, Stephan ducked, angled his sword into the first knight, shifted, plunged his weapon into the chest of another.

"We are outnumbered more than ten to one," Thomas called as he fought paces away. "We canna allow the knights outside to break through the door."

"Aye. The bastard was standing on the corner of the hatch as I raised it," Stephan spat. "Before I could kill him, he alerted the others."

"Aye, 'tis bloody luck Rónán was able to bar the chapel door," Thomas said.

Stephan engaged the next attacker. Swords screamed as they met. He twisted his weapon, locked his hilt with the assailant. As the man fought to break his hold, Stephan slid his dagger across the knight's throat.

Face crumpled with pain, the Englishman collapsed.

Another boom sounded on the thick hewn door.

Stephan cursed at the cracks in the center of the sturdy wood; with each blow a gap large enough for a man to slip inside had formed. An entry the English were taking advantage of.

A solid thud.

Wood splintered from the center, several shards as large as an ax.

God's blade. Another hit, two, and the entire door would give way. Stephen damned the decision to withdraw, that their element of surprise had been usurped. As he turned toward the next attacker, he caught the flash of gold hair from near the statue.

Katherine!

God's blade, didna the lass realize the danger she'd placed herself in? "Surround Lady Katherine!" Stephan roared as he drove his sword into an oncoming Englishman and bolted toward her.

Two English knights rushed in her direction.

Eyes fierce, she raised her blade, deflected the first attack, shifted to meet the other.

Malice flickered in the Englishman's eyes. "The Earl of Preswick will be pleased by your return, my lady."

"Go to Hades!" She angled her blade toward his heart.

The knight blocked her swing.

Alarm paled her face as she withdrew her weapon, prepared for another strike.

Another Englishman caught her from behind.

Stephan drove his dagger into the man's chest, threw him aside.

Thomas finished his man off, whirled toward the next aggressor.

Stephan glared at Katherine while his knights formed a tight circle around them. The clash of steel rang out as they battled. "You will return to the tunnel now!"

Her eyes wide with fear, she shook her head. "I was going to return to the ship, but you were hurt. Nay one was there and I—"

Shouts echoed around them.

Englishmen charged.

The sting of steel bit into his left shoulder. Furious he hadna withdrawn the men in time, Stephan ignored the stream of blood, shoved his sword into the man.

Blades hissed as quickly as curses as his men backed up, Katherine safe within their circle.

A crash sounded at the entry.

Dread crawling through him, Stephan glanced over.

Shards of wood dangled where the large door had hung. English knights stormed inside.

"Griogair," Stephan yelled through the scream of blades, "ring the bell five times!"

A tall, black-haired knight grabbed a nearby rope, pulled.

Deep notes resounded through the chapel.

At the emergency signal they'd discussed onboard ship, panic rolled through Katherine. "Stephan wants the men to withdraw?"

"We are outnumbered at least twenty to one," Thomas replied, his every word harsh as he caught her shoulder, hauled her toward the tunnel. "We must return to the galley, regroup, and plan another strategy."

With a nod, she followed. At her next step, she glanced back.

Stephan had braced himself against the wall and was battling four knights, the distance between him and any of his men widening to at least fifteen paces.

The Templar cast the rope to the bell aside and moved to help shield her, the long, deep rings resonating within the chapel like an ill omen.

With each step closer to the tunnel, armed knights continued to pour into the sanctuary, widening the gap between Stephan and any hope of his reaching them.

"Thomas," she called, "we must help Stephan before it is too late!"

Grief blazed in his eyes. "When the English broke the door, too many knights moved between Stephan and the rest of us to allow him to follow, a fact he understands," he rasped, his every word anguished. "He fights to lure the English toward him to ensure your escape, a decision any of us would have made if we had stood in his stead."

Stephan knew he was going to die? Guilt overwhelmed Katherine. Furious at herself, damning that 'twas her actions that had led to this horrific moment, she shook her head. "I willna allow him to make such a decision!"

"He told us to protect you," Thomas rasped, "and by God, 'tis what we shall do." With a firm hand on her shoulder, the Scottish knight hauled her into his arms and carried her down the ladder.

In rapid succession, his men followed.

Weakened by the blood lost, his vision beginning to blur, Stephan kept the three closest attackers engaged.

The last of his men moved out of sight.

The trapdoor slid closed.

The scrape of the bolt sounded.

Safe, thank God! They would reach the ship, sail away, and make plans for another attack.

Four more Englishmen moved toward him.

Stephan shoved his blade into the man closest to him, jerked it free. He swept out his foot, throwing the second man to the floor, then reached out, caught the third one's arm.

With a curse, the Englishman slammed to the splinter-strewn floor.

Before the two men could move, Stephan slashed both men's throats. As he started to turn, pain tore through his injured shoulder.

"Thought you would slip away from us, did you?" an English knight spat as his blade swung toward him.

Out of pure reaction, Stephan rammed his sword up. Steel clashed; the knight maintained his grip. Bedamned!

Another man caught Stephan's arm, jerked him back. Pain exploded in his face. The chamber around him spun.

Several Englishmen grabbed him, the closest withdrawing his dagger.

"Halt!" a deep voice ordered.

His body pinned, Stephan struggled to break free.

A knight to his right drove his fist into his face.

Pain shattered in his skull and Stephan fought to remain conscious.

Silence descended in the chapel, broken only by the moans of the injured and dying, wisps of frankincense tainted by the stench of death.

The hard tap of boots echoed on the weathered wood.

Through the blur of pain, Stephan glanced up. He made out a tall man, his coat of arms identifying him as of the nobility.

"I am the Earl of Preswick; 'tis my castle you attacked." His eyes narrowed. "Who are you?"

Stephan glared at the man who'd murdered Katherine's family, thrown her into the dungeon until she would agree to wed him, and claimed Avalon Castle for his king. "Who am I?" he rasped with cold violence, his burr thick, "the man who is going to end your life."

Preswick's brow rose with disdain. "I think you are far from being in a position for threats." He paused. "A Scot. A savage sent by . . ." Understanding flickered in his gaze, and a cold smile creased his face. "The Bruce. An outlaw who slayed his competitor for the crown at the Church of the Convent of the Minorite Friars to ensure he would become king."

"Become?" Stephan spat. "Robert Bruce was crowned king of Scotland at Scone by Isobel of Fife, Countess of Buchan."

"A traitor who will regret her actions." He glared toward where the knights had escaped. "How many men are with you?"

Stephan remained silent.

A knight to his left pressed a dagger flush against his neck. Stephan tried to shift; two others held him tight.

"Do not kill him," the noble said. "Take him to the dungeon. I want him alive. For now."

His body tormented with pain, two men hauled Stephan to his feet.

"Know this," Preswick said, his voice hard, "you will answer my questions. My men have inventive ways of making those who wish to remain silent talk. Once I have my answers, you will die."

Chapter Fourteen

The thud of stone sliding into place overhead plunged through Katherine like a dagger to the heart. The torch nearby flickered in a mad dance and then calmed as she fought to breathe. Stephan couldna die! *Please God, allow him to live.* If anything happened to him—

A gentle hand touched her shoulder. "Lady Katherine," Thomas said, his voice grim.

Fighting panic, she caught his shoulders. "Do-do you think they have killed him?"

Troubled green eyes held hers. "I am unsure."

She willed away her fear, the anxiety that threatened to tear her apart. Stephan needed her; now wasna the time to crumple.

Katherine refused to ponder her husband's face swelling and battered with bruises, the blood staining his mail. She focused on memories of his patience, wit, and strength. The traits of a man she was coming to know, to care for deeply.

Within the flicker of the torchlight, Aiden's troubled gaze held hers. "My lady, Stephan has fought many a battle with the odds far worse."

"Far worse?" she forced out, floundering to accept such a horrific thought.

Thomas shot Aiden a warning look, then faced her. "Stephan is a seasoned warrior. If he still lives, he will find a way to survive until we reach him."

"But the English will know we will try to rescue him," she rushed out. "They will torture him; they will . . ." If she had listened to Stephan and returned to the ship, her husband and his men could have focused on their attack. Instead, lost in her need for vengeance, she'd placed Stephan and his knights' lives at risk. She shook her head. "This is my fault, every single bit of it. I should never have disobeyed him. I—"

"You were trying to help him, Lady Katherine," Thomas interrupted, his tone firm. "Dinna worry. We will reach him."

"Odds are," Rónán said, "they have taken him to the dungeon."

"Aye," she agreed, focusing on hope. "And there is a tunnel the English know naught about that will lead us there."

Pride warmed Thomas's eyes. "That is it, lass. First we free him and then we plot the best way to reclaim Avalon."

A short while later, with a strategy devised, Katherine opened the hidden tunnel leading to the dungeon. She lifted her candle to shoulder height and nodded to the men. "Follow me."

The drip of water echoed from nearby as they made their way down the dank confines. A putrid smell tainted the air as they moved deeper.

Thomas wrinkled his nose. " 'Twould seem we are nearing the dungeon."

" 'Tis a short way now." Agonizing minutes later, Katherine held up her hand. "The dungeon is around the next turn," she whispered. On edge, she crept forward.

Ahead, torchlight streamed through the slits between the stones and illuminated the tunnel walls.

Katherine prayed they'd find Stephan alive.

Thomas squeezed beside her, gestured toward the crevices. "Can you see the entire dungeon through the openings?"

"Aye," she replied.

"Wait here." The warrior's boots scuffed against stone as he crept forward. Paces away, he peered through a gap; light fragmented into a tangle of shadows. Face taut, he returned.

Katherine released an unsteady breath. "Did you see him?"

"Aye," Thomas whispered. "He is locked in the cell to the far right."

"The one closest to the door." She took a steadying breath. "Is he . . ."

"Alive?" Thomas exhaled. "Barely."

Mary have mercy, what brutality had Stephan endured? Pressing her hand against the cold stone, Katherine focused on their immediate task. "Are any of the cells empty?"

"Several near the middle."

"Thank God." She drew a calming breath. "Eight stones to the left of where you looked into the dungeon, there is a stone with a small X centered at the bottom, along the rim. Place your finger in the depression. You will feel a notch at the tip of one of the lines. Press there. The entry will swing open into the cell."

In the dim light, an ironic smile touched Thomas's face. "The eighth stone?"

"Aye."

"And an X notched at the tip of one of the lines?"

She hesitated. "Is something wrong?"

Thomas's gaze flicked to Aiden, then met hers. "Nay, I find such detail in a secret entry interesting."

Katherine glanced back, noting surprise and disbelief in the men's expressions. "Why is the number eight and a notched X important?"

"The number eight isna important," Thomas replied, "or at least nae for our purposes." He glanced toward Aiden and Rónán. "I didna see any sign of a guard. I suspect they are finished with Stephan for now and have left a knight, mayhap two, outside the entry. In his condition, he isna threat enough to warrant more."

In his condition? She almost retched. "That the guards didna remain inside the dungeon assures me they know naught of the tunnel."

"I agree," Thomas replied. "There is no time to waste. After our confrontation in the chapel, the earl will order his knights to give chase. With the stone we secured beneath the wood of the trapdoor, a feat all but impossible, a fact he's discovered by now. Regardless, he will have ordered his ships to sail. Before his men make their way to where we are anchored, we must have fled."

Katherine nodded.

"Griogair," Thomas said to a knight several paces away, "take all but five knights and return to the ships. Pass the word to the captains that once we are onboard, we will depart."

"Aye, Sir Thomas." The knight moved to the men behind him. After a few hushed words, he lifted his taper and led the warriors away.

"Aiden and Cailin," Thomas whispered, "follow me." His gaze shifted to Katherine, and he gestured toward the two remaining knights. "Rónán and Hugh will remain by your side until you are safely aboard." His stern eyes narrowed. "Wait here. We willna be long."

She nodded.

Silently, the three knights crept forward. Where the light streamed through the crevice, Thomas counted the stones toward the rim. At the eighth, his finger skimmed over a chiseled surface, paused. He shoved.

A soft grating echoed into the silence.

Muted light streamed into the tunnel.

Thomas pushed the entry wider, waved the men forward.

Aiden and Cailin followed him into the dungeon.

Their steps faded.

Silence.

Please God, let Stephan be alive!

"Have faith, lass," Rónán whispered. "Stephan is a man of strength."

"Aye," Katherine replied. If necessary, her husband would fight until his last breath. She fisted her hands, shoved the thought aside. With another prayer she watched the entry.

Time crawled, her breathing growing more ragged with each passing second, terrified the knights would be discovered.

A faint scrape of metal sounded.

Relief swept her. "They have opened his cell!"

"Aye," Hugh said.

A thump echoed into the silence.

The scrape of steps.

Shadows muted the rays of light streaming through the opening.

A moment later, Thomas hurried inside the tunnel, half-carrying her husband, Cailin supporting his other shoulder.

Stephan! Her heart squeezed. Oh God; because of her foolishness, look at what he'd been forced to endure! "I am so sorry."

A frown lining Aiden's brow, he tugged the door shut.

"Back to the ship; hurry!" Thomas whispered.

With another prayer for Stephan, she lifted her taper and led the way.

Trembling, Katherine pressed the gash across her husband's left shoulder together while Thomas tended to him. Stephan lay so still, his eyes closed, his face a cascade of red and purple bruises still swelling and his breaths rapid and weak.

At the end of the wound, Thomas joined the severed flesh closed with his thumb, drew the needle through, then knotted the end. " 'Tis the last stitch." After smearing herbs over the neatly sewn skin, the knight grabbed a strip of cloth from a nearby pile and began to bandage the injury. A tired smile creased his face. "We are finished."

"I am indebted to you," she said, unsure how to thank this honorable man for his patience, his meticulous care in treating each wound.

As Thomas secured the cloth over the injury, he shook his head. "Thanks are unnecessary. Caring for Stephan is a task that I, or any of the others, would perform without hesitation."

A strong bond existed between the knights, one crafted by the man who led them. "My husband is fortunate to have such devoted warriors."

His expression somber, Thomas paused. "Devoted, aye."

Her husband's face twisted in pain. "Nay! To arms!"

Pushing further questions aside, Katherine laced her fingers with his. "You must lie still."

At her voice, lines of confusion deepened his brow. Stephan shook his head. "Nay! Grand Master..." He clenched his teeth. "Damn King Philip to Hades!" A shudder rippled through his body and he cursed, and then fell silent.

Confused, she glanced at Thomas. "Why would my husband call out for the leader of the Knights Templar, or France's king?"

"Stephan will be having dreams," he replied, avoiding her eyes. "I have given Stephan powerful herbs to help him sleep and to keep him from moving about and tearing open the stitches." He shrugged. "Likely the reason for his nonsensical talk."

Powerful herbs mayhap, but she sensed far more played out before her than her husband's drug-inspired ramblings.

An expression of sheer agony crossed Stephan's face. "We must sail immediately for Scotland!" he shouted, his voice strangled with grief. "God help us all!"

Mary have mercy, a potion didna feed his ramblings but memories. She leveled her gaze on Thomas.

Face ashen, he stared at her.

"I think," she said with quiet determination, " 'tis time you told me the truth."

After a long moment he nodded. He rubbed the back of his neck, sat back. "We are knights."

The ship angled up. Creaks echoed into the silence as the galley slashed through the oncoming swell.

"Who sail to foreign lands," she supplied.

He hesitated. "Warriors are needed in many places."

"Indeed, but that doesna explain why you and your men pray so often," Katherine said, watching his every reaction. "Many knights have faith, but since I joined you, I have noticed that you, along with the others, recite prayers during the canonical hours. There is but one group of knights I am aware of that adheres to such a strict, structured life built around their faith."

Silence.

"The Knights Templar," she continued, "an elite fighting force of warrior monks who have sworn their fealty to God, are revered for their bravery, and are feared for their skill in battle. Men who are forbidden to marry. But it seems from Stephan's ramblings, something has changed that. Something involving King Philip, mayhap?"

Thomas's mouth tightened as he eyed her.

"With all that I have seen, I should have guessed before now that you are Templars." A dry smile touched her lips, fled. " 'Tis obvious. The quality of the ships, the caliber of training, your skills in everything from battle to the plying of a needle to sew a wound." She paused. "What has France's king to do with the Templar knights fleeing, and why have five of your ships sailed to Scotland?"

"God in heaven, Grand Master, disbanding the Knights Templar!" Stephan clenched his teeth. Sweat beaded his brow and he fell silent.

Thomas muttered a curse.

"Disbanded?" she forced out, struggling to accept her husband's claim.

Eyes troubled, Thomas held her gaze. "You must swear an oath of secrecy that *never* will you share what I am about to tell you."

She nodded. "I swear it."

"Aye," he admitted, "we are Knights Templar."

In silence, Katherine listened as he revealed how the Templars had harbored King Philip after the riots in France earlier that year; an upheaval the monarch himself had incited by debasing the currency to a fraction of its worth to increase his revenue.

"Did France's king expect the people to meekly comply with his exorbitant greed?"

"Nay doubt he anticipated their anger," Thomas said, "but he underestimated the extent."

Disgust swept her. "King Philip is a fool to dare such a despicable tactic."

"Nae a fool," Thomas said, his voice somber, "but financially desperate, to a degree none within the Brotherhood comprehended. Never did we believe the king would turn on the Templars."

Confused, she frowned. "Why?"

"Over the years, as the Templars have done with numerous others of the nobility, we loaned King Philip significant coin to keep his interests secure. He needed our financial backing along with our fighting skills, and so we believed the Order safe from his tyranny."

A chill rippled through her. She didna want to hear more, but her question spilled out. "But you were nae?"

Thomas shook his head. "As the riots escalated, the king ordered those inciting the violence hanged. Though the sentences were carried out, the unrest continued. For his safety, France's sovereign was offered refuge in our Paris temple. But during his stay, 'twould seem the valuables within enticed him to devise a plan to destroy the Templars and seize our wealth, thereby freeing himself from his enormous debt."

Katherine listened, dreading what Thomas would disclose next.

"Desperate for peace, King Philip rescinded the currency devaluation. With the people appeased, he returned to the palace." Thomas paused, his eyes dark with emotion. "A short time later, people came forth spewing claims against the Templars; damning, heresy. None of the charges were ever tied to King Philip, but we in the Order harbor little doubt as to the origin of these false accusations."

"What happened?" she whispered.

"Armed with justifications of alleged Templar atrocities, King Philip wrote an order for the arrest of the Templars."

Horrified, she shook her head. " 'Tis despicable!"

"Aye. But for King Philip, an answer to his dire need for gold."

"How did you, Stephan, and the other knights escape?"

"The Grand Master received advance warning that, with false charges in hand, the king had written orders to begin arrests of the Knights Templar on the thirteenth of October," Thomas replied. "Unbeknownst to King Philip, under the cover of night, many of the valuables within the Paris temple were loaded on Templar galleys moored at the port of La Rochelle. Most sailed south to Portugal."

"And the remaining five," she said, nauseated by the terrible wrong, the injustice, and the king's unforgivable greed, "to Scotland."

"Aye."

Katherine shook her head. "He willna succeed. Pope Clement—"

"Willna intercede. His Grace wasna chosen as pope for his strength of character," Thomas said, his voice bitter. "King Philip ensured that the man chosen to wield the church's might was one he could bend to his will."

A shudder tore through her and she crossed herself. "King Philip has the power to sway the choosing of a pope?"

Thomas nodded.

"But . . . It doesna . . . How is such treachery possible in a position so sacred?"

Coolness shrouded the warrior's gaze. "A desperate king will do many things to save his realm," Thomas said. "Rest assured, King Philip's duplicity is known well by the Templars."

Horror filled her at the far-reaching effects of the treacherous French king's actions. Overwhelmed and saddened for the warriors who'd served for hundreds of years to protect others, she focused on her husband. "But how can Stephan marry? As a Templar Knight, he is forbidden to wed."

"As a knight within the Order, aye. But as you heard in Stephan's ramblings, with the impending arrests, the Grand Master has secretly dissolved the order. Those who remained will either be uninformed of his action or, if told, would keep the dissolution a secret."

"And—"

Thomas held up his hand. "I have explained all that I will. If you are to learn more, 'twill be Stephan's doing."

Katherine nodded, sickened by the revelations, horrified to learn that France's ruler was little better than a common thief. His hunger for power, his drive to take, to claim without care whoever he hurt, whoever he killed.

Gruesome images of her family's murder rolled through her mind; anger swelled. Her parents' deaths, ordered by yet another sovereign's quest for power. 'Twould seem nobility's virtues rose far from those they were to rule. She grimaced. Rule? Nay. Use, manipulate, lie for their own notorious gain.

Heart aching, Katherine faced her husband. "How long do you expect him to remain asleep?"

"For the next day, hopefully two."

"Hopefully?"

A hint of a smile touched the knight's mouth. "Stephan is a stubborn man."

"He is." A trait, however frustrating at times, she admired. "You know much about healing."

Thomas shrugged. "All of the men are trained in the use of herbs."

"All?" Intrigued, she studied the meticulous stitches, those of a master who knew his craft. She glanced up. " 'Tis uncommon to find so many warriors knowledgeable in the art of healing."

"The Knights Templar are highly trained," he replied, his words nonchalant, his claim anything but. " 'Tis yet another advantage we have on those we fight."

Heat touched her cheeks. "A question I shouldna have asked."

"I expect interest and curiosity from those Stephan works with," Thomas said. "As well as from a woman who loves her husband."

Love? Katherine fought the churning in her gut. He was wrong. After all she'd endured, the horrors still haunting her, never could she love a man. "Nae enough time has passed for Stephan or I to know the other, much less feel more."

"In some instances, time isna a factor in how much we care. Given your actions toward your husband, you are a woman who cares deeply, and from my observations, I believe much more."

Panic swept through her, and she grasped on to logic. "Why are you saying this?" Katherine demanded, shaken that his claim might be too close to the truth.

Thomas stared toward the lantern for a long moment and his eyes grew misty. On a slow breath, he faced her. "I see how you struggle with your feelings for Stephan. Life is too brief to nae live it, to nae risk admitting what you feel to those who matter. Take care that you dinna destroy this chance at happiness you have been given."

Pain cut through her as she remembered that never again would she have the chance to tell her family she loved them, something she would regret the rest of her life. And Stephan? She cared for him deeply, but love?

"Many years ago," Thomas continued, "I held the rank of a noble."

"You are nobility?"

"Aye," Thomas said with such sadness 'twas as if it were a weight he bore with each breath. " 'Tis a life I lived long ago. My father still lives, but due to my actions, I canna go back, ever. Yet, however foolish, a part of me wishes I could."

Shaken by the grief in his voice, she laid her hand on his forearm. "What happened?"

Thomas's expression hardened.

Nae wanting to upset him but curious to learn more, she shifted tactics. "Are you the next in line to inherit your father's title?"

"Nay, that will go to my oldest brother. My rank and holdings were minor in comparison."

He had a family. Her mind filled with questions, she withdrew her hand. "So you abandoned your nobility and joined the Knights Templar to fight in the Crusades?" she asked, the only explanation that made sense.

His mouth tight, he nodded. "Aye, but that isna why I bring up the issue. Lass, dinna make the mistake I made."

An ache built in her chest at the pain he'd suffered and, the guilt he still struggled with. "I care for Stephan," she admitted, choosing her words with caution, "but our situation is . . . different."

"Is it? Or do you want it to be so you can admit naught?" Thomas stood, his face an unreadable mask, as if but moments before he hadna shared a deep, dark secret. "I have told you what few know because your husband is an honorable man, one who has suffered greatly and holds too much inside. You are a strong, admirable woman, one I and the other knights respect. I see within the bond you and Stephan have forged an opportunity to allow Stephan to heal, and from your grief, hesitation, and pain that lingers in your eyes, yourself. A chance, however much I pray my own life will never have. Before you risk severing any possible chance for happiness between you and Stephan, consider all that you could lose."

Moved that he and his men had noticed her turmoil, more so that they approved of her, Katherine floundered. How could they believe she could tear down Stephan's walls, convince him to let go of whatever haunted him from his past, when she struggled with her own?

"You are stronger than you believe," Thomas said.

He was wrong. Strength didna drive her but fear. The loss of her family still scarred her every breath. However much she was drawn to Stephan, lured by his touch, his kiss, 'twas too soon to think of exposing herself to the possibility of so much pain.

"I will consider your advice," Katherine said, "but I guarantee naught."

He nodded. " 'Tis all I ask."

"I think you have more faith in me than I do myself," she said, her words unsteady, struggling to ignore the need her husband made her feel.

"At times," Thomas said with an encouraging smile, " 'tis enough."

Mayhap, but for her now wasna the time to dare. So she would focus on reclaiming her home. Neither was she the only one who suffered. "Thomas, I am sorry for whatever caused strife between you and your family."

"I thank you."

Thunder rumbled in the distance.

"A storm is moving in," she said.

Thomas stood. "I need to go above to help the others ensure all is secure."

"Before you go, I saw how you and the men glanced at each other when I explained there were eight stones to count in the tunnel behind the dungeon to find the hidden entry. Why?"

" 'Tis the number of points on a Templar cross."

"And the X carved onto the stone in the tunnel?"

"A Templar mark."

"Which explains your and the other men's reaction to learning of the mark's existence." Somber, she stared at this man who, like her husband, was one of honor. Humbled he'd trusted her with the secret of the Knights Templar, she shook her head. "I willna repeat what you told me."

"I know, or I wouldna have shared it. Neither did I tell you to make secrets between us, but to ask you to consider what you feel for Stephan and, when the time comes, to be strong enough to admit the truth. If I had but a day," he said, his voice a rough whisper, "even a moment to return to tell my family that I love them, I would. 'Tis better than living with regrets." With a nod, he strode from the cabin, tugging the door shut.

The quiet shudder of wood echoed in his wake.

Another rumble of thunder sounded, this time closer.

Shaken by the knight's words, she rubbed the chills from her arms. The quiet slap of waves against the bow was in stark contrast to the storm brewing in the distance, one as potent as the churning in her soul.

Rubbing her brow, Katherine turned toward Stephan. The soft shimmer of the lantern light filling the room illuminated the pallor on his face, every hard angle, the cropped brown hair that lent him an even more rugged appeal. As when she'd first met him, he looked fierce, unapproachable, a man most would avoid.

Yet she'd come to know him, had discovered that behind the cool façade was a man driven to protect, a man who battled his own demons. And as a Knight Templar, a devout man who put others before himself.

How he must have struggled to accept the dissolution of that elite force. The grief, the sadness in his eyes now made sense. She ached for him, for those he'd lost. A fate Katherine well understood.

Life wasna fair; 'twas ruthless in its demands and none escaped its touch. Happiness was fleeting against the reality of pain delivered by the loss of those one loved.

Shaken, Katherine settled beside where her husband lay, caught in a restless sleep filled with nightmares.

Help him? How could she allow herself to care for this man, to love him, when her grief was still so raw?

Memories of their kiss sifted through her mind. Of how the soft breeze had encircled them as if a force of its own, his hesitation, and then the way his mouth had claimed hers.

And, God help her, she'd wanted him. The feel of his body pressed against hers had left her yearning for more, a need that made her ache with wanting, a hunger that blurred the memories of her assault.

A tear rolled down her cheek, slid to her chin, wobbled and dropped to the floor. She stared at the blur of wetness upon the aged plank, how it soaked into the weathered wood, absorbed into a dark blemish that would linger. On the morrow the stain could vanish, but traces might remain, as did the tender memories of their first kiss.

She sniffed.

Aye, she cared for Stephan. He was a man who made her feel more than she'd ever believed possible. Her attraction toward him was incredible considering her fear of men since the attack. Was

Thomas right? So afraid to care, was she ignoring the depth of her feelings for Stephan?

As if a gift, warmth touched her heart, a slide of emotion that settled over her in a warm haze. And she understood.

She loved Stephan.

Katherine stared at her husband, ached with what he made her feel. How was this possible? She was broken inside. Never could she come willingly to his bed. After her hesitancy at his touch, how much time would pass before he grew tired of her? As if she could blame him for seeking the warmth of a woman's bed when with her he would find naught but coldness? But having realized that she loved him, to see him in the arms of another would leave her devastated.

Katherine struggled to catch her breath. Stephan must never learn how he made her feel. To allow her husband such hope would be cruel when he was a man who deserved a wife who would willingly join him in his bed. His children should be born of love, nae created beneath the icy terror of his touch.

Her husband shifted and agony lined his face.

"I am here," Katherine said as she lay a cool cloth on his brow. She stroked the dampened linen over the firm sweep of his jaw. "Sleep now."

His entire body stiffened. "Nay!" Stephan tried to sit.

She caught his shoulders, pressed him against the bed. "You are safe; go back to sleep."

"The Templars . . ." In the lantern's glow, his face tightened, his breathing quickening. "God, nay! Johanna, run!"

She stilled. Who was Johanna?

"They are coming!" His mouth pressed together until his lips grew white. "Johanna!"

Another nightmare. " 'Tis fine now," she said, keeping her voice soft.

He gave a strangled cry. "God's blade, so much blood, too much." He shuddered. "Come back to me. Damn you, damn you to hell, live!"

Frantic to stop him from tearing out his stitches, she held him tight, unsure how long she could keep him still. " 'Tis a dream."

"Nay!" Stephan twisted. "They are all dead!"

The scrape of wood sounded behind her.

Katherine turned.

"What is wrong?" Thomas asked as he ran to her side and helped her keep her husband still. "I could hear Stephan's shouts from above."

"He is having another nightmare." As for her feelings toward her husband, that she would have to explore later. At this moment, whatever she had left inside, she'd give to Stephan.

Chapter Fifteen

The rumble of thunder echoed from far away. Stephan shifted and agony streaked through his body. God's blade, what had happened?

Memories stormed him: their attack on Avalon Castle, the battle, discovering he and his men were greatly outnumbered, and Katherine's arrival. Terrified for her life, he'd discarded attempts to reach his men and turned to providing a distraction for the English until his knights had ensured her escape.

Pain still burned his body at the inventive methods used by the Earl of Preswick's knights in their attempts to pry information from him. With every brutality, he'd focused on the fact that Katherine and his men were safe.

Broken images flashed in his mind. Arms hauling him up, assurances that he was safe, the splash of oars in water, and then blackness.

Thunder exploded nearby. A rush of wind slammed against the hull, and the bed gave a violent lurch.

Stephan groaned.

"I think he is beginning to awaken," Katherine whispered from his side.

"Aye," Thomas agreed from nearby. "You have remained with your husband for the last two days, my lady. Go and rest. When he is fully awake, I will tell you."

"You are as tired as I," she said, stubbornness clinging to the exhaustion in her voice, "while I have caught naps here and there."

His friend scoffed. "Falling asleep in your chair far from meets the criterion of a nap."

"You worry too much," Katherine said. "Truly, I am fine."

Stephan peered at his wife from beneath hooded eyes.

A smile touched her lips.

His lids grew heavy and he closed them.

"Thomas," she said, "your standing here is helping naught."

"Stubborn you are," his friend grumbled. "At sunrise, if I havena heard from you, I will return. By God, you will go and rest then if I have to cart you to your bed myself and tie you there."

"Aye, Sir Thomas," she replied.

With a soft mutter, his friend departed.

Wood groaned as the ship angled up. Thunder rumbled, this time louder. The rough howl of wind filled the chamber.

A thud.

Clothes shifted.

A quiet sigh.

Curious, through the twist of pain, Stephan again forced his lids open.

Murky light from the lantern shrouded Katherine as she knelt, the golden spill flickering over her face as if it were dust sprinkled by the fairies and he ensnared within its spell.

Fatigue marring his wife's brow, she bowed her head and pressed her hands together in prayer. Quiet words fell from her lips.

The Lord's Prayer.

Emotion filled Stephan as she whispered the Paternoster, each word heartfelt, each verse as if dredged from her soul. Humbled, in silence he followed along.

"Amen." On an unsteady breath, Katherine made the sign of the cross. Blue eyes lifted, stilled. Relief filled them, and then darkened to concern. "You are awake."

"I . . ." He tried to speak, but his mouth was dry, his throat refusing to comply.

"Wait, you will be thirsty." She poured him a cup of water, lifted it to his mouth.

He savored the coolness sliding down his throat.

After several sips, she set the drink on a nearby table. "For now, you will only have a little at a time. Once you are better, you can drink your fill." Katherine pressed her palm against his brow. Her mouth relaxed. "Good, nay sign of a fever."

"Ho-how long have I been asleep?" He swallowed and then winced, his throat burning from the enemy's many strangleholds. His arms and chest ached. Even the muscles across his back were sore from the repeated beatings.

"Thanks to the potion Thomas gave you, almost three days."

He grimaced. "Thomas is known for his concoctions."

"With how long you slept, I can understand why," she said, a touch of humor in her voice. "And your friend has a fine hand with a needle as well. I helped him while he sewed a large gash in your shoulder."

Stephan skimmed his fingers over the well-crafted stitches. "You helped?"

"I did, and," Katherine said, as if sensing his unease, "you are nae the first warrior I have tended after battle. Neither will I be asking how you feel. With the bruises covering your body, I expect 'tis as if a battering ram has hit your head."

He shot her a wry smile. "Close."

Thunder boomed overhead. Rain pounded the ship with torrential force.

She frowned. " 'Tis worse than the squall several hours ago."

"How long has it been storming?"

"Since yesterday morning. Thomas and the others dropped anchor in a bay hidden behind trees. With the fierceness of the winds, we are thankful for the shelter."

"Where are we?"

"In one of the secret coves the fishermen from the village recommended if ever we had need to hide."

"All four of the ships are here?"

"Aye."

Their cargo was safe, thank God. Neither could they remain here for any length of time. Even in this downpour, after their attack, the English would be searching for them. Stephan gritted his teeth, swung his legs off the bed, and sat up.

Katherine caught his arm. "What are you doing?"

"Getting out of bed."

"You need to lie down. If you start moving about, you risk tearing open your stitches."

He scowled. "I have slept for several days. Time enough for my wounds to set."

"Sunrise isna for a few more hours. If you go above deck now, you will see none but the watch."

He hesitated.

"Thomas warned me that you would be stubborn."

"Nay, determined."

She blew out a rough breath. "Call it what you will. If you stand up now, 'twill be to prove you can. Foolishly, may I add."

Stephan held her gaze, irritated he would hesitate at her caution, but her actions along with her words exposed one thing.

She cared.

Need rippled through him, the potency leaving him floundering. Somehow, without his wanting to, Katherine had breached his defenses. Regardless of his desires, of his intention to keep distance between them, 'twas too late.

He swallowed hard, wanting her, damning his need. "You look tired," Stephan said, wishing more than a hand's width separated them. With a slight pull, their bodies would touch, and he could draw her to him, taste her mouth against his, nuzzle the silken flesh along her throat.

God's blade, what was he thinking? Mayhap it wasna his feelings for her that had changed but the herbs Thomas had shoved down his throat that skewed his mind with such unwanted thoughts.

But he knew he lied.

Knew he wanted her.

Knew to reach out to her now, with his defenses weakened, would be a mistake.

"Lie back," his wife urged, "at least until the sun begins to rise."

He complied, if for naught more than to encourage Katherine to put distance between them. "From the fatigue in your eyes, you need rest as well."

Red touched her cheeks. "I will, once Thomas returns."

"I am nae a child in need of a nursemaid! Now off with you; there is little cause for you to remain." She stiffened, and he muttered a curse.

"You had nightmares," she rushed out. "Several. If you fall asleep and have more, I must be here to prevent you from causing damage to a wound."

He stilled. "Nightmares?"

"Aye."

Shame crawled through him as memories of his horrific dreams knifed through him. "What did I say?"

Without meeting his gaze, Katherine stood, walked to stand before the lantern. "For the most part, naught but unintelligible ramblings."

He damned the guilt resurrected by his past, a penance that would forever haunt him. "And those you understood?"

She turned, her eyes guarded. "You . . . You called out for Johanna."

The image of his sister as she'd fled from their attackers ripped through his mind. Her screams, the fear in her eyes. She'd reached the wall walk before they'd caught up to her, before, in an attempt to escape, she'd slipped and fallen to her death.

"Is Johanna a woman you loved?"

At the worry in her voice he paused. She was jealous? Grief crumbled to pain; he was horrified his wife would learn the truth. "Aye," he rasped. "She was my sister."

Sadness darkened her eyes and she walked closer, covering his hand with hers. "I am so sorry."

Her sincerity stole his breath, made him ache at all he'd lost, left him terrified of the woman he'd found, one who didna understand that with mere words she could hurt him. Never had he known a lass who moved him, one who touched his soul. Katherine did both.

However much he wanted her, if she discovered the truth behind that fateful day, how could she nae be horrified? More, he feared if she learned of her father's heinous acts, she would completely withdraw, and any chance for their marriage to be more than one of convenience lost.

Stephan cleared his throat. " 'Twas a long time ago."

"Mayhap," she whispered, her words raw with sadness, "but you still bear the pain, grieve your sister's loss. How can you nae?"

Her compassion left him floundering with how to reply.

"What happened?"

Wanting to strengthen their bond, Stephan found himself needing to share, so he would tell her portions. The rest would forever remain hidden. "When I was seven summers, our castle was attacked," he said, the memories of the screams of the dying, the terror, recalled with complete clarity. "My family was killed, and the castle . . ." God's blade! He couldna say more.

Her face had paled to a deathly white. "Oh, God, you have suffered so much."

" 'Twas a long time ago." Red-rimmed eyes met his, and he damned himself for weakening and explaining any part of his past. "You need to go to your bed and sleep," he stated, his words harsher than he'd intended, but if she stayed, he worried that he'd do something foolish like share more secrets, ones he'd sworn never to reveal.

"Steph—"

"Go!" His order boomed into the storm-fed night.

Any remaining color on her face fled, but beneath the uncertainty was determination. "Dinna think harsh words will have me fleeing. I am nae afraid of you. Neither," she said, bending closer with a scowl, "will you push me away because you hurt."

Without warning, anger slammed him. "You dinna know how I feel!"

Fury blackened her eyes. "I watched my family die, murdered as pawns in a political gain," she shoved out, her every word raw. "I wasna given the choice to look away as those I loved were slain, swords plunged into their hearts. I was held tight, made to—" She whirled, but he caught her body's shudder.

Blast everything to bloody Hades! Wincing with pain, Stephan shoved off the bed, stood. "Katherine," he said, keeping his words soft, "you dinna have to tell—"

She whirled, her eyes brilliant in their fury, mesmerizing in their passion. "I will finish, by God." Her gaze narrowed, as if daring him to speak.

He remained silent, understood her need to explain, something he'd almost given in to moments before.

On an unsteady breath, Katherine exhaled. "The Earl of Preswick stood by my side, held me as the blade was removed from each body, forced me to watch the life in their eyes fade, empty until their gazes were blackened by death."

"Katherine—"

"And then," she pushed on, tears streaming down her cheeks, "the earl explained that I would marry him, my life spared for such an honor." She gave a cold laugh. "But I escaped, thwarted his contemptible plan. And as I fled, I swore that I would do whatever it took to reclaim Avalon Castle, a promise that even if it meant skirting the truth to a king, I will keep."

As would he.

For her.

For them.

A fact he'd never share.

The moment passed, and Stephan understood. After her heart-rending confession, their relationship had changed. He'd known of her family's murder, the attempted forced marriage, and her escape.

He'd thought her a resourceful woman, mayhap clever. On both counts he'd underestimated her. Katherine was a woman any man would want, one who cared, fought for what she believed in, and would face any challenge for those she loved.

Humbled by her ferocity, moved by her passion, he stared at her. How would it feel to be loved by such a woman? When they'd met, he'd nae wanted a wife, had been furious she'd sailed with him and his men. God help him, now he couldna envision a life without her.

Shaken by what she made him feel, want, he stepped toward her. "The bastard will die," he said with the force of fury pouring through him, "by my blade."

"Nay, by my hand."

"Taking a life solves naught but leaves blood on your hands, memories in your heart to later regret," he said, humbled by this woman who, after such a horrific experience, refused to crumple. Though he'd seen her in quiet moments, her grief, the woman alone, one too terrified to trust. He lifted his hand. "Come here."

"Why?" she demanded.

"Must everything between us be a challenge?" he asked, fatigue riding his voice.

Doubt flickered in her gaze. Katherine glanced toward the door and then turned back to him. "The sun will be up soon."

"Nae for another hour or more."

She didna move.

"Please."

With hesitant steps, she walked toward him.

Stephan took in this amazing woman, doubting she'd think of herself as such, and wrapped her hand within his.

Her eyes grew wary.

He slipped his hand around her waist. An easy pull brought her against him.

She stiffened. "What are you doing?"

"I wanted to hold you."

Panic flickered in her eyes. " 'Tis unseemly."

The absurdity of her statement made him chuckle, at odds with the pain tainting his every breath. "Lass, we are wed. You have remained in the same chamber with me on many a night."

Red swept her cheeks. "That is nae a good reason."

"Because I need you," he whispered, shaken to find his words true.

The wariness on her face melted to hesitation.

Needing to touch her, he lifted her chin, their mouths but a breath apart.

Her lower lip trembled. "Why are you doing this?"

The desperation in her voice shattered the hold on his will. "Because I, you, need this." Stephan brushed his mouth against hers, her soft moan sliding through him, igniting a desire so fierce it smothered his anger of moments before, until all he could do was sink into the kiss, into all that she made him feel.

Her mouth worked hesitantly against his. Slowly, her body relaxed, and after a long moment she was kissing him back.

Of every dream in his life, none had surrounded him with such fulfillment. He shuddered against the potency of his desire, the heat of her body against his, and how Katherine fit so perfectly within his arms.

As her tongue met his, awareness tangled inside until his every touch, his every taste was filled with her. He ignored his aches, drew her with him to his bed, caressed her face as he pressed a kiss against each lid, the curve of her jaw, doubting he'd ever tire of touching her.

"Stephan," she breathed.

On a groan he claimed her mouth, took the kiss deeper.

Katherine shifted beneath him, her body pressed against his, and he felt each curve, the way each fit intimately against the other. He skimmed his mouth along the silky skin of her throat.

"Stephan—"

"I want you," he rasped, moving lower while his hands began loosening the bindings of her gown. "And when I—"

"Nay!" Eyes raw with torment, she shoved him away.

Stunned, he stepped toward her, and the room spun. Furious at his weakness, he halted. "What is wrong?"

She shook her head. "I am sorry. God help me, more than you will ever know. You are a good man, one any woman would want in her . . ." Her eyes filled with regret, Katherine stepped back. "I canna ever be the wife you wish."

Shaken by the depth at which he wanted her, fighting back the desire, he stepped forward. "We have time."

She remained silent.

Bedamned. As if he didna have his own secrets? "Katherine, there is much each of us needs to learn about the other. Things I need to tell you but canna."

Her eyes softened with understanding. "I know."

He stilled. "Know?"

"When you were asleep, you spoke of your being a Knight Templar."

Chapter Sixteen

His pulse racing, Stephan held Katherine's gaze and fought to quell the mounting panic. God's blade, he'd exposed the Brotherhood! Worried eyes watched him. "Stephan, what is wrong?"

Wrong? A pathetic word for his unforgivable transgression. He'd given his vow to the Grand Master, was responsible for keeping the fact that the Templars had fled France a secret, for protecting treasures for which many a king would kill.

"Stephan, talk to me."

"I believe you are mistaken," he said with as much calm as he could muster.

"Thomas admitted 'twas true."

Bedamned! Why had his friend confirmed anything? He should have owed his ramblings to the herbs he'd given him, to loss of blood. Still, his wife had proven herself to be a woman he could trust. Confident he could salvage the precarious situation, he nodded. "How much did Thomas tell you?"

"Enough to make sense of what you were saying in your sleep."

"Such as?"

"He explained King Philip's false charges, the Grand Master dissolving the Knights Templar, and how you and the others boarded your galleys in the port of La Rochelle and fled."

Bedamned! He struggled to decide how to best proceed. Disclosures in the wrong hands could destroy all that was holy.

"And," Katherine said, interrupting his thoughts, "discovering you and your men were Knights Templar answered many questions that had perplexed me from the first."

God's blade. With her intelligence, he should have anticipated his wife would notice variances in the lifestyle of him and his men from other knights.

" 'Tis sickening that King Philip abuses his power to where nae even the church dares to intervene against false charges." Her hands fisted at her sides. "Damn him to Hades! His treachery willna go unpunished. In the end, he must answer to God."

"King Philip will," Stephan rasped, sickened that valiant men, warriors of God and ignorant of the French king's foul intent, would pay for a king's greed. He banked his fury. However upset, he needed to ensure that her enlightenment of his and his men's presence in Scotland remained a secret.

That Thomas had acknowledged their being Templars assured Stephan she'd earned his friend's trust. A feat accomplished by few. Given the sensitivity of their mission, neither would Robert Bruce have selected her to be Stephan's wife if he'd held any doubts of her character.

"What Thomas divulged," Stephan explained, his voice grave, "is information that in the wrong hands could lead to the death of many men."

"Never would I breathe a word of this," Katherine stated. "On my honor, I swear it."

The sincerity of her claim eased any doubts.

"The vows you swore upon becoming a Templar explain why even after the Grand Master's dissolution you dinna wish to marry."

"It wasna you," he whispered, "never you."

A sad smile touched her mouth. "I know that now, but the reason changes naught between us."

Confused, he stepped toward her.

"Dinna come closer." Her voice wavered.

"Katherine—"

"That I know the truth is enough." She moistened her lower lip. "Neither will I question you further about the Templars. I am unsure of the reasons why my godfather found it necessary for us to wed. Your being forced into such an agreement was wrong."

He should be thankful she was pushing him away. Wasna this what he'd wanted? She'd earned his trust. Now she knew his secrets. 'Twould make their life ahead simpler.

Once Avalon was seized, she would remain while he sailed off to support their king. Naught would change except that with a wife in name only, he could remain free from worry about the complications of intimacy.

The words in his throat shattered against the lie they'd become. "Mayhap the start of our marriage wasna what either you or I would have wished, but having come to know you, I canna find regret in Robert Bruce's decision."

Katherine's eyes darkened with a blend of emotions he couldna fathom. "Nor I."

Her admission scraped through his mind, unlocked yearnings he'd fought to suppress. Needing to touch her, to hold her, Stephan ignored the pain and stepped closer.

"Dinna," she whispered, her voice breaking. "However much I want you, I canna be the wife you need." Regret darkening her eyes, she turned and fled.

Shrouded in moonlight, Stephan climbed the rocky bank toward the entry to the secret tunnel. "After a sennight and unable to find us, the English will believe we have long since fled."

The quiet tap of rocks echoed below his boots as Thomas stepped up behind him. "Aye. Though Katherine is far from pleased to be left onboard."

An understatement. She was furious. Neither was her anger the biggest complication between them. After her shocking revelation that she knew he and his men were Templars, he'd overridden common sense and admitted he was satisfied with their marriage. Ever since, she'd avoided him. When forced to meet his gaze or talk to him, she ensured that their time together was minimal.

Stephan stepped around the next rock. A fitting punishment for ignoring his training and allowing his emotions to rule his decisions.

Still, he couldna understand the rationale behind her stating that she couldna be the wife he needed. With his sworn vows as a Knight Templar, since their marriage he'd left her untouched. Except for the kisses.

Neither had he forced her. Despite her claim, for a moment passion had flared between them, a merging of desires, needs, that had spilled out beneath the moonlight and left him aching for more.

He rubbed his brow. God's blade, 'twas a mess, one, with his losing sight of his mission, he deserved. The lass was wise to keep her distance. At least one of them had blasted sense.

"With you ordering Lady Katherine to remain onboard, she willna be giving you a smile anytime soon," Thomas said, drawing him from his thoughts.

Stephan shrugged, climbed higher. "She is safe; 'tis what is important." And what he needed to remember. "Now that we are aware of the secret tunnel's location and how to enter, her presence is unnecessary. As well, her knowing we are Knights Templar allows us to speak freely. Never had I planned to tell her. Nor would I have if nae for the potion you mixed."

"You needed to sleep," Thomas said. "And I hold nay regrets. The lass is trustworthy."

"She is. Given his insistence on our marriage," Stephan said, "a belief our king shared."

Gaze shrewd, his friend studied him. "I know that look; something is troubling you."

"Aye; your prying into what isna your affair."

" 'Tis, when the reason concerns you, my friend. I . . ." Disbelief, then humor touched his friend's face. " 'Tis the lass who has you floundering. You like her."

"She is my bloody wife. 'Twould be ill advised if I didna."

A smile curved his lips. "If asked, I would be saying that you *more* than like her."

"I didna ask."

"You didna," Thomas said, his voice ripe with pleasure, "but against your every wish, 'tis obvious. A fact that pleases me." The tinge of humor faded as he glanced at the tunnel entry. "As for your plan for our attack, I agree. A fire in the stables will serve as a solid deception until everyone moves into place."

"Indeed," Stephan agreed, refocusing on their mission, where his mind should have remained. "This time we will seize Avalon." He opened the passage, led his men inside.

A while later, shouts echoed from the bailey as the Englishmen passed buckets of water to throw on the blaze.

Pressed into the shadows, Stephan nodded to Cailin.

The Templar angled a polished wedge against the sun. Glints of light reflected toward the church where more knights awaited the signal.

The bells began to ring.

As expected, Englishmen broke away from trying to smother the flames, withdrew their blades, and charged toward the chapel.

"Now!" Stephan shouted.

One of his men sounded the horn.

Yelling as they ran, Stephan joined his warriors as they flooded the castle from several strategic directions.

The knights slowed, stumbled back, whirled to face the charging force.

Stephan's archers quickly dropped the leading line of the Englishmen.

Realizing they were trapped, several men began to retreat but were quickly overwhelmed and surrendered.

The soft moans of the dying echoed through the bailey as Stephan scanned the stronghold. Though weather-beaten, the turrets, along with the remainder of the castle, stood solid. Avalon would provide a secure stronghold for the future.

His men, a few bearing minor injuries, separated the few prisoners for which they would demand a ransom.

Stephan sheathed his weapon, glanced at Thomas at his side. "Put all of the captives in the dungeon. On the morrow, I will send a ransom demand to Edward of Caernarfon."

Thomas gave him a rueful smile. "The young king willna be pleased. He struggles with his nobility as he fights to claim a country that was his father's desire to rule, nae his."

"The English king's struggles are his to fight. What matters is the gold he will pay, which will aid King Robert in his fight to reclaim Scotland."

Thomas nodded.

"As for the Earl of Preswick," Stephan said to a knight nearby, "have him brought to me."

"Aye." His man hurried off.

Moments later, a curse rang out, then a scuffle.

" 'Twould seem," Stephan said with disgust, "they have found the earl."

Struggling to break free, the lanky lord fought the Templar's hold as he half-dragged him forward. " 'Tis outrageous. Release me!"

Several paces away, the knight stopped and hauled the man to his feet.

His face red, he glared at Stephan. "Have you any idea who I am?!"

"Aye," Stephan replied, "a pathetic choice to select to keep this stronghold safe."

Outrage darkened his face. "I am—"

"The Earl of Preswick," Stephan cut in, "the English lord who seized Avalon as well as kept the previous earl's daughter alive in hopes to wed."

" 'Twas by royal decree," he blustered.

"And did your king order you to force the lass to watch as you murdered her family?" Stephan seethed, "or was that for your own twisted pleasure?"

The man's face paled. "I—"

Fury pouring through him, Stephan caught the noble's throat, squeezed it. "You are the basest form of life. Nae fit to breathe."

The noble gasped, struggled to break free.

"I should slice open your gullet and spill your worthless blood into the earth. But 'twould do naught but stain it, for I doubt even the maggots would want you." He shoved the man to Cailin. "Throw this murderous bastard into the dungeon."

"You cannot!" the earl roared. " 'Tis an act of war!"

Stephan clasped his dagger, trembling with the urge to slay the bastard. "Your attack and seizure of Avalon initiated that." He nodded to his knights. "Take him away."

Spewing oaths and threats as the guards hauled him across the bailey, the earl met Stephan's gaze. "You will regret this. I will be back to slay your arse, and your men, and rape any women left behind."

The calm in Stephan's mind snapped. "Halt!" Aye, he should ignore the noble, focus on the ransom, but his threat toward Katherine severed any thought of mercy.

With cold precision, Stephan strode to a slain Englishman sprawled nearby. He jerked the knight's bloodied sword from his hand, nodded to his guards. "Release the earl."

Cailin shoved Preswick forward.

The noble stumbled, recovered. Wary, he eyed the surrounding men.

"Here." Hilt first, Stephan tossed him the weapon.

The earl caught the sword, scowling at the knights making a wide circle around them before leveling his gaze on Stephan. "Am I handed a sword so you can kill me and claim you were defending yourself?"

Stephan grunted. "The fight will be fair. Unlike you, I meet my opponent face to face, nae like a coward hiding in the shadow of a king."

The earl's mouth thinned. "At least I fight for a king who ascended to his rightful place on the throne, nae a noble who changed his fealty with each battle, and slayed Red Comyn, the rightful claimant to the Scottish throne."

"Strategy is the sign of an effective leader." Banking his fury, the need to end the worthless bastard's life, Stephan emptied his mind of emotion, lifted his blade. "Nae like the king you serve, whose preference is carpentry or digging a ditch."

"Damn you!" Preswick lunged.

Pain screamed through Stephan as he swung. Honed steel scraped.

Confidence gleamed in the Englishman's gaze. "You were a fool to give me a weapon, a fact you will soon learn." He lowered his blade, thrust it forward.

Stephan stumbled back.

The earl drove forward.

Stephan sidestepped, angled his sword, and blocked the Englishman's blow. Stephan's arm trembled as he held the earl back.

A cold smile touched Preswick's face. "There is blood on your shoulder, Scot. You are weak, wounded, and a fool to believe you could ever defeat me."

The pad of footsteps echoed nearby.

Katherine stepped into view and paused alongside Thomas, her eyes wide with shock.

The earl's gaze cut to her. "Lady Katherine," he said with contempt. "You came to speak your vows and seal our marriage. A ceremony we will complete once I have dealt with this pathetic excuse for a knight." He focused on Stephan, jerked his sword up.

Honed steel loosened in Stephan's hand, and he kept his grip, barely. Furious he'd allowed his wife's presence to distract him, he focused on the noble, welcoming the surge of anger.

Preswick charged, his every blow brutal, the gleam of victory in his eyes bright. "Cede and mayhap I will spare your life."

"The only way you will leave here is with your remains hauled away."

Red mottled the nobleman's face. With a curse, he drove forward, each blow punishing, each swing meant to destroy.

His body exhausted, aware he'd returned to battle too soon, Stephan held his own, refusing to quit, determined to give Katherine the justice she deserved.

As the earl made to swing, Stephan feigned a shift to the right.

His attacker swung.

Stephan ducked. Steel swung inches above his head. Feet braced, he stood and drove his blade into Preswick's heart.

Chapter Seventeen

Wind tugged at Katherine's hair as she stood on the wall walk, the battlements crafting a formidable outline against the swath of gold smearing the sky.

Pride filled her.

Home.

Far below the castle, waves rumbled ashore. She savored the taste of the sea, the peaceful rush that filled her whenever she'd scanned the vast horizon over the years.

Weeks ago she'd stood alongside her father at this exact spot. Excitement had filled her as she'd told him of her dreams, the travel and all she'd hoped to accomplish in life. He'd smiled, pride in his eyes, and had assured her that in addition to her heart's desire, she would achieve so much more. To him, all in life was possible if one but believed.

Now he, along with her family and dreams, were gone.

Aching at the loss, she lay her hand upon the cool stone, took in the crash of waves assaulting the land. Like life, a battle never ending. Turmoil would continue to reign. However powerful, dreams could be shattered, hopes destroyed until one struggled for every breath.

" 'Tis a formidable stronghold," Stephan said. "One that I will do whatever is necessary to keep."

At the fierceness of his claim, she faced him. Solemn eyes held hers, concern dark within. He'd nae comment on her upset, but neither would he ignore her grief. If her husband saw the need, as he had hours ago, he would hold her until, by her choice, she stepped away.

Images of him slaying Preswick flickered in her mind. A part of her had been sickened at witnessing the Englishman's death, another satisfied the merciless bastard would never hurt another.

Why was there so much evil? How could people believe status or wealth would bring satisfaction? Dinna they realize that regardless of whether they achieved their goals, they couldna find warmth in a gold coin at night, nor would a castle or country conquered offer anything but duty.

Immersed in their need to keep their spoils from all who sought to claim their power or wealth, the vicious cycle would begin again. In the end, those who held riches earned naught but the burden of defending all they amassed.

A sad life indeed.

Stephan's brow furrowed. "You were nae meant to witness the earl's death."

"I know. Only after word reached the ships that Avalon had been taken did your men allow me to disembark." Katherine laid her hand atop his. "Preswick deserved his fate."

"He did, but England's king willna be so understanding. We must prepare for retaliation for the earl's death."

Katherine shrugged. "I am nae so sure. He will be pressed by his nobles for such reprisal, but Edward of Caernarfon isna a man who wished for the crown. He bears the title but lacks the drive for power of his father."

Stephan nodded. " 'Tis whispered that after his coronation, one of the king's first acts wasna to resume his father's campaign to conquer Scotland but to invite Piers Galveston, Earl of Cornwall, to the palace." A wry smile touched his lips. "A man his father had exiled."

"A move that nay doubt sent whispers of discontent throughout the palace."

"Aye," her husband agreed. "Those who surround the king are a jealous lot. Edward's actions willna encourage their loyalty. In the short time since he has taken the throne, anger has brewed within his countrymen that the young king's focus is on his own desires, nae the needs of England."

"If so, a godsend for King Robert."

"Indeed." Stephan paused. "Neither do I think the young sovereign is foolish enough to ignore Scotland. He is a man of considerable knowledge and intelligence. Regardless of his yearnings to pursue more provincial interests, I believe to stay his noble's unrest he will make the motions of wanting to claim Scotland, mayhap on occasion order troops sent north. Or, if pressed, take part in a campaign."

"Until Robert the Bruce can reunite Scotland, we will never be safe."

Silence fell between them.

The lonesome cry of a seagull echoed as it glided nearby on currents of air.

Her husband's gaze darkened.

Shaken by the heat in his gaze, she stepped back. "There is much to do before we sup."

"There is."

For a long moment he watched her, the need on his face shaking her to the core. Though she loved Stephan, how could she make him understand her fear of a man's touch without admitting her shame? After their time together, Katherine wanted to believe he wouldna be repulsed to learn she was tainted, her innocence lost. What if she was wrong? Neither would she take the risk. "We will have more days together in the future," he said.

They would, and that was what terrified her the most. She stepped back. "I must go."

Frustrated as Katherine rushed toward the turret, Stephan muttered a curse. After their kiss and all that they'd shared throughout their journey, he'd begun to believe their bond had strengthened. Instead, with each day she seemed to withdraw further.

However much he wanted to owe her retreat to her suffering of the last few weeks, 'twas but an excuse. Neither did he have any idea how to repair the growing distance.

With a sigh, he departed the wall walk and turned his attention to Avalon. After the battle this day, there was much to rebuild. The weeks ahead would be busy. As for Katherine, over the next few months he would find a way to mend the breach between them.

He descended, the slap of his feet upon the turret steps empty companions. A short time before he'd been furious at Robert Bruce's insistence that in addition to securing Avalon he must wed Katherine. Now he'd grown fond of the lass, enjoyed their time together, and in truth, desired her in his bed.

With his vows taken as a Templar, never had he believed he

would entertain notions of having a woman in his life, much less an intimate relationship. At the time of the Grand Master's dissolution of the Brotherhood, along with his encouragement to merge with the Scots, had fallen on deaf ears. Now he found life without Katherine impossible to consider.

A woman like her would want more than a simple marriage. She was filled with passion, a lass who held dreams, desires of love. Love he didna have to give. Neither could he forget that she didna know of his past, his shame, or of her father's having slain his family.

At the bottom step, a pool of blood from the day's battle lay congealed in the late afternoon sun, darkening as if it were an ill omen.

So caught up in preparing for the siege, he'd lost track of the time. God's blade, 'twas October thirteenth.

Fury poured through him as he thought of the Grand Master and the Templars who'd remained in France, ignorant of King Philip's sordid intention.

God help them all.

Stephan shoved his hand against the stone wall, fought to breathe. His body trembled as grief slashed his heart. With the arrival of midnight, hours before, the arrests had begun.

Damn King Philip to Hades!

On wobbly legs, Stephan strode to the chapel. Inside, he knelt before the cross, bowed his head. Anger burned his soul as he recited the Lord's Prayer over and again for his Templar brothers.

The quiet scrape of the door echoed behind him.

His body tense, he continued to pray.

Paces away, Thomas knelt, his whispers joining Stephan's as he, too, began to recite the Paternoster.

Another muffled thud of the door sounded, followed by several more soft swishes.

Whispered prayers filled the chapel.

With each repetition, Stephan damned the fact that hundreds of miles away, innocent men, those who had sworn their lives to God, warriors who protected the innocent, were now subject to the very devil himself.

With the candles inside the church nearly gutted after hours of prayer and grief still weighing heavy on his heart, Stephan made the sign of the cross and departed. The night cloudless, a near-full moon hung in the sky as he stepped outside. With the stroke of midnight, the powers the Templars once had wielded, like the moon, began to wane.

On a curse, Stephan closed his eyes.

The scrape of the door sounded behind him.

Thomas paused at his side, his eyes dark with anguish. "Never will I forget the treachery King Philip has wrought this day."

"Nor I," Stephan rasped. "He will pay for his transgressions."

His friend muttered a curse. "Nor will our brothers be forgotten."

"They willna."

In silence, Thomas departed.

Pain from his injuries pummeled Stephan as he strode to the keep. His wounds would heal, but King Philip's perfidy set into action this day couldna be undone.

With his mind a tangle of emotions, halfway across the bailey he'd walked numerous times as a child, memories of his father watching him spar rolled through his mind. Then he'd longed for the day when he'd hold his own blade, had anticipated the moment he would become a knight.

But weeks away from being presented with his first sword, one he'd spied the blacksmith crafting as his father had looked on with pride, had come the attack.

As the assailing force had begun climbing over the walls, his father had ordered him to hide. A lad of seven, terrified, he'd complied. Frozen with fear, with stroke after pitiless stroke, he had witnessed Katherine's father slay his own.

Groans from the father he loved as he lay dying haunted him still, a potent reminder of how he'd clutched his dagger, and of how, with tears streaming down his face, he'd remained concealed, shielded by naught but cowardice.

Blades had clashed nearby as Stephan had begged God to save his mother, who'd run between his father and the next swing. But when he'd peered through the crevice a moment later, he'd seen her sprawled upon the ground, her fixed gaze staring skyward. His chest tightened. Then his sister Johanna's scream had split the air as she'd fallen from the wall walk and died.

When 'twas clear his home was lost, their knights crumpling against an overpowering force, when he should have fought to preserve his legacy, one his father had given his blood to keep, he'd fled.

A wolf's cry echoed in the distance.

On a curse, damning the memories, Stephan strode across the bailey. He wouldna sleep this night. If he did, with his mind fertile with horrific and shameful memories, 'twould be filled with naught but violent dreams.

He walked to the stable. Far from comforted by the fresh smell of hay and horses, he grabbed a currycomb and walked to the first stall. A soft nicker welcomed him when he moved to a steed's side. With smooth, efficient strokes, he brushed the destrier. Once finished, he moved to the next stall, finding solace in the mundane task that allowed his thoughts to blur.

"Stephan?"

At Katherine's voice, he glanced toward the stable door.

Framed within the mix of moonlight and the lantern's golden glow, she looked like a fairy cast from the other world.

" 'Tis late," he stated, his words gruff, wanting to be alone. "You should be abed."

"I-I spoke with Thomas," she rasped. "He explained that this day, the arrests have begun."

Bedamned! "He should have said naught!"

"Dinna blame him." Sorrow tore her words until they fractured like ice. "Like you, Thomas keeps his emotions hidden deep inside, something I learned during our time at sea. When I saw him on the wall walk, his expression held such distress, I couldna leave without seeking to discover what caused his upset or trying to help."

"Why were you on the wall walk?"

"I . . ." A tremor rippled through her. "I was looking for you."

Stephan closed his eyes. Nae wanting Katherine to see him in his moment of weakness, he damned his yearning to draw her into his arms, hold her until her sadness faded. An act he would have performed in other circumstances, though with his emotions fragile, if he went to her now, he was terrified he'd confess his own turmoil.

He cleared his throat, turned his attention to the next steed, and drew the currycomb over the horse's neck. "You have found me. Now you can return to the castle and sleep."

Footsteps on hay crunched closer.

"Go," he whispered.

She paused at his side. "I canna."

Furious at himself for being so weak, he glared at her, praying she'd retreat.

Katherine angled her jaw toward him, her look as fierce as it was fragile. "I know you are angry, hurt, how could you be otherwise? An atrocity has been committed. Innocent men will die because of King Philip's greed."

Her heart-torn words shattered the formidable wall he'd built around himself. Stephan shoved the currycomb onto the top of a post, drew her against him, giving solace, accepting the same. For a long while she stood within his embrace, her body soft against his, the calls of the night a solemn backdrop.

On an unsteady breath, she exhaled. "I dinna know how to comfort you, or what words to offer. After learning why Thomas was distressed, I couldna let you be alone."

Humbled by his wife's strength, her caring, Stephan met her gaze. "I understand how to deal with the casualties of war. A battle you can prepare for. You have expectations, understand that there will be loss. But when duplicity arises from those you have protected, watched others die to defend . . ." He shook his head. " 'Tis the most contemptible form of betrayal."

She gave a shaky nod, the sadness upon her face almost bringing him to his knees.

His fingers trembling, he wiped away a tear from her cheek, found comfort in the act, strength in her caring. "I thank you for coming to be with me."

"I could have done naught else."

She could have, but her action bespoke a woman of honor, one with whom any man would be blessed to share his life. Without warning, need roared through him, and he lowered his mouth, halted a whisper above hers.

Shaken by his action, Stephan released her; aware the kiss wasna from desire, but his need to believe that from this moment of darkness, hope could arise. Still, in his mind, the reason excused naught. "I am sorry. 'Twas wrong."

"I—"

"Say naught." He took her hand. "The day has been a difficult one for us all. 'Tis time to rest." In silence he led her toward the door.

* * *

Stephan tipped the bucket over his head. Water splashed onto his face as he turned into the cold stream.

At his side, Thomas scrubbed the dirt from his body, tossed the crumpled cloth aside. "The last man is buried."

Stephan nodded as he dried his face, appreciating the cool freshness against the layers of sweat and dirt from the grueling work of the last few hours. A gruesome deed, one thankfully behind them. "With a messenger sent to deliver our ransom demand to Edward of Caernarfon, we can begin rebuilding Avalon, as well as shoring up its defenses."

His friend lifted another water-filled bucket and poured. Thomas shook his head, set aside the wooden container, and grabbed a cloth.

Across the bailey, a woman, her face weathered, her silver hair hanging in a long braid over her shoulder, shuffled toward the keep, a basket in her hand.

Stephan watched her slow but determined steps as memories crashed through him. It couldna be. He'd thought anyone he would have known from his youth had gone or long since died.

He glanced at his friend. "Thomas, make a list of what needs to be done, and then make assignments for the men. There is something I must do."

Through the side of the wadded linen, his friend glanced over. "What is it?"

Stephan shook his head. "I will explain later." Tightness squeezing his chest, he strode after the woman, quickened his pace when she disappeared inside the keep. As he entered, he caught a wisp of her gown as she entered the turret. He lengthened his stride, hurried up the curve of smoothed stone.

Several steps up, Stephan caught sight of her. "Eufemie?"

The elder turned. Torchlight from the sconces illuminated the furrows on her aged brow. Disbelief widened her eyes, and the hand carrying her basket grew white. "God in heaven. Lord Stephan?"

Happiness filled him as memories came back, of her tending him as a lad, of the stories she would tell. "Aye," he replied, his voice rough.

The elder wiped the tears from her eyes, stepped down. A smile wobbled on her lips. "You have come home."

He glanced down the steps. Confident nay one was about, he nodded. "Where are you headed?"

"To bring herbs to one of the wounded knights." Shrewd eyes studied him. "He would be your man, aye?"

"He would."

Pride glowed on her face. "I knew you would return. Your da would have been so proud."

He had his doubts, nor would he speak of this further. "I need to talk to you in private."

Sage eyes held his. "I know of a place." Basket secured on her arm, Eufemie headed up the steps.

In the privacy of an empty chamber, Stephan explained that, after the attack so many years ago, he'd escaped. Upon reaching the home of a distant uncle, he'd learned the man was dead.

The thick folds on her brow sagged. " 'Twas too much for a lad to face alone."

His mouth tightened. " 'Tis in the past."

"Mayhap, but those terrible times haunt you."

"Memories, naught more," he stated, keeping his voice empty, refusing to allow the pain, the hurt, to take hold. "Now I am back, rightful heir to Avalon, a legacy I will keep."

"Rightful heir?" A frown edged her mouth. "I spoke with Lady Katherine earlier this day and she said . . ." Shock, disbelief, and then acceptance flickered on her face. "You wed your enemy's daughter?"

Guilt washed through him. "She doesna know of her father's actions. Neither do I intend for her to ever discover the truth."

The healer tsked. " 'Tis a burden to keep such a powerful secret from the lass."

"Mayhap, but on this I willna be swayed."

Troubled eyes held his, and she made the sign of the cross. "You must tell Lady Katherine. If she discovers that her father murdered your family—"

"She willna. Her father's actions were his sin to bear, nae hers."

Aged eyes held his. "Regardless of whose wrong, I beseech you, tell her."

He damned this convoluted mess. Katherine was innocent of the crimes tangled in the past. "We willna speak of this further."

Eyes blazing, she glared at him. "You may be lord of the castle, but you will listen to me."

Respect filled him at her spirit, the way her eyes held his as if on a dare. He nodded in deference, finding himself curious at what Eufemie would say. " 'Twould seem I will."

The anger in her eyes faded. "You were always a wise one."

Humbled by her praise, one he'd far from earned, Stephan remained quiet.

"Like you," the healer began, "I watched the lass grow. As well, she was an inquisitive child, asking questions one atop the other." Melancholy filled her gaze, yet she chuckled. "Countless times she appeared at my door at first light with fresh milk, eggs, or a loaf of bread still steaming hot."

"She loves you," he said, moved by the image, one easy to imagine given Katherine's compassion.

"And I her." She shook her head. "It broke my heart how the English noble murdered her parents, forcing her to watch." She hesitated. "I assume she told you?"

Stephan nodded.

Her hand on the basket tightened. "Though slight of build compared to the Earl of Preswick, she held her own when he threatened to lock her away if she refused to marry him. As he towered over her, instead of cowering she spat in his eye."

As stunned as he was proud of his wife's daring, Stephan nodded. "An act for which the king's man incarcerated her in the dungeon."

"Aye. The lass is intelligent. Once alone, she somehow escaped. Miraculously, somewhere in the mayhem after, she met and married you."

"She did."

Shrewd eyes studied him. "Katherine is a good woman, a strong lass any man would be blessed to have as a wife."

"Indeed."

A fragile smile touched her lips like the first bloom of a morning rose. "I was so upset, I missed the obvious. You care for her."

Startled, Stephan struggled for a reply. How after so many years could Eufemie deduce the truth in but moments? He owed her ability to the close bond they'd had when he was a child. Whatever the reason, he was thankful for the unexpected link to his past, to the friendship she offered, one that remained strong.

Warmth touched his heart as he pondered her claim. "I care for Katherine very much," he admitted, finding peace in the admission.

"But . . ." Frowning, he strode to the arched window, watched the breakers roll in.

Unsure how to explain, desperate to find a way to break through the barrier his wife had erected between them, Stephan turned. Beneath the healer's inquisitive gaze, he tried to find a way to admit he'd failed to build more than a simple bond of trust with his wife.

Her mouth settled into a firm line and she set aside her basket. With quiet steps, the elder walked to him. "You have always been able to talk to me."

"When I was a child. Years have passed. Times are nae so simple."

"Nor were they ever," she replied. "Now you are a noble with responsibilities, one who has returned to his legacy, and a man now bound to his wife. Though somehow I sense 'tis nae the responsibility that has you worried but the woman."

Stephan curled his hands into fists.

"Can you nae speak with Lady Katherine?" she asked.

He relaxed his hands. "Nay."

Sadness settled in her gaze, and then the elder gasped. "God in heaven, you dinna know?"

"Know?" At the dismay in her eyes, he braced himself against whatever the healer alluded to.

"When she was fifteen summers, Katherine was attacked," Eufemie explained. " 'Twas an awful time."

"Attacked?" he repeated, focusing on the single word. "You mean defiled?"

"Aye," she replied, a waver in her voice.

Fury roared through Stephan, an anger so deep 'twas like blackness smeared upon his soul. And explained why on their wedding night, when he'd avoided their marriage bed, her eyes had filled with relief. "Is he dead?" he demanded like a man possessed.

"Aye. Her father tracked him down, gutted him, and tossed his body into the sea."

Stephan grunted, approving of the blackguard's demise.

"As one would expect," the healer continued, "the lass withdrew. Months passed. Slowly, she began to speak. With more time, ever so often, a flicker of a smile appeared on her face." The healer wiped at her tears. "One day I heard her laugh. From then on, most believed she had moved past the attack."

"But she hadna," Stephan supplied, understanding too well how a person could smother horrific events, bury them so deep as to nae face the shame.

Eufemie nodded. "When she first told me that she'd married, after I moved past my shock, I'd assumed she'd finally let the pain, suffering, and fear go. From your words, I realize she hasna." She sighed. "The marriage wasna her choice, was it?"

"Nay. 'Twas King Robert's decree."

A sad smile flickered across her face. "She was always his favorite."

"Did the king know of the assault?" he asked, wondering why her godfather would keep Stephan ignorant of such an important fact.

"He did and understood that 'twould take a man of honor, kindness, and great patience to win Katherine's heart." She paused. "Our king must regard you highly indeed."

Far from flattered, Stephan remained silent.

"But a wedding doesna a marriage make, does it?" the elder asked, her voice soft with understanding.

As if he had anything to lose by admitting the truth? "Nay."

"And with the way you feel for your wife, 'tis what you are wanting, is it nae?"

"I . . ." He rubbed the back of his neck. "She refuses to let me close."

"As I would expect for the reason I explained."

A reason he hadna known of until now.

" 'Twill be difficult for you to break through her defenses."

"I would never harm her."

"I am sure she knows this, but," Eufemie said quietly, " 'twill take a patient hand, one I believe you have, as does our king."

Patience. A blasted bushelful. "You think it can be done?"

"Aye."

Hope ignited. "How?"

A twinkle sparkled in her eyes. "As any man would do who wants to win a woman's heart. You must woo her."

Sweat broke out on his brow. "Woo her?" he strangled out.

"Flowers, kind deeds, and the words of a lover."

Heat touched his face.

"I have embarrassed you now," she said with a chuckle. "It wasna my intention. I am too old for such whimsies to affect me any longer, but there was a time . . ." Her eyes misted and she shook her head. " 'Tis nae me that we speak of but Lady Katherine. Take your time with the lass; let her come to you. If you push her too fast, she will continue to withdraw."

A fact he'd experienced firsthand. Though he'd nae known why.

She arched a brow. "I would think if a man of your wit and handsome looks puts his mind to it, he could woo any woman off her feet. Dinna tell me after all these years, you have nae left a trail of lasses in your wake."

He stiffened. His life as a Templar barely left him time to think of a woman, much less woo one.

When he didna reply, her aged eyes grew tender. "Have faith in yourself; I do."

Faith, of that he had nay doubt. His ability to woo and win Katherine was another matter.

Chapter Eighteen

To keep her mind off the destruction left in the Englishmen's wake, Katherine scrubbed a window in the keep with a damp rag. She glanced at the sun beginning to set, wiped the sweat from her brow, and continued to clean.

The rap of hammers against wood, the voices of the men, and every so often the bells of the chapel echoed from outside.

She'd reclaimed her home, one she would rebuild with pride, and the penance of marriage, one she would bear. Penance. A harsh word and, considering she loved Stephan, unfair. Though coerced to wed, he was a man any woman would want. And she did, as a friend. With her tangled past, to believe their union could be more was but a fool's wish.

That her body had ached for him when they'd kissed changed naught. Though gentle, his caresses had brought back her tormented past. Overwhelmed, she'd run. Nay doubt she'd left him confused. How could he nae be? Though a Knight Templar, he was still a man. However much Katherine wished otherwise, she couldna give him the intimacy he desired.

Frustration churning inside, she lifted the damp cloth to the next pane, scrubbed. Memories of her assault would forever haunt her. At times they were far away, hidden in some distant part of her, but there they waited, lurked until her mind was relaxed, and then they would again attack.

Destroy her momentary peace.

Shatter any belief that she could overcome them.

However much she wished, nae even a man of Stephan's ilk could smother the memories.

Tears burned in her throat. Why could she nae discard the horror or shame? Mary have mercy, hadna enough years past? Would there ever come a time when she could move beyond the scarred recollections, relax her defenses, and welcome her husband into her bed?

Her body shuddered at the thought of a man's touch, and she lowered her head against the windowpane. There was nay hope.

"Katherine?"

At the concern in her husband's voice, she straightened, his arrival throwing her further off-balance. "Aye?" Katherine replied as she continued to clean, providing herself more time before she must face him.

"You are upset?"

Hand fisted on the damp cloth, she lowered the rag to her side. "I find it hard to be otherwise. Since our arrival, even with your knights working from dawn 'til dusk, we have barely made progress on all of the necessary repairs. 'Twill take months to rebuild everything."

"It will, but it is time we have."

Time? Aye. Time for his subtle yearnings to turn into his reaching out for her and, in return, her only offering disappointment. "Do we?" she asked, allowing frustration to fill her words. "Once Edward of Caernarfon receives the ransom demand, outraged by our brazen demand, he willna forfeit the coin but order a force to attack."

"Mayhap, but I believe the king has more pressing problems."

"The death of the earl is nae an act he will dismiss. He will be furious."

"He will be, and we will prepare for retaliation," Stephan said, "but 'tis only war. Men fight. Men die. 'Tis nae pleasant but the way of things."

The situation wasna that simple. Before, she'd anticipated the day Avalon was rebuilt; then her husband, along with a strong contingent of men, would sail to fight for their king. Now thoughts of Stephan leaving, of his mortality, left her shaken. If anything were to happen to him . . .

"Though much remains to be done, however overwhelming it appears, I am pleased with our progress. The larger renovations will be finished in a sennight, mayhap a few days more. Then, our attention will turn to smaller, more intricate repairs. The reason I am here . . ." He paused. " 'Tis time I began going through the castle's ledgers."

A part of her dreaded this moment, the familiar surroundings, the writings in her father's hand, the small chamber where she'd visited him often over the years. "Follow me." Bracing herself for the rush of emotions entering the room would bring, Katherine set the damp cloth aside and started down the corridor.

Her husband's steps firm but quiet, he kept pace at her side.

As they walked, the wavering of torchlight cast a mixture of shadows and light throughout the hallway. Too aware of the man beside her, her thoughts tumbled to her inability to share intimacy. Why had she dared to give in to the urge to accept his kiss? How could she have deluded herself into believing that even though she loved him, she could accept such?

Upon the smoothed stone of the turret, their steps echoed as one, a muted tap that broke the silence.

An ache built inside. How long would Stephan wait? How long before the desire in his eyes faded? How long until through sheer frustration her husband turned to another?

On her next step, lost in her thoughts, she stumbled.

Stephan caught her.

Her emotions fragile, Katherine stiffened. "I thank you. I wasna paying attention."

Gentle fingers lifted her face to his. In the wash of torchlight, concern darkened his eyes. "More than worries of King Edward's retaliation concern you."

Mary have mercy, after everything, aware she could never have him, she again wanted his kiss. " 'Tis that . . ." Nay, she couldna speak. She stepped back, gave herself much needed distance. "There is still so much to repair."

His mouth tightened, as if far from convinced.

Too aware of him, she remained silent.

After a long moment, he nodded. "Let us go."

Thankful he'd nae pressed as they continued up, once they reached the corridor, she fell into step at his side. Vacant places that had once held paintings she'd loved over the years tore at her heart. Down the hallway, the tapestry from Portugal her father had gifted to her mother was gone. Damn the English. At the end of the passageway, Katherine halted before a finely crafted door. She turned the handle. "My father's private quarters."

*   *   *

Stephan moved past Katherine, glanced around the small chamber where her father had worked. A place nay doubt she'd visited many times over the years. This was the reason for her upset, nae thoughts of their kiss or how she'd pulled away from him.

With mere weeks having elapsed since she'd witnessed her parents' murder, each turn within Avalon and every chamber would incite fresh waves of grief. Memories of his own life inside the castle, though they hurt, had been muted by the years.

"If you would like," he said, "you can return to—"

Blue eyes leveled on him. "Nay. 'Tis my home." The scrape of wood echoed as she closed the door behind them, but he caught her slight tremble. Nor would she welcome further concern. He focused on the reason for coming to the chamber.

A short while later, after thumbing through the castle ledger, pleased by the meticulous documentation of purchases, daily household uses of food, ale, and the details of castle life, Stephan closed the cover.

Anxious eyes held his.

"Impeccable records, ones I am sure impressed the English."

Pride flickered in her gaze. "My father's entries were always meticulous."

Indeed, his accounting skills rivaled those of the Templars. Nay wanting to find anything admirable about the man, Stephan couldna find fault with how he had run Avalon. Neither would he linger. Sadness filled Katherine's eyes. If he was to woo his wife, it wouldna be in a chamber that brought her sadness.

He stowed the ledger inside a drawer, stood. "I have something to show you."

His wife frowned. "You but scanned the records."

"So I did. What I saw assures me that when I perform a more careful review, my remaining questions concerning details of the castle will be answered." He took her hand.

Her fingers tensed within his.

A reaction he'd expected, but if the lass was to become used to his touch, 'twould begin now. " 'Tis growing late. There is something of importance I need to show you before the skies grow too dark."

Though he'd made preparations, anxiousness rumbled through

him as he led her toward the gatehouse. Wooing and women were nae his expertise.

As they exited the stronghold, wisps of clouds slid across the sun, an orange ball in the sky.

"Why are you bringing me beyond the castle walls?" she asked, worry straining her voice.

Why indeed? He felt like a fool, but when he'd visited Eufemie that morning, the healer had assured him that in addition to the little things he'd begun to do for Katherine each day, once he believed they'd made significant progress, 'twas time to strengthen their bond. Confident she was ready for the next step, he'd made his decision.

"You will like it," Stephan said.

Doubtful eyes met his and his wife's step slowed.

He drew her forward, prayed he'd judged the time right. If nae, he'd shift the topic and allow their evening to be that enjoyed by two friends.

As he led her down the twist of rocks, the soft rumble of the surf grew. After they rounded a large boulder, a hidden cove came into view, the pebbles smoothed by waves over time. He released her.

Delight shimmered in her eyes. "It has been years since I came to this inlet. 'Tis well hidden." She smiled. "I am surprised you found it."

When he'd pondered where to take her, an area where they could be alone and away from prying eyes, this hidden cove had come to mind. A place he'd often visited as a child, one he'd believed only he'd known of. 'Twould seem they had yet more in common. "I discovered it when I was making note of the island's shoreline."

"As you are a Knight Templar, I shouldna be surprised." Katherine slowly turned, taking in everything. A smile touched her lips as she met his gaze. "Let me show you something." She walked to the far wall of rock.

Intrigued, Stephan followed.

At the base, she knelt beside a smaller boulder, half hidden beneath a time-worn ledge. With care, she pried away the stone.

A miniature cavern lay before her.

" 'Tis still here." She reached in, withdrew a small wooden galley. Happiness glittered in her eyes as she stood. She handed him the carving.

Impressed by the detail, he turned the vessel against the lingering shine of light, frowned at the Templar cross emblazoned upon the sail. "Whoever crafted this had a fine hand."

"My father brought the replica to me from one of his journeys. When I received the miniature, I held reservations of ever playing with such a finely crafted gift." Her expression softened. "Then he brought me here and set the ship upon the waves. As the galley rocked its way down the length of the shore, he'd tell me stories." Memories warming her eyes, she sighed. "I always loved our visits here."

The tenderness for her father in her voice warred with his loathing for the man. Stephan shifted his thoughts to a safer matter. "Do you know why the sail is emblazoned with a Templar cross?"

She shook her head. "But whenever we sailed the ship, Da would tell me tales of the Knights Templar. At the time, I never questioned his stories. Now I find myself intrigued that in a sense, 'twas as if a premonition of my meeting you. Odd, is it nae?"

A shiver wove through Stephan, an unease he dismissed. "Nay doubt from his travels, your father gleaned many tales of Templar battles. Ones," he said relaxing a degree, "that tend to grow with the retelling."

"Indeed." With a twinkle in her eyes, Katherine walked to the shore and set the boat on the tip of an incoming swell. The ship bobbed with abandoned glee on the wave, ascending to the foam-tipped crest, then sliding into the oncoming trough. As the replica continued to bob on the water down the shore, she walked alongside. Paces from the edge of the cove, she lifted the craft into the safety of her palm.

Red dusted her cheeks in a flattering hue. "You must think me foolish."

Enchanted by the sight of her with sunlight on her face and joy in her eyes, he stepped forward, wove his fingers through the soft flow of her hair. "I canna think you foolish when this brings you such happiness."

Awareness flickered in her gaze, quickly smothered by panic.

But now Stephan understood her hesitation. Refusing to rush her, he stepped back. "I have a surprise to show you."

Katherine watched him for a long moment. After replacing the replica in the secret cavern, she returned.

The crunch of sand entwined with the soft rumble of waves as he led her to where a tree had washed ashore years ago. Sun-bleached branches poked skyward with feeble twists. He reached over the trunk, lifted a covered basket.

The amazement in her eyes made his efforts worthwhile, but the surprise guaranteed naught. Neither did he hold the skills to stir a woman's desire. But he cared for his wife, and with each moment Stephan found himself wanting more. In addition to the pleasure touching her gave him, there was also the peace being with her brought. In her presence, the emptiness haunting him since he'd fled Avalon so many years before had vanished. His hand tightened on the edge of the basket.

He stilled.

God's blade, he loved her.

Never had he believed he'd find a woman who touched his heart, one who could ease the grief of his past. But here, now, he realized Katherine had.

Humbled by such a blessing, Stephan focused on his task, this moment of great magnitude. In the many battles he'd fought, none had been of more importance.

By the attention she took with her dress since they'd arrived at Avalon, her smile given at his approach, and the tenderness in her eyes when they met his, he believed she cared for him. He'd also caught her shy looks, the undeclared yearning within her gaze. And he recalled the hungry way, if only for a moment, she'd responded to his kiss.

Orange rays melded with purple streaks overhead like a tangle of power, a potent play as night slowly claimed the sky. In the growing darkness, he placed the basket on a flat rock, determined to do whatever was necessary to win her heart.

With the shimmers of fading light surrounding them, curious as to what was inside the wooden container, Katherine waited as her husband lifted the cloth.

Nestled inside were bread, wine, two goblets, and several wedges of cheese.

Confused, she glanced up. "Why are these here?"

"After the day's hard work, I thought you would enjoy watching the sun set while we ate."

The unsureness of his gaze left her charmed, his thoughtfulness more so. He lived his life wielding a blade, a warrior whose life was on serving those in need of protection, nae such a mundane task. Nor had she missed how he'd grown more attentive toward her.

Since they'd seized the castle, at night he took care to ensure that all was secure, check on his men, confirm the people living within were taken care of, and had established a new routine. After finishing their evening meal, he now escorted Katherine to the wall walk, where they discussed a myriad of issues from the mundane to the universal.

In addition, instead of departing at first light to join his men, Stephan now had food sent to their bedchamber. Earlier this day he'd broken his fast with her; then a short while later, he'd surprised her with dried wildflowers.

Caution smothered Katherine's secret wish for him to love her. He was being thoughtful, nay more. "I would, I thank you."

His gaze lifted to hers.

Prepared for their time together to be one of friendship, the need in his eyes stole her breath away. A tremor whispered through her body, then another. Like magic, the soft ebb and flow of the incoming tide filled her with a steadiness, with strength. Wrapped in this moment, far from prying eyes, she pushed aside her worries.

With each shaky breath, her love for this valiant warrior intensified. That he'd taken time to make her feel special bolstered Katherine's belief that one day he could love her. If their time together this night ended with a kiss, 'twas an intimacy she could accept.

With efficiency, he spread out the fare, and then filled her goblet.

Katherine took a sip, savoring the warm tang on her tongue. "I had thought the English destroyed all of the wine during the attack."

"When they knew they were to be defeated, before we seized Avalon, they gutted every barrel. This had been stored in one of our ships' holds. 'Twas made in France, as was the cheese. The bread," he said with a smile, "came from the kitchen."

"You mean from Godit." A rueful smile touched his lips, and she gave a soft laugh. "I have seen how the cook eyes you."

"And how is that?" he asked, relaxing beside her on the smooth stone.

"Like you were a ripened apple, one she would like to eat."

He chuckled; emboldened, she met his gaze. "Why is that?"

Though whispered, the potency of his voice tingled upon her skin like a caress. She lowered her gaze to his mouth and her awareness grew. Struggling against another shot of anxiety, she forced herself to reply. "Because you are fair to look upon."

Hazel eyes darkened like emeralds glistening in the fading light. "As are you." His touch tender, he lifted her face. "I would be liking a kiss," he said, his every word quiet, rough with yearning.

Tingles brushed her flesh, but she didna withdraw, the stakes too high for cowardice. "As would I."

His nostrils flared, but he didna move.

She waited a moment longer.

He remained still.

Heat warmed her cheeks and she started to shift back.

"Lass, tis your kiss to give," he said with infinite tenderness. "I willna be taking what you dinna freely offer."

Hers? Elation filled her, and then her heart plunged in shame. Horrified, she jerked free and scrambled to her feet. Only one reason existed for his compassionate offer. "You know of the assault!"

With slow, controlled movements, Stephan stood. "Katherine—"

"St-stay back!"

"The sin wasna yours," he said, his words quiet, "nor will what happened change who you are in my eyes."

"How can it nae?" she demanded, outraged that he knew, furious that from this moment he would look at her as if she were scarred, stained, unfit to touch.

"I would be a fool to label you for the atrocity of another."

On a sharp breath, she looked away, aching inside. 'Twas naught but words. If only he could. Her breath hitched and she took another step back.

"Katherine, stay. Please."

Her entire body trembled and she wished she could curl up and die. She faced him. "I canna."

"You can. This moment the choice is yours." Solemn eyes held hers. "With me you are safe. Always. Forever. Trust me."

She exhaled, clung to his declarations as if they were a lifeline, fought to bury the horrific images from her youth.

"Never would I hurt you."

"I know."

"Please, come and eat." Stephan walked to where the food was spread out on the stone.

"Wh-what if I wanted your kiss?"

He stilled. A moment passed, and then another, as if he gathered himself. He turned, his gaze hot but tempered with controlled calm. "As I said, 'tis yours to give. Before you ask, I would be liking it, but I willna push you. When we kiss, 'twill be your decision. When we make love, 'twill be your choice as well. Nor am I a man experienced," he admitted, his voice quiet, "but for you I will offer what I can, give you any tenderness I have."

As a Templar, he would be untried, but so caught up in her own terrible memories, she'd nae considered his own experience with women, or lack of. But he'd empowered her to choose, even at the risk of his pride.

Humbled by his offering, to prostrate himself before her to help her heal, she stepped forward, her decision made.

She wanted this kiss. Before her worries built, swayed her decision, Katherine rose on her tiptoes and pressed her mouth against his.

Stephan remained still as she moved against his lips, but desire burned in his eyes as they held hers.

Becoming braver, she deepened her sensual foray. His mouth brushed across hers, slow, savoring, heat igniting, luring her to take the kiss deeper.

His taste filled her, hazed her doubts until she was lost in the moment. She plunged headlong, savoring the rightness of it, how they each fit against the other.

Stephan's hand skimmed the back of her neck, drew her forward until his muscled chest pressed firm against her softness.

A fissure of panic swept her; she stilled.

" 'Tis only me," he whispered as he pressed delicate kisses on her mouth, along the curve of her cheek. "Look at me."

Trembling, Katherine met his gaze, the warmth, and tenderness there eroding her nervousness.

"Kiss me, lass," he whispered. "Trust me to be gentle, to make love to you as you should have been from the first."

"I-I dinna know if I can."

He brushed a windswept lock of hair from her cheek. "You are a strong woman, one who wields a sword without hesitation, one who dares to face her aggressors boldly. I canna believe you willna follow your heart."

"My heart?" she whispered.

The first twinkle of stars shimmered in the sky as hazel eyes held hers. "Do you care for me?"

"A-aye."

He skimmed his lips against hers, drew her to him slowly, his fingers doing magical things against her skin until she was kissing him back. When the slide of heat ignited, he drew away, his own breathing unsteady. "I believe you feel more."

"Stephan . . ."

Eyes dark with conviction held hers, the stars dotting the sky like a promise. "Trust me with the truth."

Her entire body stilled as the words trembled on her tongue. "I am afraid."

"As I am. Caring about someone, wanting you, is nae a charge I take lightly."

"You care for me?" she asked, hope filling her words.

Tenderness creased his expression. "Indeed. I love you, Katherine."

"You love me?" Happiness filled her until she thought she would burst.

"Aye, I love you, and will tomorrow, and forever."

"I love you as well," she rushed out, "I had hoped—"

" 'Tis naught to hope for. What we have is real, what few ever feel."

Elation stormed her, swept away the blackness shrouding her soul. The doubts, the fears that had haunted her over the years began to fade. She nodded, unsure what to do, what to say.

Stephan swept her into his arms, carried her to the blanket he'd spread upon the sand. As she stood before him, he pressed a kiss upon her mouth, teased her with light flicks of his tongue until she moved into the kiss, tasting, taking, her whole mind focused on this moment.

On him.

While his fingers glided over her arms, released the first tie of her gown, she kept her mind on the pleasure of this moment, on the joy he brought to her life.

His every touch seduced her, lured her to forget, to only feel. Her soft sighs melded with his moans as his hands gently skimmed over exposed flesh with teasing strokes. When she thought she couldna feel more, with her nakedness covered by the shimmer of starlight, he proved her wrong.

"Stephan," she gasped while his fingers toyed, teased until deep inside she began to tremble, to ache with the need of something more. "I want you," she said on a moan.

He pressed kisses up her thigh, brushed his fingers across her sensitive flesh until she arched beneath him. "You must be sure."

"Never have I been so sure of anything in my life."

Under the moonlight, Stephan moved his body over hers. "I love you, Katherine." He sank deep.

She stiffened beneath the pressure.

"Trust me." He claimed her mouth, teased her until all she could think of was him.

When she began to relax, began to kiss him back, he moved within her, and the fire that had burned before scorched. Her needs spun to desperation until she arched against him, met his every stroke.

Then her world exploded into a myriad of colors and she was floating, suspended in a magical place where naught existed but bliss.

Stephan called out her name as he filled her. His breaths coming fast, he drew her against him.

Infused with a sense of completeness, she rested her cheek against his heart, the rapid beat slowing.

"You are amazing," he whispered.

She shied away.

Her husband caught her chin. "Never be ashamed of what we do, how we love."

"I . . ." Katherine shook her head. "You must think me absurd."

His hand cupped her face as he brushed his lips over hers. "I think you are beautiful, intelligent, and incredible."

A sigh fell from her lips.

"You like that?" he asked as he nibbled along the curve of her neck.

"Aye, how your mouth moves over me feels wondrous."

"On that I agree." He inched lower, his tongue working miracles across her flesh.

Tingles of scandalous pleasure rolled through her, and she arched against the deftness of his touch. "What are you doing?"

"I"—Stephan drew her nipple into his mouth, and then inched lower—"am going to again make love to my wife."

Chapter Nineteen

Stephan shifted in the bed, his body bumping against skin. Reflex had him reaching for his dagger, then he stilled, opened his eyes. A smile curved his mouth as his gaze fell upon Katherine's nakedness. Bolts of need shot through him as he took in her soft, full curves until he ached to touch her, to make love to her again.

Yesterday, while he'd carried the basket of food to the secret cove, his intention had been to strengthen their bond in the sharing of a meal. He'd hoped for a slow kiss, mayhap two. Only in his wildest dreams had he believed they would make love and, upon their return to their chamber, that their intimacy would continue through the night.

But as she'd stood before him, outlined in the fading sun's glow, Katherine's shyness, her fear of a man's touch, had driven him to help her move past the nightmares that haunted her still. Through the first crucial moments, he'd held misgivings she would dare to allow him close.

Then she'd moved her mouth over his.

Her softness, her taste had done away with his uncertainties. And when she'd returned his kiss 'twas like a dam breaking free. Her every response to his touch, his kiss, had emboldened him to dare more. Until, wrapped in each other's arms and embraced by shimmers of moonlight, her cries of release had driven him to find his own.

Through the window, the first light of dawn sifted through the skies. Content, Stephan drew her closer. With her in his arms, her hair streaming over his chest, 'twas as if he held the world.

They were man and wife in every way. A fact that before he'd sailed to Scotland would have left him terrified. Now, with love for

Katherine filling his heart, he couldna think of life without her. From this day forward, he would do whatever was necessary to keep the smile on her face, and love for him in her heart.

None would harm her.

Ever.

Unbidden, memories of witnessing his family's death rumbled to the fore. Angry at the thought, he smothered the gruesome images against the life he'd found. Her father's murderous deed was in the past, an incident she would never discover.

Since his youth he'd carried hatred for the man, had sworn revenge. Now his animosity paled against the happiness Katherine had brought him. Peace lay within his life, within his heart. Nevermore would black memories of his past mar his future.

Steadier, Stephan skimmed his hand along her shoulder, across the soft swell of her breast.

On a lazy sigh, she shifted, her fingers reaching to lace with his.

Humbled by this amazing woman, he drew her against him, whispered that he loved her in Gaelic.

Caught within the shimmer of candlelight, her lids lifted. Blue eyes met his. Cloudiness cleared to warmth. A slow and wondrous smile curved her mouth. "I thought 'twas a dream."

"What was?" he asked, pressing kisses along the curve of her jaw.

"My loving you. Your loving me in return." Desire burning in her gaze, she moved over him, brushed her mouth against his, then with slow, heart-stopping pleasure, deepened the kiss until his body hardened and screamed its demand. Mischief danced in her eyes as she shifted, scraping her teeth against the muscled flat of his stomach, then edged lower.

"What are you doing?" he groaned.

"This." And destroyed his every last thought.

Katherine winced against the sun's rays and tugged the covers over her head. Memories of last night sifted through her, drawing an appreciative sigh, more so at how a short while ago she'd devastated Stephan by initiating intimacy, her daring surprising them both.

Aches rippled through her body, but the discomfort was well worth the hours they'd made love. After his passionate response to her boldness, to lure him to remain abed a while longer shouldna be difficult. Her body humming in anticipation, she turned.

Rumpled sheets sat piled atop the place where Stephan had lain.

She glanced toward a smaller chamber that adjoined theirs. "Stephan?"

Silence.

With a frown, she slipped from the bed, crossed to the opening. Except for several chests that held her clothes and his, one filled with herbs, and another for valuables, the chamber stood empty.

He'd left without saying goodbye?

Why? He'd enjoyed their lovemaking, had he nae? Or had she failed him in some way? Worry built as she tugged on her garb. By the time she reached the turret, she was half-running to the great room.

The scent of baking bread and stew bubbling in a large caldron over the fire in the hearth filled the large chamber. Several men sat at the tables breaking their fast, but Stephan was nowhere in sight.

"Good morning, my lady."

At Aiden's cheerful voice, she looked over.

Green eyes held hers with respect as the knight walked toward her. "I see you are awake."

Heat touched her cheeks. "Have you seen my husband?" she asked, refusing to dwell on her tardiness to her morning duties. Last night had held magic, a beginning for them both and, for her, a start to moving past her fears.

"I have," the knight said. "He is in the tunnel below the chapel."

Unease trickled through her. "Why would he be there?"

Surprise flickered in his eyes. "I thought you knew."

She forced herself to smile. "Nay doubt he told me. I was half asleep when he left." With the way her mind was still a blur of fatigue, 'twas more than likely the truth. Still, what had been so urgent that he would work with the men in the tunnels with little rest? "Are you heading there now?"

Aiden glanced toward the tables. "Aye. Would you like to break your fast before you go?"

She shook her head.

"Fine, then. You are welcome to join me if you wish."

"I thank you." Sunlight blinded her as they stepped into the bailey and she shielded her eyes.

"Nae a cloud in the sky," the knight said with appreciation, "but there is a bite of winter in the air."

Soon the snow-filled wind would keep them inside, the hearth ablaze to ward off the chill.

Before she'd dreaded returning to her chamber alone, the flickering flames leaving blackened nooks that would lure her to darker memories. With Stephan sharing her bed, the wondrous things they could do throughout the night, and the special moments that would fill her heart, hope filled her mind.

Distant voices melded around them: children playing, women near the well, knights carrying broadswords headed toward the lists.

The familiar sounds brought comfort, and her earlier worries at Stephan's having left before she'd awoken eased. She glanced at the Knight Templar. "How do you find life in the Highlands?"

"As I grew up nae far from here, 'tis a life I am familiar with."

"You were raised nearby?" she asked. With his brogue, she'd nae considered the possibility.

Pain flickered in his gaze. " 'Twas many years ago. Since, I have remained away."

"Do you nae miss being near your family?"

Aiden reached for the door, tugging the entry open. "We are here."

She noticed that he'd ignored her question. Neither did she have the right to pry. Still, during the journey to Avalon, he'd become her friend. "If ever you have a need to speak about your past, I am known for having a good ear."

A wry smile touched his lips. "I thank you for the offer, but my past and my life then are but distant memories."

Sadness touched her that he would view his youth so, nor with the sadness haunting his eyes did she believe his assertion. The hurt, regardless if he admitted it, bothered him still. She frowned.

Neither had Stephan mentioned his past. With their relationship growing stronger, 'twas a matter of time before he did.

She followed Aiden into the chapel, the scent of frankincense and myrrh lingering inside. The familiar items within, a crucifix behind the lectern, ewers, a basin, and several gilded vessels, brought a touch of peace.

Katherine skimmed her hand over a pew as they walked past, the time-worn surface honed by the hands of the many parishioners who'd entered over the years to pray. "I thought most everything had been destroyed during the battle."

" 'Twas a fair amount of destruction," Aiden replied, "but several of the knights are skilled in woodworking. Whatever they couldna repair, they rebuilt."

She paused. Upon closer inspection, several of the benches didna have an aged look. "Their craftsmanship is incredible." Impressed by the workmanship, she ran her hand over one of the newly built items; polished wood slid beneath her palm. "They have even stained the new pews to match the old. If you hadna told me, I wouldna have noticed."

The knight nodded. "Stephan wanted to surprise you before he informed you that the work was complete."

Tenderness filled her. This was the reason her husband had kept her away from the chapel. Moved by his thoughtfulness, any lingering concerns faded. "Then 'tis time I thanked him."

Aiden led her down the ladder, the coolness of the tunnel after the warmth from above making her shiver.

Faint voices echoed in the distance.

At their approach, Stephan looked up. Surprise, then warmth filled his eyes. He met her halfway, took her hand. "I thought you would still be abed."

Heat touched her cheeks as the knight strode past. Alone, Katherine moved into Stephan's arms. "I woke up to find you gone."

He brushed his mouth against hers. "I told you I was leaving, but you didna move. You looked so peaceful, I couldna wake you."

All of her worry for naught. As he held her against him, awareness slid through her. "I am awake now."

His gaze darkened. "If I could leave right now, I would."

Curious, she glanced toward his men. Several held torches, while others ran their hands along the walls. "What are they looking for?"

"Cracks in the wall that may be the outline of hidden doorways to the catacombs, ones we desperately need to hide the goods still onboard the ships. None but the Templars must know what we transported."

She recalled the whispers of treasures held by the Templars: gold beyond what any man could envision, the Ark of the Covenant, the Holy Grail, and even more. Were the rumors true? Could the crates contain these coveted artifacts? However much she wished to know, these warriors were willing to give their lives in order to keep the secrets safe. She refused to dishonor their sacrifice.

"Mayhap there is documentation of the hidden chambers in one of my father's ledgers?"

Frustration darkened his gaze. "I thought the same, but I searched through them all." Stephan paused. "Onboard ship, you mentioned the catacombs. Can you recall anything about how your father entered them?"

Memories of following her father through several rarely used tunnels into large caverns came to mind. A child, she'd paid scant attention to the way they'd arrived there, a fact she now regretted. She shook her head.

"We have to find them. Everything must be safely hidden before I depart."

Her throat went dry. "Depart?"

Regret touched his gaze. "However much I wish to remain, my agreement with King Robert includes training his knights, along with supporting his efforts to unite Scotland, a missive requesting our support could arrive at any time."

Panic flared. "What about Avalon?" *What about me?* Katherine silently added.

"A contingent of trusted knights will remain to guard the castle." On a frustrated sigh, he gathered her close. "When we wed, I couldna wait for the day I sailed away. Now I curse what I canna avoid."

Shame swept her. 'Twas nae only she who struggled with his leaving. "Come back to me, Stephan."

His eyes rough with emotion, her husband cupped her face. "I swear it."

"And I will keep you—" Memories stormed her mind. She pulled away. "Mary have mercy!"

Concerned by his wife's pallor, Stephan frowned. "What is wrong?"

"I . . ." Katherine's lips curved into a smile. "I canna believe I didna think of the hidden room before."

Hope ignited. "Hidden room?"

"Aye. Follow me."

"Wait a moment. I need to tell Thomas where I am going."

She nodded.

A short while later, his anticipation growing, Stephan followed his wife into the chamber his parents had used, a room nay doubt hers had slept in as well, one since his return he'd ignored. His wife believed he'd left the quarters untouched as her pain of loss was so fresh. Never would he share that this room held sad memories for him as well.

Against the back wall stood a large bed, the woven cover atop emblazoned with a Celtic design. A wool rug lay angled on the floor, and several chests stood stacked to the right.

As she neared the bed, Katherine slowed. A tremor ran though her.

Stephan stepped to her side, far from surprised at the sadness clouding her gaze. " 'Tis difficult."

"Aye. When I was a child," she whispered, "I would crawl beneath the thick covers with my da, and he would tell me stories of the fey and, every so often, King Arthur."

He grimaced, nae wanting the tender vision, to think of her father as a man who cared. Stephan drew her against him. "You will always have their love." Too well he knew that the thoughts of a lost loved one did not ease the pain or allow them to live on. Time and sheer determination did that. With the blur of years one could look back with tenderness.

"You are right, but I am blessed because now I have you."

Guilt collided with pleasure. That he could be there for her left him humbled, but he damned the secret of his past, which could destroy everything.

"Looking back," she continued, "I find it sad that never did I find my mother sharing his chamber."

"There could be many reasons."

"Indeed," she said, "but I dinna want to sleep elsewhere but at your side."

A belief he held as well. Nae wanting to linger, he glanced around. "You said there was another chamber here?"

"Aye." Katherine walked to a hanging tapestry woven with an intricate design depicting Jesus and Mary Magdalene.

He frowned at the wall hanging, one her father must have purchased, shifted his gaze to the outline of the door. He remembered the room beyond. Too small to contain anything substantial, his father had kept naught but the most important items from his travels. "I dinna recall there being a—"

A frown wedged Katherine's brow. "What?"

He silently cursed at his slip and shook his head. "I am surprised to find a space for storage built within the lord's chamber. 'Tis unusual."

"Indeed, but so is the hidden room behind this chamber."

A hidden room? Disquiet edged through him. Yet another mystery he hadna known of. What else had his father nae informed him of before he died? "Has it always been there?"

"Nay, my father had the chamber built."

His shoulders relaxed. This explained his ignorance of the room's existence.

"Once, as a child, I asked my father if he would show me the entry to the secret room," she continued, ignorant of Stephan's turmoil. "He would smile and change the topic. One day, after I had gained twelve summers, he brought me here. His voice somber, he said if anything were ever to happen to him and my mother, I should know how to enter. I was to take the book with the letters embossed in gold to Robert Bruce; he would know what to do."

A strange request. "Robert Bruce? Why-how does . . ."

" 'Tis perplexing to me as well. At the time, so caught up in learning the mystery of how to enter, I didna think to ask or realize the responsibility my father passed on to me. Then, with the siege of the castle, the turmoil, and my escape, his instruction about the book and the hidden chamber slipped my mind."

A shudder fell from her lips as she began to lift the finely woven image.

Stephan stepped forward.

"Let me enter first," she said, her words rough. " 'Tis something I must face."

With a grimace, he nodded. As upon their arrival, with each room through which they'd made their way, she'd wanted to enter first, a request he respected, understanding she struggled with the memories each chamber invoked. At least he was there, and she didna have to face the pain alone.

With a deep breath, Katherine shoved. "Mary have mercy!"

Withdrawing his dagger, Stephan stepped past her, stilled.

The small room stood in shambles. Shards of destruction lay strewn about like a sea of chaos. Books were scattered, shelves splintered, and shards of glass littered the room.

"Wh-why would the English do this?" She took a cautious step forward. "They have destroyed everything!"

He secured his blade. "A show of power," he spat, "or simply because the English bastards could."

" 'Tis a disgrace."

"Aye." As if the English had shown respect for human life with their razing of Berwick, or the way they'd lured Scots to a false eyre-court in Ayre, and the numerous other atrocities that had left uncountable Scottish men, women, and children dead.

Outrage built inside, a rough fury that he'd nae experienced since he'd witnessed his family murdered.

Katherine bent over, picked up the bottom of what once was a decorated box, and tears filled her eyes.

With a silent curse, Stephan drew her into his arms. Her quiet sobs shuddered against him, each one breaking his heart. "I am sorry." And he was, for her grief, for her pain, and for what little remained of those she loved. Nae even something as small as a box was left untouched.

Long moments passed and the soft trembling of her body stilled, but he held her, gave her the sympathy she needed, compassion absent in his life for so many years.

"I will ensure everything is repaired," he whispered.

"I thank you," she said, her words unsteady. "My father would have liked you."

Of all she could have said, her claim wasna one he'd expected. Neither did he reply. His feelings toward her father didna match her beliefs.

On a sigh, Katherine stepped away, turned over the bottom of the destroyed wooden box. "The English didna discover it."

"Discover what?"

Pride filled her gaze. "This." She slid her nail into an indentation that he hadna noticed, and pried.

The bottom of the box separated, exposing a key secured inside.

In disbelief, he stared at the finely crafted metal, a uniquely fashioned piece similar to but a handful that existed, all held by the Knights Templar. God's blade, what was this?

Ignorant of his turmoil, Katherine stepped over the twisted debris, halted before the wall. She glanced back. "One of the stones is false."

She slid her fingers along the crevice of rock, paused. "Here." With pressure, the stone shifted.

The soft shimmer of light from the outside chamber exposed the lock.

Metal scraped as she slid the key inside, turned it. The sound of a catch opening echoed in the silence. Katherine pushed.

The door whispered open.

Through a window light filled the massive chamber, illuminating polished shelves filled with ledgers, leather-bound books. Several he'd read, those coveted volumes having belonged to the Grand Master.

Unease built inside as he scanned the numerous tomes. One on Templar training, another holding notations on their system of banking. On the far end, a glint drew his attention.

He struggled for calm as he recognized a volume bound in the finest tooled leather, the inscription inlaid with gold.

" 'Tis nae what you expected?" Katherine asked, her voice rough with pride.

"Nay," he said, unable to pull his gaze away from the book. To his knowledge, there was but one in existence. Before him stood proof there was another.

Why hadna the Grand Master told him? More important, why did Katherine's father possess books of such importance to the Brotherhood?

Bits of white from where a chest had been propped open caught his attention. Heart pounding, he walked over, stared at the pentagram carved on the cover.

Dread roiled through him as he raised the lid. Folded inside lay a white surcoat emblazoned with a red cross. Beneath lay a white mantle.

'Twas impossible.

A sacrilege.

Until this moment he'd dismissed the Templar markings he'd seen within Avalon as those created by others outside Katherine's family. But before him was the proof. Her father had been a Templar!

Chapter Twenty

Stephan's hands trembled on the lid of the chest. Impossible! Katherine's father couldna be a Knight Templar. He had married and fathered a daughter, both actions forbidden to anyone within the Order.

How could he explain the unprecedented collection of Templar records, those rivaling the Grand Master's? If ignorant of the situation, Stephan would deduce that whoever held the contents of this chamber played a significant role in the Knights Templar.

" 'Tis a white surcoat emblazoned with a red cross," Katherine said with confusion at his side.

God's blade, he was so caught up in his shock he'd forgotten his wife's presence. As if it was unimportant, he tucked the garb into the box, secured the lid. "So it appears."

She frowned. "What is wrong?"

Wrong? Coldness swept Stephan. A gross understatement of the caliber of inappropriateness here. As if his every fiber wasna in shock, he shrugged. "I am surprised by the size of the chamber. Upon entering the castle, one would never suspect this existed."

Pride beamed on her face. "My father had the room built with such in mind. From outside, the window appears to belong to another chamber."

A false assumption he'd made as well. He stood.

"And over here is where my father kept his ledgers."

Dragging his gaze from the chest, Stephan took in the carved desk, simple yet ornate, the craftsmanship exemplary, then focused on the book she'd picked up.

"If there are . . ." Her eyes dark with emotion, she looked away.

"Katherine—"

"Nay." She met his gaze, her face composed. "If there are maps of the tunnels and hidden chambers, they will be found here."

"I thank you." However much he longed to begin his search, 'twas too important to rush and risk missing anything. However much he wanted to deny it, evidence assured him that her father had been a Templar.

Confused and upset, he set the book aside and pocketed the key. "Let us go. On the morrow I will review the ledger." In mere hours he would start reviewing the tome with the gold inscription, along with the numerous other volumes that filled the room. Within them he should find his answers.

Desire slid through Katherine as Stephan carried her across their chamber and lay her on their massive bed. Flames within the hearth illuminated her husband's nakedness, the taut curve of muscles, and the tenderness of his gaze.

He made love to her with infinite care, his every touch sending her higher, his words rough with passion, as if she was his entire world. When she found her release, he followed, then lay beside her and drew her into his arms.

She sighed within his warm embrace. "I thank you."

"I have nae done aught but make love to my wife, one whom I adore."

Warmth swelled inside. How could she have missed the depth of this man, his caring? When they'd first met, foolishly she'd seen the warrior and considered him little more. Now she knew and was blessed to have him in her life. "You love me and you make me happy."

Pleasure softened his gaze, and he drew her into a long, slow kiss that made her ache for his touch all over again. As he deepened the kiss, she rolled on top of him and sat up.

"What are you—oh . . ." he groaned as she took him deep.

Emotion swirled within her as his hands skimmed over her flesh, took her higher until their bodies merged in a blissful release. Sated, her body humming, she lay flush atop him with a happy sigh. "I canna move."

His chuckle ended in a happy moan. "I canna either."

Katherine laughed, never having felt so good. "I could remain like this forever."

"And I," he agreed, his gaze darkening with heat. "If I die, I will go a happy man."

Her laughter faded.

With a silent curse, he grimaced. "I am sorry. I didna mean—"

Katherine shook her head. " 'Twas said in jest. With the recent events in my life, I am overly sensitive."

"Never would I hurt you," Stephan whispered. His wife's soft breaths fell upon his skin like a caress, and he savored each one. Never had he imagined his life could be so fulfilling.

Though 'twas temporary.

Any day a missive from the Bruce would arrive, orders to fulfill promises made. However much he wished otherwise, for the near future, his time with Katherine was drawing to a close.

Her even breaths against his skin assured him she slept. What if she carried his babe? A son or daughter to hold, a child with her eyes and one who someday would inherit Avalon.

His heart ached as he stared at her in the tumble of golden firelight. How could he leave her? With the responsibility of the Templar treasures and his word given to a king, how could he stay?

A distant rumble had him glancing toward the window. Torn, he slipped from the bed and walked to the opening.

Shards of clouds shielded the waning moon. Silver rays slipped through a break, illuminating the castle.

Pride filled him at the progress made in rebuilding his home. He glanced at Katherine, smiled. *Their* home.

A cool breeze brushed his skin.

With a grimace, he secured the window. The sounds of the night smothered, the snap of the fire in the hearth echoed with cheerful abandon, the flames illuminating Katherine lost in sleep.

After the hours they'd made love, and with little remaining of the night, he should return to bed. Questions of the Templar garb, along with the numerous volumes addressing life within the Order, haunted him.

Regardless of the proof, he rebelled against the idea of her father being in the Brotherhood. Given her father's nobility and marriage, 'twas hard to believe. With more questions than answers, Stephan began to pace.

As he reached the hearth for the third time, he rubbed his brow. God's blade, he needed answers, ones he wouldna find here. Stephan walked to the bed, drew the sheets up to Katherine's shoulders, and then pressed a kiss upon her cheek. With quiet steps, he slipped from the chamber.

Torchlight flickered on the walls with errant scrapes as he strode down the corridor, conjuring shadows as if an ill omen. Ignoring his unease, Stephan lit a taper, and then entered the small room. He walked over and slid the key into the lock, pushed.

The slide of the door whispered into a softness punctuated by thunder.

Through the window, lightning cut across the storm-blackened sky. Another blast of thunder echoed, this time closer.

He grimaced. A fitting night for a storm, when his own thoughts churned as dark. He stowed the key, stepped inside, and pushed the door shut. Within the candle's somber light, he scanned the volumes of books, ledgers, and the desk he'd seen earlier this day, and then walked to the chest.

Stephan removed the white surcoat and mantle, both slightly smaller than his own.

A Bible lay beneath them.

Curious, he set the garb on a chair, lifted the worn tome, and opened the cover. He frowned at the Latin inscription.

Arcana imperii—Jacques de Molay, Grand Master.

Secrets of the empire.

An odd inscription. Perhaps it held the reason why Templar records and items were hidden within this chamber?

Confused, he skimmed through the holy book, found naught but pages worn from the Bible's frequent use. Frustrated, he searched the volumes on the desk.

Naught.

Candlelight shimmered over one of the other tomes on the bookshelf.

He retrieved the leather-bound book emblazoned with gold lettering. As with the other volume in the Grand Master's library, each page noted every detail of the history and foundation of the Knights Templar, along with the secrets they guarded.

Unfathomable. How did the previous Earl of Dunsmore, a man who'd killed his family, come to have custody of a book of such significance? How could he be a Templar? Nothing he'd seen answered the question of why one of the Brotherhood would be allowed to live a life so far out of bounds of their strict rule.

Frustrated, he set aside the tome, withdrew the ledger to its left. In order of joining, the inked names of Knights Templar were listed since the beginning, when Hugues de Payens had recruited several knights and formed the Order. Stunned by the meticulous detail, Stephan shook his head in disbelief.

'Twas as if Katherine's father had built this hidden room for the sole purpose of storing a complete copy of Templar records. Then, if a crisis befell the Brotherhood and the records in Paris were destroyed, the loss would matter little. Exact copies of the most important Templar books filled this chamber.

Far from understanding anything, Stephan shelved the book, withdrew the next. Important Templar events filled the pages. He skimmed the notations, paused at a date written in bold at the top of the next page. Candlelight wavered over the skillfully penned words; his blood turned to ice.

Let it be recorded by order of the Grand Master, for his crimes of treachery against Scotland in plotting with King Edward to advance his intention of seizing Scotland, Finguine MacQuistan, Earl of Dunsmore, has been slain.

I regret to post that as we stormed the castle and made to apprehend the earl, his wife ignored several warnings not to intervene, and his daughter lost her balance as she fled upon the wall walk. Both died. I was informed, before I departed France, that they had a son. Upon questioning the residents, they explained he had drowned earlier this year.

As of the seventh of March in our lord's year of 1286, as instructed and secretly bestowed by King Alexander III before his death earlier this year, I shall claim the title of Earl of Dunsmore, and ensure Avalon Castle remains secure.

Yours in service, Sir Cainnech MacIssac

The parchment trembled in Stephan's hand. His father had conspired with King Edward? Revulsion warred with disbelief at the horrific accusation. They were wrong. His father had lived with honor, loved Scotland, a country he had served with pride. Though he had led with a firm hand, his father's every act had been backed by care.

Yet from his years of working at the Grand Master's side, Stephan had learned their leader did naught without proper cause. In the past, when incidents had arisen, instead of passing immediate judgment, Jacques de Molay had researched the issue, if possible, questioned numerous people regarding the case, before making a ruling.

With a curse, Stephan tossed the ledger on the desk. Shame burned inside him as he strode over, snatched the volume up again, and reread the entry.

Nay doubt remained.

His father had been a traitor.

On unsteady legs, he collapsed in the chair, fisting his hands against the rawness burning in his chest. His entire youth—a lie. The honorable man he'd believed his father to be, the warrior he'd always admired was a traitor.

What of his mother and sister: had either of them known? He doubted his sister had had any idea of their father's perfidy; her death was described as naught but a tragedy. What of his mother? Had fear of their treachery being uncovered spurred her to run to his father's aid?

Stephan muttered a curse. He wanted to believe his mother was innocent, yet at this moment, with every fragment of his youth tossed in chaos, he wasna sure.

Overwhelmed, he took in the room filled with Templar information never intended to be viewed by those outside the Order. A way of life he'd fought for since he'd fled Avalon so many years before.

Katherine.

God's blade. Shame twisted into a blackened wash. She believed him a good man, one she loved. What if his wife discovered his father's duplicity? How could she look at him with anything but revulsion?

Fear cut through him, and Stephan shoved to his feet, wanting to seal the room, deny the chamber's existence, along with the facts logged within the books. Yet when a man whose entire life was dedicated to God, to making the right choice even if the decision brought him shame, he couldna hide the truth.

Last eve he'd made love to Kathryn and dreaded leaving her. Now, as when he'd first met her, 'twas unthinkable to remain. His heart ached. If she carried his child, 'twould be one he would never know. As much as he loved her, wanted her forever, he wouldna stay to bring further dishonor to her family.

Through the window he stared at the storm-blackened sky. Mayhap this turn of events was for the best. Never had he intended for their marriage to be more than a façade. Foolishly, he'd mistaken desire for duty. But a part of him couldna find regret that if only for a while, they'd shared something extraordinary.

With a curse, he reopened the ledger to the damning page, stared at Jacques de Molay's signature. If the Grand Master had known of his father's treachery, he wouldna have sent Stephan to Scotland to meet with . . . He frowned. But as the leader of the Knights Templar, how could he nae have known?

Upon entry into the Brotherhood, as with each man, Stephan had given his name, his history, sworn upon those facts. Records Jacques de Molay would have reviewed prior to allowing him to enter the Order, and again with each leadership role he'd achieved.

Yet, with ruin descending upon the Templars by King Philip's decree, the Grand Master had entrusted Stephan to lead five ships and a contingent of Templars to Scotland. Why would the grand master have selected him when he knew his father had betrayed Scotland? Or what if by some incredible chance, the Grand Master had never connected his father's name and title to Stephan? He found the idea dubious, but 'twas the only explanation that made sense.

"Stephan?"

Guilt sweeping him, he slammed the book shut, glanced toward the entry.

Sleep-tousled hair framed eyes hazy with fatigue as Katherine stared at him.

She'd never looked so beautiful. He wanted to go to her, forget the horrific discovery of moments before, carry her to their chamber and make love with her as if the remainder of their life together lay ahead.

"What is wrong?"

The concern in her voice sent another wash of shame through him. "I couldna sleep."

She stepped inside, glanced around. Her gaze rested upon the ledger. "Did you find something?"

He shrugged. "There is a great deal of information to review."

"There is." She walked over, pressed her body flush against his. "I woke up wanting you."

Her sultry voice had him weakening. Needing to taste her, the goodness of her soul, for a second to lose himself in his love for her, Stephan claimed her mouth.

On a moan, she wrapped her arms around his neck, took the kiss deeper.

Lost to her taste, he skimmed his hands along the softness of her skin, over her supple curves until his blood pounded hot. Needing her, he pressed her against the wall, his hands skimming across her flesh.

"Make love to me, Stephan, here, now."

He stilled. Horrified he'd almost taken her within this chamber that held secrets of such importance, he released her, stepped back. She didna know all that stood between them. "There is much to do before I depart."

Confusion darkened her eyes. "You sound as if you are leaving soon?"

He'd planned to wait until he'd received a writ from the Bruce. With what he'd just discovered, how could he remain? "My men and I leave within a sennight."

Katherine's face paled.

" 'Tis imperative that I find the map of the catacombs," he stated, willing his mind to forget the silkiness of her skin, her potent taste lingering on his tongue. "Before we leave, all of the cargo within the ships' holds must be hidden. After we break our fast, until I discover the hidden chambers below Avalon, the men and I will begin transferring the goods into the secret tunnel."

" 'Tis the middle of the night. More than enough time for us to return to our bed."

His body tightened. "I must continue the search."

A seductive smile upon her lips, she walked to him, began pressing kisses over his jaw. "A few hours will make little difference."

Against his every wish, he caught her shoulders and gently held her away. At this moment he needed to accept the deeds of his father and to somehow find a way to move on—without her. "Nay."

The smile faded. "I see."

She didna, nor ever would. 'Twas his shame to bear, nor would he taint her with the knowledge he'd learned this night. In the end, her upset served him best. When he sailed from Avalon and didna return, her hurt would eventually fade to anger. Over time, she would erase him from her mind. But he would never forget her.

"I will inform you once I have found the map," Stephan said, his voice devoid of the pain churning inside.

"I . . ." She hesitated, took a step back. "As you are remaining awake, I will bring you a tray to break your fast."

"Return to bed. I will eat when I am hungry."

She angled her jaw, a gesture of protection he'd seen before.

Turning to the desk, he sat, opened a different ledger, and flipped the pages as if engrossed in his search.

Moments passed.

A sigh.

The tap of her footsteps faded.

Shaken, Stephan closed the unread book and called himself every kind of bastard. He'd hurt her and, God help him, if she learned the truth, he'd hurt her more.

Chapter Twenty-one

A fternoon sunlight illuminated the ledger as Katherine turned to the next page. She noted each entry, pleased by the detailed accounts of the running of Avalon since the English had seized the castle. However much she'd despised the Earl of Preswick, his meticulous records ensured a smooth transition in retaking the stronghold.

She turned her attention to the last few lines; the words again blurred. Frustrated, she closed the book, leaned back in her chair, and rubbed her temple.

Since she'd found Stephan in her father's secret chamber that morning, their confrontation and his subsequent withdrawal had left her shaken. Mayhap she fretted for naught? A Knight Templar, his concern in hiding the cargo in a secure place was tantamount. Yet part of her worried more than the urgency of their leaving provoked his brusque manner. Her husband seemed more distant, as if he was pushing her away.

A low throbbing continued in her temple. Why could she nae rid herself of these foolish notions? Hadna Stephan's lovemaking been tender throughout the night? She skimmed her finger along the edge of the page. Instead of searching for disquiet, she should be thankful that although she wed out of duty to preserve her home, she'd found love.

Confident naught but her own doubts created illusionary distance between them, she returned the ledger to the drawer and departed.

Outside the keep, enjoying the warmth of the sunlight, she walked toward the chapel.

Aiden came out of the holy sanctuary. Green eyes warmed as they met hers. "Lady Katherine."

She nodded. "Is Stephan still working below?"

"Aye." A frown touched his brow. "I caution you, he is as prickly as a wounded badger."

Her disquiet returned. "What happened to make him so?"

The knight shrugged. "None of us knows."

The reason for her husband's withdrawal became clear. "Mayhap his annoyance is because soon he, along with many of his men, will sail away."

Surprise flickered in Aiden's eyes; his face quickly masked his reaction.

She stilled. "He didna tell you of the impending departure?"

"The decisions of when we are to sail are Stephan's to make."

But the news had caught this warrior off guard. Loyal to her husband, he wouldna admit otherwise. "Indeed they are." She started to walk past.

"Lady Katherine . . ." Aiden shook his head. " 'Tis naught of importance." He strode toward the keep.

What had the knight intended to tell her? Unsettled, Katherine entered the chapel, climbed down to the tunnel. Faint echoes of men's voices guided her to where they worked.

Crates from the vessels lay stacked along one side of the tunnel. 'Twould seem Stephan was frustrated that the catacombs' location eluded him, and with his plans to sail imminent, he'd decided to store the cargo here until their return.

Her husband's voice calling out commands echoed down the passage. A moment later he strode into sight, helping to carry a large crate. Hands pressed against a corner, his muscles bunched as he and several knights shoved. It settled against the wall with a thud. "Hold!"

The men stepped away.

"Next we—" Her husband's gaze met hers. "Retrieve the next crate from the ship," he ordered. "I will be there in a moment." Expression taut, he strode to her.

She forced a cheerful smile. "You look tired."

"We *all* are," Stephan replied, his voice cool.

"You and the men must be hungry. I will have food and water sent below."

"We need naught."

She held a burst of anger in check; he was tired, concerned because soon he had to leave. "I understand there is much to do prior to your departure, but you have been pushing yourself and your men since first light." Ever since she'd found him in her father's secret room . . .

"There is work to be done. 'Tis my priority."

Nae her. Though he'd nae spoken the words, his meaning was clear. "You said little this morning of the reason you must leave. Did a runner from King Robert arrive?"

Silence.

Her worry built, the reasons for his hasty departure numerous. "Something has happened, has it nae?"

"The reason for our departure is nae one that I will discuss."

" 'Tis my castle as well," she said, her anger slipping out, "and as mistress, I will know why."

"A contingent of men will remain behind to keep Avalon secure from any threat."

Katherine stepped closer. "You didna tell me why."

The echo of men's voices neared.

"Aye, I didna." With a curt nod, Stephan strode past without looking back.

She clenched her fists, wanting to stop him, to demand answers. Neither would she embarrass herself or him before his knights.

For her husband to have such a fierce response, whatever news he'd received must be dire. Still, it didna excuse his brusque manner. If he thought he could push her away after they'd joined in the most intimate of ways, after he'd confessed his love and after she'd shared hers, he was wrong. However upset, Stephan would learn that she would always be there for him; his battles were hers, they'd fight them together.

Candlelight flickered through the chapel as she stepped from the ladder. She knelt before the cross, prayed for strength and patience.

A soft scrape sounded from the entry.

Katherine made the sign of the cross and turned.

Eufemie entered. Warmth shone in the healer's eyes. "Lady Katherine."

She forced a smile for the woman she considered a friend and stood. "I had planned on visiting later today."

The elder walked closer, paused. "What is bothering you, child?"

" 'Tis naught."

"Lass, I have known you too many years to be believing that. Come." Eufemie moved to a pew, patted the empty space at her side. "You have always been able to talk to me; naught has changed."

"It has; now I am married."

"Indeed," the healer said with a smile. "Your husband is a fine man."

Surprised by her sincerity, she walked closer, settled beside the elder. "I wasna aware you had met him."

The healer sat back. "We have talked many times."

Many times? Never had Stephan mentioned they'd spoken. "I admit to being surprised," Katherine said. "He is a man frugal with his time."

"And with good reason."

"What do you mean?"

"He has endured much in his life," Eufemie said. "More than most."

"He told you of his past?" she rasped.

" 'Tis a long story, one I have given my word nae to reveal."

Hurt, Katherine started to rise.

The elder caught her arm. "Sit, please," she said, her voice gentle.

"I . . ." She settled on the bench. "St-Stephan has told me naught of his past. How can I nae be upset when he refuses to share such things with his wife yet confides in a stranger?"

Sadness darkened the elder's eyes. "As much as I wish to explain, 'tis his story to tell."

"It is," she agreed, temper coating her words. "My husband is wrong to withhold such an important part of his life from me. He has claimed to love me, you would think he wouldna hesitate to share his past."

Surprise, then joy warmed her friend's face. "He told you that he loves you?"

She hesitated, confused. "Aye."

The healer placed her hand on Katherine's arm. "I wish I could make you understand what he has had to overcome to admit his feelings for you."

"Then tell me! I deserve to know."

"You do, and however much I want to explain, 'tis nae my place." She paused. "Know this: He has made significant strides in overcoming his past, and I am confident that with time he will share all."

"He is leaving," she blurted out, her fear of losing him shoving out the words.

The healer raised a brow. "He has received a missive from King Robert?"

"All Stephan will tell me is that he and his men will depart within a sennight."

The elder's gaze darkened.

Disquiet ran through Katherine. "What is it?"

"I promised that I wouldna tell you of his past," Eufemie breathed. "Neither can he allow this to continue."

"What to continue?" she asked, more confused than ever.

The elder made the sign of the cross. "The answers you seek are within your father's ledger."

She frowned. "His ledger?"

"Aye." She gave a heavy sigh. "I already regret telling you, but your husband is wrong to keep his past from you, more so when you love each other."

Emotion stormed through her. "I am determined to see our marriage succeed."

The healer gave her arm a gentle squeeze. "And so you shall."

"Where is it?"

She shook her head. "Sadly, I dinna know where your father kept his private records."

But she did; in the secret chamber where she'd found Stephan early that morning. "I thank you." With a quick embrace, Katherine looked at the crucifix hanging on the wall. 'Twould seem her prayers had been answered.

Exhausted after a long day of moving cargo off the galleys, Stephan knelt at the altar in the chapel, bowed his head, and began to pray. Guilt weighed heavy on his mind, each Our Father far from penance enough for the secret he withheld from Katherine, one that, if known, would destroy the precious bond between them.

Bond.

He grimaced. After his harsh words to her earlier that day, he'd jeopardized even that. As if he had a blasted clue of how to deal with what he had learned. God's blade, 'twas a bloody mess! Shadows flickered across Stephan. He glanced up.

Thomas knelt beside him, bowed his head, and began to pray.

As he whispered the Paternoster, Stephan followed along in silence.

After several repetitions of the Lord's Prayer, his friend made the sign of the cross and then sat on the pew.

Stephan remained kneeling.

"We need to talk."

At the irritation in his friend's voice, he stiffened. "I am nae finished with my prayers."

A bell tolled, the harmonic sounds fading against the distant voices of the men in the bailey.

"Does Lady Katherine know we are leaving?" Thomas asked.

"Aye."

"Does she know our meeting with King Robert is by *your* choice?"

Stephan shot his friend a hard look. "I gave my promise that we would train his men."

The knight crossed his arms over his chest. "I thought you were happy here."

Frustrated, he sat back. " 'Tis a long story."

"Over the years," Thomas said, "you have shared your past with me. Things I believe would come as no surprise to your wife."

"There is something new."

His friend arched a brow.

In a hushed voice, Stephan explained the ledger and the discovery of his father's guilt.

Thomas's eyes widened. "God in heaven!"

"Now you see why I canna stay."

"Lady Katherine loves you. I believe if you tell her—"

"If I do, I will lose her!"

"As if by leaving you are keeping her close?"

Bedamned!

Solemn eyes held Stephan's. "Do you love her?"

"Aye," he replied.

"Then go to her. Explain."

" 'Tis nae so simple," Stephan said, his words quiet.

" 'Tis nae."

"What of the evidence supporting her father being a Templar?"

Stephan grimaced. "How do I accept that as possible?"

"It doesna make sense. 'Tis forbidden to have a wife and child and have remained in the Order. Was there anything else in the ledger that might give a hint of how this came about?"

Stephan rubbed his neck. "I was so upset at learning my father was a traitor, I didna read more. A fact I will remedy now." He stood.

"I pray you find the answer you seek," Thomas said.

"An entreaty I share." For if he didna try, indeed, he would lose his wife.

Horrified, Katherine stared at the page. Mary have mercy, her father had killed Stephan's family! Tears burned her eyes for the child Stephan had been, for the suffering he'd endured.

When she'd found her husband this morning, he'd been reading this ledger. His withdrawal had naught to do with his feelings toward her, but rather guilt at discovering his father had been a traitor to Scotland.

She ached for Stephan, needed to assure him that she still loved him, wanted him in her life forever. But a man who wrapped himself in his pride, a warrior who fought for what was right—could he move beyond learning of his own father's treachery?

With these few lines, all on which he'd based his entire life had been destroyed. Even if her husband wanted her, before he could allow anyone close, he must accept and move past all he'd learned this day.

If he ever could.

Katherine wanted to help him but doubted he'd accept her offer. Neither was his stubbornness the worst of her worries. With her father having killed his family, how could he ever want her?

A tear rolled down her cheek, then another. Oh God! The words on the page blurred. She closed the ledger, sobbed until nay tears remained.

Empty, exhausted, she forced herself to reopen the journal. If any hope existed to repair their marriage, she needed to discover the full extent of what stood between them. Through sheer will Katherine reread her father's inscription about following the Grand Master's orders, then of his being a Knight Templar.

She stared at the words. How could her father be of the Brotherhood and wed? Marriage and children were forbidden.

Perplexed, she scanned the detailed accounts of her father's actions, along with his reports to Robert Bruce and Jacques de Molay, the Grand Master of the Knights Templar.

Odd. Why would her father report to both men? Intrigued, she continued to read. A line halfway down the page caught her attention.

She stilled.

Impossible? Hands trembling, she returned to the top of the page she'd skipped and read each word, each sentence, as a slow pounding built in her head.

Mary have mercy, Robert Bruce was a Knight Templar!

Dates alongside entries chronicled how, over the years, Robert Bruce had been in contact with the Grand Master. The Templars' escape, in addition to where to hide their cargo, were plans long since made.

With King Philip's written order to begin the arrests of the Templars, the Grand Master had set the plan into action. The reason Bruce had welcomed the Templars, and why he'd bestowed Avalon Castle on Stephan.

Parchment scraped as she turned the page. Flickers of candlelight wavered across the top entry, penned in a bold hand. She gasped and the ledger slipped from her hand and slammed to the floor.

Nay, the words couldna be true!

Fingers trembling, she recovered the worn ledger, thumbed to the page she'd read moments before.

The words remained.

The words stamped with the king's seal.

The words penned with but a few letters that had changed her entire life.

As of this day, Sir Cainnech MacIssac is charged with the care and protection of Lord Robert Bruce's daughter, Lady Katherine of Annandale.

'Twould seem that Robert the Bruce was more than a king.

More than a Knight Templar.

He was her father.

Chapter Twenty-two

Numb, Katherine stared at the incomprehensible script. It seemed that penned within this secret journal, within a passage stamped with the king's seal, lay truth.

Finger trembling, she pressed the tip to her sovereign's name. "King Robert is my father."

Dust motes sifted through the stream of sunlight as her whispered claim faded.

He'd visited Avalon numerous times over the years. Under the guise of being her godfather, his frequent visits had raised nay suspicions.

With the innocence of a child, she'd accepted their closeness without question. A familiarity the Bruce had used to build a strong bond between them, one that existed to this day, a trust he'd used to convince her to wed Stephan.

Katherine closed her eyes, trying to catch her breath, and then opened them. The chamber remained unchanged, while her life's foundation, the image of the family she'd wrapped her life around, was shattered.

The ledger lay open beneath her hand. Katherine hesitated, unsure whether she should read more. How could she nae?

Fighting for calm, she turned the pages to the life-changing script. To the right of the disclosure of her true lineage lay Robert Bruce's seal, dated and signed, his signature attesting to the statement's truth. She continued on, paused at the next entry.

I, Sir Cainnech MacIssac of the Knights Templar, swear to Robert the Bruce to guard his daughter Katherine. Through special permission of King Alexander III, and with the Grand Master's approval, I will assume the title of Earl of Dunsmore.

"Cainnech MacIssac," she whispered, needing to say the warrior's name, to make this real in her mind.

The next paragraph revealed that the woman who would play the part of the Templar's wife had in fact been Sir Cainnech's sister. Beaten to near death by a ruthless husband, she'd escaped and agreed to share the responsibility of raising Katherine in exchange for protection. It explained why Katherine had never seen the people she'd believed were her parents sleep within the same quarters.

Though nae her real mother and father, Sir Cainnech and his sister had raised her with kindness, ensured she received a wonderful education and, over the years, had given her their love. Humbled by their kindness, Katherine continued to read, skimming the pages for the one name still missing.

She reached the end of the ledger, and a knot tightened in her throat. Why was her mother's name missing from the entries? Her hand unsteady, Katherine shut the ledger. How long before Robert Bruce arrived at Avalon? He would come, of that she had little doubt. The questions she needed to ask him built inside her. Who was her mother? Had he loved her? Would the full truth ever be disclosed? Or had the king's intent for her return home been for her to discover her royal heritage?

Katherine dismissed the latter. A skilled tactician, a man of strength and honor, if the king had intended for her to know of her parentage, he would have explained upon her arrival at Urquhart Castle after escaping the English.

Unsure what to think, what to believe, she walked to the window. She stared at the churn of clouds moving in, the sun's rays steadfast in a valiant attempt to slip through the breaks to reach the earth.

Where could she begin to figure everything out? She shook her head. How foolish to worry about the details. At least she had a father who lived, one she loved, a man who'd earned her respect.

Stephan had naught.

But from the first, her husband had known Scotland's king was a Templar. Imperative information he'd withheld, even after she'd learned his true identity, and that of his men. He'd decided the truth about the Bruce wasna worth sharing.

Bedamned, she wasna a lass who needed tending, though her mule-headed, pea-brained husband believed otherwise. Mary have mercy, what else had he nae told her?

What of Stephan's claim that he loved her? Was it true or part of the grand scheme? With the revelations of moments before, she was unsure what to believe.

Needing time to think, Katherine ran from the chamber, walking into Stephan's chest as he started to enter.

Strong hands caught her.

"Let go of me!" She struggled to break free, hurt, aching, and at this moment needing to be alone.

"Katherine, what is wrong?"

A tear rolled down her cheek. "I know."

At his wife's pain-filled words, shame smothered Stephan. God's blade, she knew her family's death had been served by his father's hand. Never had he meant to hurt her. As if burned, he released her, stepped back, and turned away.

"Look at me," she rasped.

He remained still, wrestled at what to say, doubting any hope existed to save their marriage.

"Do you love me?" she asked.

Of all questions he'd prepared himself for her to ask, he'd nae expected that one. "You read the entry in the ledger."

"I-I did, but I need to know if your claim that you loved me was true, or if I was but a pawn to reclaim your heritage?"

Furious, he whirled. "You believe I married you for Avalon?"

Blue eyes darkened. "Did you?"

"Aye . . . at first," he admitted. "When I ran away, with my parents dead, never did I believe I would hold my father's title or rule Avalon Castle. Even if I wanted to, once I had given my vow to the Brotherhood, 'twas forbidden by Templar rule. With the dissolution of the Order, and with King Robert's offer, 'twas a chance to reclaim a forbidden legacy."

Hurt streaked through her eyes. "And why you wed me?"

"In part, but a very small one. I assured our king 'twas unnecessary to marry you when 'twas only the stronghold the Templars needed. But he knew I was desperate, that I had promised the Grand Master I would do whatever was necessary to protect the goods the ships carried. The Bruce pressed. In the end, I agreed."

A blush crept up her cheeks. "Neither can I find condemnation. I, too, married to reclaim what I believed was my home."

The sadness in her voice piled atop his grief. "I am sorry, Katherine."

"As am I." Unsure eyes held his. "Where do we go from here, or can we?"

With knowledge of his father's shame enshrouding him, Stephan shook his head. "I am unsure," he replied, aching, terrified he'd lost her and wanting her forever.

"Is what you read this morning why you have decided to sail to Urquhart Castle?"

Guilt-ridden, he glanced toward the ledger, cleared his throat. "Aye."

"I admit I am struggling to accept everything." She blew out a rough breath. "Regardless of what we both learned this day, it doesna have to change anything between us. That is, if you still love me."

Hope ignited, faded to caution as he stared at her in disbelief. "How can you still want me after learning my father betrayed Scotland, put our country's freedom at risk?"

"Did you know of your father's actions?"

"How could I? I was but a child at the time."

"Then how can you cast blame upon yourself for any part of your father's dealings?"

Sadness weighing heavy on his soul, he shook his head. " 'Tis nae so simple."

"Only because you will nae let it be."

He ached inside, a deep keening that threatened to tear him in two. "You dinna understand."

Katherine walked to him. "Then help me."

Mortified, however much he didna wish to expose his cowardice, he had to tell her the truth. "As a lad, during the attack, I hid. Watched as my parents were slaughtered, my hand curled around a dagger I didna dare to wield. I detest cowardice, yet at the moment when my family needed me most, I acted with naught but dishonor."

Sympathy darkened her gaze. "You were a child. Afraid."

He gave a cold laugh. "Afraid, aye, but angry as well," he stated, holding her gaze, needing to see her eyes as he bared his soul. "At the onset of the attack, my father ordered me to hide. Like a spineless fool, I obeyed."

"You did as you were told," she said, her words firm.

"I could have fought. Instead, I watched those I loved die."

"And have paid with guilt ever since." Katherine lay her hand atop his. "You were a loyal son, one strong enough to obey his father instead of allowing your emotions to endanger your life."

"It changes naught!"

"It changes everything! You dinna owe a penance for yielding to your father's request. If we had a son and our castle was under siege and the odds overwhelming, would you nae order him to hide and then escape? Allow hope that in the future your child would find a way to reclaim his heritage?"

Remorse weighing heavy on his mind, Stephan assessed her every word. Her reasoning made sense, yet shame and condemnation lingered. "I dinna know."

"I think you do."

He shot her a cool look. "Mayhap, but 'tis nae a simple task. Years have passed that I have lived with my disgrace."

Her hand gently squeezed his. "Years have passed with you condemning yourself for a false belief. 'Tis time to accept that the guilt wasna yours to bear."

"I . . ." He muttered a curse.

" 'Tis much to take in, but if you still love me and want me, we can move forward. Together."

If he still loved her? He did, but she deserved more in life than a man whose father left dishonor as his legacy.

At his silence, hurt darkened her gaze. "I see." She stepped back. "As you know where the catacombs are located, you and your men can move everything within them before you depart."

Still trying to accept that she'd still want him, Stephan caught the last of her words. "Know where the catacombs are? How could I?"

"You read the ledger, saw the map hidden within the pages."

"Map?"

A frown touched her brow. "You didna see it?"

He shook his head.

With quiet steps she retrieved the ledger, turned the pages. Near the end, she paused. "Here." Parchment crinkled as she opened it.

Stephan stared at the drawing, awaited the exhilaration of knowing where each hidden chamber was located with details of how to enter. In addition to securing the Templar treasure, leaving a force to keep this strategic stronghold secure, he and his men could sail without worry in support of King Robert's efforts to reclaim Scotland.

Pain twisted inside him. Stephan set the book aside. "I always dreamed of one day reclaiming Avalon. Never did I believe 'twas possible."

" 'Twould seem you have your wish," his wife said, her words remote.

"Mayhap, but now I find that 'tis nae my wish after all."

Wary eyes held his.

Stephan stepped closer. "You asked me if I loved you."

Eyes wrought with turmoil held his. "A question you didna answer."

"Because you leave me humbled," he said, his words rough. "I canna understand how you could want a man whose father was a traitor."

Tenderness softened her gaze. "Do you think me so shallow that I would hold your father's duplicity against you?"

"I prayed you wouldna." Taking the greatest risk of his life, he set aside the map and cupped her chin. "I love you, Katherine; you are my heart, my life, and I canna live without you."

"You still love me?" she asked, as if nae daring to believe his claim.

"After everything," he said, aware he needed her to say the words, "I need to know if you still feel the same."

Her eyes warmed with love. "How could I nae? You are the man I have given my heart to."

Humbled, Stephan drew her into a kiss, one layered in passion, steeped in need, and rich with his love. At her soft moan, he drew her against him, held her tight, because he could, because she let him. "I-I thought I had lost you."

"Never." Dismay flickered in her eyes. "Mary have mercy."

"What is wrong?"

Face pale, Katherine withdrew from his arms. "You said moments ago that you hadna read all of the entries."

He nodded.

"You dinna know?"

"Know what?"

Katherine hesitated and then handed him the ledger. " 'Tis best if you read them yourself."

Dread spilled through him as he continued reading from where he'd stopped earlier. God's blade, what else was there to learn? He thumbed past a page, then another.

Stilled.

In disbelief, Stephan reread the finely crafted lines, lingered on the seal signed by their king.

Incredible.

Unbelievable.

But true.

His fingers tightened on the page as he lifted his eyes, noted the worry in her own. "Your father is King Robert."

"I never knew," she whispered. "I always believed the people who raised me were my parents."

"I-I dinna know what to say."

The soft tap of footsteps echoed from outside the chamber. "Stephan," Thomas said as he halted at the entry, urgency in his voice.

Body tense, he glanced up. "What is it?"

"King Robert's ship has been spotted on the horizon," he said.

At Katherine's gasp, Stephan folded his hand around hers. "Ensure all is prepared to welcome him. We will join you momentarily."

With a nod, Thomas hurried out.

The soft tap of leather upon stone faded.

Katherine looked at him. "My . . . father is here."

Stephan smiled. "Aye. Your father. And nay doubt to discuss plans of an upcoming attack."

"He knows me, but in the guise of my godfather." She withdrew her hand, walked to the window, and turned. "I—I canna act as if I dinna know the truth."

"Nor would your father expect you to," Stephan said, confident of his assessment. "Our king is nae a man who abides pretense. Once he knows you are aware of your parentage, he will expect questions, and answer them in kind."

"I agree, but 'tis still difficult. All my life I have thought of him as a friend of my parents, a man I could turn to, one I could trust."

"Neither has that changed."

The worry in her expression eased and she nodded.

"Come." He drew her with him as he walked toward the entry. "We must welcome our king."

* * *

A short while later, with the formalities of greeting their sovereign complete and settled within the solar, Stephan handed King Robert a goblet of wine and then moved to sit beside Katherine. " 'Tis an honor to welcome you to Avalon Castle, Your Grace."

"I had planned to visit prior," the Bruce said. "Due to complications, I was delayed."

Scotland was embroiled in a civil war and their sovereign struggled to reunite clans divided. *Complications* hardly described the gravity of the difficulties he faced.

The king glanced toward Stephan's hand covering Katherine's. A smile touched his lips, and then his gaze shifted to her. "You are happy?"

A blush swept her cheeks. "I am, Your Grace."

The king nodded to Stephan. "And how do you find marriage?"

"Agreeable. In truth, I love her," he said, curious at her father's reaction.

Surprise, then happiness, warmed the Bruce's face. He arched a brow at Katherine. "And you?"

"I love Stephan as well." She paused. "Is that what you sailed to discover?"

A smile curved the king's lips. His laughter, warm and rich, bubbled through Katherine like waves of hope. "I admit seeing how you were faring was one of the reasons for my visit. Neither am I too proud to admit that I prayed that you and Stephan would grow close."

"I know the truth," she said, her words unsteady. "I know that you are my father."

Silence crashed around them, broken by the muted voices in the bailey below, the wind outside, and errant sparks in the hearth.

The king's face whitened. "How?"

"I found a ledger, one kept in the secret chamber my fath—" she paused—"Sir Cainnech MacIssac built."

The Bruce studied her. "You read all the pages?"

"Aye," she replied, her words tight. "Sir Cainnech MacIssac was a Knight Templar, and 'twas his sister who pretended to be my mother. But the entries mentioned naught of my real mother. Who was she?"

Grief darkened the Bruce's eyes, a deep sadness that revealed that whoever the woman was, her father had loved her. " 'Twas many years ago, long before my first marriage. Her name was Mariote. A cart drew up where I was staying and she climbed down. However impossible it sounds, when I saw her, I fell in love."

Happiness touched Katherine's heart. "And did she love you in return?"

Tenderness softened his face. "Aye."

She leaned forward. "What happened to her?"

The warmth in his expression faded. "Our time together was fleeting. Duty demanded my attention and I was forced to depart. Months later I learned Mariote had given birth, fallen ill, and died."

Sadness swelled inside Katherine. Never would she meet the woman who had stolen her father's heart. "I am so sorry."

"Never will I forget her." Melancholy touched his gaze. "You have the look of her, as well as her stubborn determination. A trait that will indeed offer challenges to your husband."

"Challenges I shall forever cherish, Your Grace," Stephan said. "But..."

The king arched a brow.

Now wasna the time for hesitation but truths. "You are aware of my father's treachery?" Stephan's question thundered between them.

The king nodded. "I am."

"I dinna understand... How could you..." He shook his head. "God's blade, how could you allow your daughter to wed the son of a man who'd betrayed Scotland?"

"Your father's decisions were his own," the king said. "In Urquhart Castle, when you believed Katherine's father had murdered your family; before you departed, you told me that 'twas wrong to take your anger out on someone who was innocent, nor would you hold the sins of her father against her. As to your father's choices, 'tis a feeling I share. Stephan, you are your own man, one who over the years has carved a legacy of pride, honor, and respect. Indeed, you have earned mine. In Urquhart Castle I believed that circumstance brought you both before me. Now I understand 'twas fate. That you and my daughter have fallen in love is a blessing."

" 'Tis," Katherine said, moved. "When you first stated your wish that Stephan and I marry, I was furious. Now I understand that your decision was nae only made for love, 'twas guided by wisdom. For that I thank you. And I must admit that although I will always love Sir Cainnech MacIssac and his sister for raising me with kindness and compassion, I have always loved you as well."

The king walked over and embraced her tenderly, then pressed a kiss on her brow. "You are a blessing in my life, Katherine. Always remember that."

Happiness filled her, but shadows lingered. "Why did you send me to Avalon and never tell me why?"

Sadness filled his eyes. "Given the political upheaval at the time of your birth, along with my having to swear fealty to England's king, 'twas unsafe to allow King Edward to become aware of you. With his drive to claim Scotland, had he learned of your existence, discovered your importance to me, he would have done all within his power to abduct you. And with you in his grasp, King Edward would have held the ability to force me to heel beneath his rule."

"Which is why you turned to the Grand Master," Stephan said.

Bruce nodded. "After long discussions, we agreed 'twas best to place Katherine under Templar protection. We met in secret with King Alexander III, who due to the circumstance, agreed to bestow the title of Earl of Dunsmore upon Sir Cainnech MacIssac. The rest you know."

She nodded. Her father's explanation eased misgivings of why he'd kept their blood tie a secret. A shiver swept her. "Had King Edward learned of my existence, with him merciless to all, Scotland would have long since lay beneath his rule."

Lines furrowed the king's brow. "A distinct possibility. Thank God he never did. Still, the challenges of reuniting a torn Scotland are many. Neither can I forget England's new sovereign. Though inexperienced, Edward of Caernarfon is a man of intelligence, one to proceed against with caution."

"Mayhap," Katherine said, pride in her voice, "but I have faith in Scotland's king."

A smile touched Bruce's lips. "I believe you might be partial."

With a soft chuckle, she smiled. "Mayhap."

A sennight later, standing on the wall walk with the first light of dawn shimmering through a thick layer of fog, Stephan pressed a kiss to his wife's brow as the last Templar galley faded from view. "I should have sailed with Thomas, Aiden, and the other Templars."

"Our king needed a warrior he could trust to ensure Avalon Castle remained safe." Katherine smiled. "I believe my father chose well."

Pride at her words filled him, and he skimmed his mouth across hers. "I believe," he said, his burr thick, "your father wants a grand-child."

In the soft morning light, she entwined her fingers in his. "He did hint at that."

Stephan laughed, never so happy in his entire life. "'I need a grandson on my lap' is far from a hint."

Her eyes twinkled with mirth as she pressed her body flush against his. "And I do believe you are just the man to fulfill the task."

Need seared him, and he lifted her in his arms, thankful for her love, the happiness she'd given him, and the promise of their life ahead.

Katherine's laughter spilled between them. "What are you doing?"

"Taking you to our chamber to make love to my incredible wife, who I love with my every breath. And"—Stephan gave her a wink—"giving a king his wish."

Keep reading for
A sneak peek at the next book in
The Forbidden Series,
FORBIDDEN KNIGHT
Available June 2017
From Lyrical Press

Chapter One

Scotland, late fall 1307

Wind sharp with the edge of winter battered Alesone MacNiven as she ducked beneath the thick limb of an oak. She scanned the surrounding trees, her body aching with exhaustion after two days of hard travel.

Withered brown leaves scraped across the snow-smeared ground like harbingers of death. She shuddered, damning the images haunting her mind. Although she'd nae seen Comyn's men since last night, his knights hadna given up searching for her.

Fingers trembling, she withdrew the ring from a hidden pocket in her cape. A flake of snow settled on the ruby embraced by the carved gold figure of a lion.

> *"Give this to King Robert," Grisel Bucahn rasped. "Tell him—" Her body rattled as she'd coughed.*
>
> *"Dinna try to talk," Alesone pleaded to the woman who'd raised her.*
>
> *Her beloved mentor placed the ring in Alesone's palm, curled her fingers over the circlet. "Lo-long ago I saved Robert Bruce's life. He said if ever I had need of his assistance to bring him this ring. 'Tis too late for me, but he will protect you."*
>
> *"Grisel—"*
>
> *"Our enemy returns any minute. Go!"*
>
> *Tears burning her eyes, Alesone hugged Grisel, slipped the ring into her pocket, and fled.*

Sunlight shimmered off the ruby as if to mock her heartbreak. She stowed the ring. Aye, the bastards would pay!

After taking a drink, she secured her water pouch and continued on. Beyond the stand of fir and oak, a field came into view. Alesone kept to the woods. As much as she needed to put distance between herself and her pursuers, 'twas safest to travel under cover.

A pain-filled scream sounded nearby.

She ducked behind a clump of bushes.

"Tell us where King Robert is!" a man's rough voice demanded.

Dread ripped through her. *Sir Huwe!*

Another agony-laden scream.

Pulse racing, Alesone looked whence the voices had come in search of the knights. She spotted the clump of firs a distance away.

Go! 'Twas tempting death to linger. And yet, if she left, whoever suffered Sir Huwe's brand of twisted brutality would die. Like Grisel.

Crouching low, she crept to the thick boughs. Between the breaks in the needled branches, she caught sight of the burly knight's back.

From her limited view, neither could she see if his detestable friend helped him with whomever he tortured. Alesone grimaced. Little doubt the vermin was near. Like wolves, bad blood traveled in packs.

Her bow readied, she crept closer.

Another knight, ill-kempt, stood paces away.

Her skin crawled with disgust.

With a curse, Sir Huwe hauled up the man who lay sprawled at his feet. "The king is camped nearby; tell us where!"

Blood streaked the prisoner's half-swollen face. He remained silent.

"Let me kill him," the scrawny man spat. "He is naught but a traitor to Lord Comyn."

"Ki-King Robert is Scotland's rightful king," the stranger rasped.

"Rightful king," Sir Huwe grunted. "The Bruce murdered his rival at the church of the Greyfriars to ensure he received the crown." His fingers tightened on the man's garb. "Tell us where he is or die!"

The bastard! Alesone stepped into the opening, drew back the bowstring, aimed. "Leave him."

Sir Huwe's gaze shifted to her. Surprise darkened to recognition. His eyes narrowed. "You are a fool to dare to threaten me."

"Move back," she ordered, praying he didna see her trembling, "and I will allow you to walk away, unlike what you allowed Grisel."

A cold smile iced his gaze. He shoved the wounded man to the ground, strode toward her. "Unlike the healer, before you die beneath my blade, with your spirit you will make a fine piece to bed."

She released the shaft.

The arrow drove through the knight's heart. On a grunt, Sir Huwe stumbled back, collapsed.

Outrage reddened his accomplice's face. He withdrew his sword, charged.

Her second arrow plunged deep into his chest.

Face ashen, he stumbled back, dropped to the ground.

After ensuring nay others were in sight, Alesone secured her bow, and hurried to the injured man's side. "I am a healer." She knelt, tore a strip from her garb, and pressed the cloth against the large gash across his shoulder.

Pain-filled eyes held hers. "You must leave!" the stranger urged. "A large contingent of Comyn's troops wait over the ridge. I was on my way back to warn . . ." The stranger's face paled.

"King Robert. I heard you. Dinna worry," she said as she secured his broken arm. "I am loyal to the Bruce."

Relief swept over the man's face. "The king must be warned of the threat."

"Aye." She helped him as he struggled to his feet. "Can you walk?"

He nodded. "My name is Sir Deargh."

"I am called Alesone." With one last look around, they hurried into the shield of trees.

Firelight illuminated the powerful sovereign's face, that of a warrior, a man renowned for his tactical expertise. Fighting to steady her nerves, Alesone curtsied before Scotland's king. " 'Tis an honor to meet you, Your Grace."

"Rise, Mistress Alesone," Robert the Bruce said.

Exhausted, she stood, relieved they'd arrived before the last rays of sunlight faded.

The crackle of the campfire melded with the murmurs of the men outside the tent as the king settled in a sturdy but unadorned chair. He motioned for her to sit on a nearby bench. "You saved the life of one of my knights. For that I thank you."

She clenched the ring in her palm. "I am a healer. I did naught but come to the aid of a wounded warrior."

"Which explains your actions in part, though my knight could have been a criminal."

"A worry I would have considered, Your Grace, but I heard his attackers demand he reveal your camp's location. I recognized the knights as well. Both men served Lord Comyn."

Surprise flickered in his eyes, and then his gaze narrowed. "How would you know their allegiance?"

"My loyalties lie with you, Your Grace," she rushed out, aware that with but a word he could name her a traitor and order her hanged.

The Bruce rubbed his chin. "From my man's account of the event, a claim I believe." He paused. "You are brave to have faced down two knights alone."

Brave? Nay, furious.

"Tell me, why are you in the forest without protection when Scotland is at war?"

She drew an unsteady breath. " 'Tis complicated."

A frown worked his brow and he leaned back. "I have time."

Against the snap of the fire, Alesone met the king's eyes, found sincerity, patience, and intellect. Grisel's dying words roiled through her. Though the healer had saved King Robert, would his pledge given to her those many years ago override Alesone's blood tie to his enemy?

As smoke curled from the flames, Alesone explained how, two days before, she'd returned to her home and found the woman who'd raised her beaten, and dying. And how, with her last breath, she'd revealed who'd attacked her.

"What did she do to incite their outrage?" Bruce asked.

Tears burned in Alesone's eyes as she struggled with the loss, that she'd never again see Grisel. "I found one of your knights wounded, hid him in our home. Until Comyn's men charged, we believed no one was aware of his presence. Before they stormed the hut, she helped your knight slip away through a secret passage. Loyal to you, Grisel remained to stall the men so he could escape." She paused, angled her chin. "Neither will I apologize for killing either of Comyn's men this day."

"Nor should you." With a dark frown, he set his cup aside. "You are alone and on the run, then?"

"I am."

"You travel to relations?"

"Nay." Alesone damned that her voice wavered.

"Friends?"

She shook her head. Hand trembling, she held out the ring. "Grisel Bucahn said to bring you this and you would offer me protection."

Recognition flared, and his hands tightened on the arms of the chair. "God's teeth," he rasped.

At the emotion in his voice, her throat tightened. "I will never forget her."

Eyes dark with sadness held hers. "Nor I; she was a fine woman, one to whom I owe my life." For a moment he studied her, and then gave a curt nod. "I will honor my promise to her and offer you my protection. And your arrival is fortuitous. I am in need of a healer, one to tend to me personally as well as the injuries of my men. A position I offer you."

Overwhelmed by his generosity, she nodded. "I thank you. 'Twould please me to serve you, Your Grace."

The king grimaced. " 'Twill nae be easy. Life on campaign is difficult at best."

"I am well aware of the demands necessary and more than prepared for the task. In addition to understanding how to use herbs, I am skilled with a bow and a dagger," she stated, proud of her skills, which had saved her life many times over.

Satisfaction filled the king's eyes. "Mistress Alesone, 'twould seem we have a bargain."

Dread eroded her happiness. Though he'd offered her a position as well as his protection, neither did he know of her own circumstance. Terrified of admitting her bond to his enemy, she refused to be labeled a spy. "There is one more thing, Sire. I fear when you know the truth of my lineage, you will withdraw your offer."

The king's eyes narrowed. "Go on."

"I am . . . Or rather, my mother was . . ." Bedamned! "Lord Comyn is my father."

The howl of wind against the tent filled the silence.

A tremor slid through her. *Please let him look past my heritage.*

His mouth tightened. "You said as a newborn you were left with Grisel?"

Shame warmed her cheeks. "Aye. My mother was a noblewoman.

While her husband was away on Crusade, she went to Comyn's bed. Horrified at learning she was with child, she begged Comyn to aid her, but he cast her out. After she gave birth, she brought me to Grisel." A tremor slid through her. "Then my—" Alesone paused and inhaled, lifting her chin. "My mother threw herself from the cliffs. She preferred death over a lifetime of shame. As I grew, my father, along with those within the castle shunned me. Though I hold a blood tie to Comyn, I swear to you, I loathe the very name."

A cinder snapped within the dance of flames as Alesone awaited the king's reply.

Face taut, Bruce exhaled. "My offer for you to serve as my healer remains. But," he said, his words firm, "you must swear fealty to me, and never shall you disclose to those loyal to me who your father is. All who serve me might nae be so tolerant."

Thankful, she dropped to her knees. "Until my death, Your Grace, I swear my fealty, and I shall keep my blood tie a secret."

The king lay his hand upon her shoulder. "Mistress Alesone, I welcome you."

The churn of water filled the crisp morning air and a light mist clung above the land as Sir Thomas MacKelloch glanced toward his knights at the river's edge. "While you finish watering your mounts, I will go atop the hill and ensure nay one is about."

His men nodded.

Unless King Robert had moved, they should reach the sovereign's camp by midday. Thomas tugged his fur-lined cape closer and led his bay up the steep incline.

The frozen ground crunched beneath his steps as he searched each shadow where an enemy could hide.

Overhead, gray clouds began to smother the sun.

Snow was coming, a storm paltry to the tempest raging within France.

Two months had passed since the Grand Master had secretly dissolved the Knights Templar, a decree Thomas still struggled to accept. In but a breath, the Order, a way of life he loved, had ceased to exist. A decision few of the brotherhood who'd remained within France knew about. For the sake of ensuring their treasures were safely removed and hidden, it was a secret he and the others who had sailed away must keep.

Thomas clenched the reins as he contemplated the arrests of the Knights Templar in France. Charges included claims of heresy, idol worship, sacrilegious acts, and more.

All lies.

Falsehoods spewed by malcontents who'd been cast from the Order.

However despicable the allegations, all within the Brotherhood understood their nefarious origin.

King Philip IV.

A royal plummeting toward financial disaster.

So deep in debt, in his desperation to replenish his coffers, France's king had sacrificed the elite warriors who'd protected him over the years.

Thomas jammed his boot into the hard ground and shoved up. Naught could change the king's atrocious act. Thank God the Grand Master had received warning of the charges, allowing Thomas and many Templars to flee.

Still, too many knights remained in France, including the Grand Master, honorable men falsely defamed. He swallowed hard. Mere weeks had passed since the arrests had begun, and many Templars had been killed. And before 'twas over, many more would die.

A branch cracked beneath his boot.

He cursed, tugged the reins and pushed on, ready to reach Scotland's king, to wield his blade once again for right.

Fragments of sunlight slipped through the clouds, illuminated the few stubborn leaves clinging to their branches overhead. For a moment, the ice-laden shells danced within the current, the fragile brown shimmers warming to amber. The gust abated, and the leaves hung limp like forgotten promises.

Thomas grimaced. Watching a bloody leaf. A fine way to get oneself killed with the enemy about. He tugged his mount forward.

As he rounded the next tree, the break in the clouds thickened. Gloom settled upon the forest. With a wary eye, he scanned the ridge above. Once he reached the top, he could—

A flash hissed past, a finger's width before his heart.

An arrow lodged in a tree to his left.

God's teeth! Thomas clasped the hilt of his sword.

"Withdraw your blade and die!"

Furious, he glared at the slip of a woman emerging from the tree line paces away. With her skill, neither had the lass wanted him dead. A bird's cry sounded from behind him.

Relief edged through Thomas. His men had heard him, understood trouble was about. Now to keep the lass talking until his warriors seized her. Then, by God, he would have answers. "I am nae a threat."

"Remove your hand from your weapon, state your name and your loyalty."

Bloody damn. Unsure if her fealty was to Comyn or the Bruce, a wrong answer could hold a fatal consequence. "Sir Thomas MacKelloch."

"Release your sword and state your loyalty!"

A hand flashed to his far right, alerting him that his knights had surrounded her and were closing in. "Lass, I am but passing through."

Another arrow whipped past, slicing the first straight down the center.

In disbelief he stared at the severed shaft. An expert archer, he was proud of his ability and could match her skill, a proficiency held by very few. Who was she? More important, why was she so close to King Robert's encampment? God's teeth, if her intention was to kill the Bruce, with her accuracy, the lass would need only one attempt.

With quiet steps, his knights moved behind the lass.

"I would be asking for your loyalty as well," Thomas said.

With a panther's grace, the slender lass drew back the bowstring.

His knights lunged.

The lass screamed as Rónán caught the woman's hands, jerked them behind her back. "Release me," she demanded, her legs kicking out with dangerous accuracy.

Rónán held tight.

Aiden retrieved her bow, while Cailin made a quick search and removed several daggers hidden within her garb.

Cailin held up the dagger she'd hidden in her boot, grimaced. "*A sgian dubh*. The lass is well armed."

Furious at placing himself and potentially his men in danger, Thomas stormed over.

Blond hair tugged free from her braid and whipped against his adversary's comely face. Furious eyes held his.

"Who are you?" Thomas demanded.

Bewitching moss green eyes narrowed.

Impressed by her daring, neither would his questions go unanswered. "Your name."

The lass tried to free her arm; Rónán held tight.

"Alesone MacNiven."

"Why did you threaten me?"

"I only sought your name and loyalty."

Thomas grunted. "You have an interesting way of asking. Who are you loyal to?"

Fear edged her eyes.

A dose of nerves would serve him well. "Tell me, by God, or I will haul you before King Robert and state your plans to assassinate him."

At his words, her face paled. "Never would I harm Scotland's king."

"You are loyal to the Bruce?"

She nodded. "I am his personal healer and beneath his protection."

An untruth. He'd received a detailed brief on those of importance who traveled with the king. Never was a woman mentioned, certainly not one who was a healer. "Indeed?" he said, his voice ripe with suspicion. "With Scotland at war, I find it odd that the Bruce would allow a woman under his protection to leave camp without a proper guard."

"He doesna know I left," she said, her words unapologetic. "I needed but a few herbs. I was returning to camp when I heard you tramping up the knoll."

Tramping? Thomas bit back a smile at her daring. "'Twould seem a fortuitous day." He nodded toward his men. "We are en route to meet with the king. 'Twill be interesting to hear our sovereign's response to your claim." Thomas glanced at his friend. "Cailin, how many weapons did the lass carry?"

"Nae counting the bow and arrows, seven."

"'Tis dangerous away from the encampment," she said, temper sliding into her voice.

"Aye, but nae for a mercenary intent on killing the king."

Shock widened her eyes, and then they narrowed. "I told you my reason for being here."

"You did, a claim I find of great interest." Thomas caught her wrist, damning a shot of awareness. He nodded to Rónán. "I will escort Mistress Alesone, if indeed that is the lass's name."

His friend released her and stepped back.

Alesone struggled against his hold. "I dinna need an escort!"

"What you need is yet to be determined," Thomas warned, far from pleased by the delay, even less so at being saddled with a stubborn lass he couldna trust. "If you continue to fight me, you will be tied and carried to camp. How you meet the king is your choice."

Outrage flashed in her eyes. "How dare you treat me with such disrespect, you . . . you ill-bred lout! I am nae a criminal."

"A decision I will allow our king to make." Though beautiful, this woman promised to be naught but trouble. With a muttered curse, Thomas tugged her with him and headed toward their sovereign's encampment.

ABOUT THE AUTHOR

A retired Navy Chief, AGC (AW), Diana Cosby is an international bestselling author of Scottish medieval romantic suspense. Diana has spoken at the Library of Congress, appeared at Lady Jane's Salon NYC, in *Woman's Day,* on *Texoma Living! Magazine, USA Today*'s romance blog, "Happily Ever After," and MSN.com.

After retiring from the navy, Diana dove into her passion—writing romance novels. With thirty-four moves behind her, she was anxious to create characters who reflected the amazing cultures and people she's met throughout the world. Diana looks forward to the years ahead of writing and meeting the amazing people who will share this journey.

Diana Cosby, International Bestselling Author
www.dianacosby.com

"Diana Cosby is superbly talented."
—Cathy Maxwell,
New York Times Bestselling Author

HIS CAPTIVE

Divided by loyalty,
drawn together
by desire...

DIANA COSBY

First Time in Print!

HIS CAPTIVE

With a wastrel brother and a treacherous former fiancé, Lady Nichola Westcott hardly expects the dangerously seductive Scot who kidnaps her to be a man of his word. Though Sir Alexander Mac-Gruder promises not to hurt her, Nichola's only value is as a pawn to be ransomed.

Alexander's goal is to avenge his father's murder, not to become entangled with the enemy. But his desire to keep Nichola with him, in his home—in his bed—unwittingly makes her a target for those who have no qualms about shedding English blood.

Now Nichola is trapped—by her powerful attraction to a man whose touch shakes her to the core. Unwilling and unable to resist each other, can Nichola and Alexander save a love that has enslaved them both?

"Diana Cosby
is superbly talented."
—Cathy Maxwell,
New York Times
Bestselling Author

His
Woman

Some passions are too powerful to forget...

DIANA COSBY

HIS WOMAN

Lady Isabel Adair is the last woman Sir Duncan MacGruder wants to see again, much less be obliged to save. Three years ago, Isabel broke their engagement to become the Earl of Frasyer's mistress, shattering Duncan's heart and hopes in one painful blow. But Duncan's promise to Isabel's dying brother compels him to rescue her from those determined to bring down Scottish rebel Sir William Wallace.

Betraying the man she loved was the only way for Isabel to save her father, but every moment she spends with Duncan reminds her just how much she sacrificed. No one could blame him for despising her, yet Duncan's misgivings cannot withstand a desire that has grown wilder with time. Now, on a perilous journey through Scotland, two wary lovers must confront both the enemies who will stop at nothing to hunt them down, and the secret legacy that threatens their passion and their lives . . .

His
CONQUEST
DIANA COSBY

HIS CONQUEST

Linet Dancort will not be sold. But that's essentially what her brother intends to do—to trade her like so much chattel to widen his already vast scope of influence. Linet will seize any opportunity to escape her fate—and opportunity comes in the form of a rebel prisoner locked in her brother's dungeon, predatory and fearsome, and sentenced to hang in the morning.

Seathan MacGruder, Earl of Grey, is not unused to cheating death. But even this legendary Scottish warrior is surprised when a beautiful Englishwoman creeps to his cell and offers him his freedom. What Linet wants in exchange, though—safe passage to the Highlands—is a steep price to pay. For the only thing more dangerous than the journey through embattled Scotland is the desire that smolders between these two fugitives the first time they touch . . .

DIANA COSBY
His DESTINY
"Medieval Scotland roars to life in this fabulous series."
—Pam Palmer, New York Times Bestselling Author

HIS DESTINY

As one of England's most capable mercenaries, Emma Astyn can charm an enemy and brandish a knife with unmatched finesse. Assigned to befriend Dubh Duer, an infamous Scottish rebel, she assumes the guise of innocent damsel Christina Moffat to intercept the writ he's carrying to a traitorous bishop. But as she gains the dark hero's confidence and realizes they share a tattered past, compassion—and passion—distract her from the task at hand . . .

His legendary slaying of English knights has won him the name Dubh Duer, but Sir Patrik Cleary MacGruder is driven by duty and honor, not heroics. Rescuing Christina from the clutches of four such knights is a matter of obligation for the Scot. But there's something alluring about her fiery spirit, even if he has misgivings about her tragic history. Together, they'll endure a perilous journey of love and betrayal, and a harrowing fight for their lives . . .

DIANA COSBY

His SEDUCTION

"Medieval Scotland roars to life in this fabulous series."
—Pamela Palmer, *New York Times* bestselling author

HIS SEDUCTION

Lady Rois Drummond is fiercely devoted to her widowed father, the respected Scottish Earl of Brom. So when she believes he is about to be exposed as a traitor to England, she must think quickly. Desperate, Rois makes a shocking claim against the suspected accuser, Sir Griffin Westcott. But her impetuous lie leaves her in an outrageous circumstance: hastily married to the enemy. Yet Griffin is far from the man Rois thinks he is—and much closer to the man of her dreams . . .

Griffin may be an Englishman, but in truth he leads a clandestine life as a spy for Scotland. Refusing to endanger any woman, he has endured the loneliness of his mission. But Rois's absurd charge has suddenly changed all that. Now, with his cover in jeopardy, Griffin must find a way to keep his secret while keeping his distance from his spirited and tempting new wife—a task that proves more difficult than he ever imagined . . .

DIANA
COSBY

"Medieval Scotland roars to
life in this fabulous series."
—Pamela Palmer, *New York
Times* Bestselling Author

His
ENCHANTMENT
The MacGruder Brothers

HIS ENCHANTMENT

Lady Catarine MacLaren is a fairy princess, duty-bound to eschew the human world. But the line between the two realms is beginning to blur. English knights have launched an assault on the MacLarens, just as the families of Comyn have captured the Scottish king and queen. Now, Catarine is torn between loyalty to her people and helping the handsome, rust-haired Lord Trálin rescue the Scottish king . . .

As guard to King Alexander, Lord Trálin MacGruder will stop at nothing to defend the Scottish crown against the Comyns. And he finds a sympathetic, and gorgeous, ally in the enigmatic Princess Catarine. As they plot to rescue the kidnapped king and queen, Trálin and Catarine will discover a love made all but impossible by her obligations to the Otherworld. But a passion this extraordinary may be worth the irreversible sacrifices it demands . . .

THE
OATH
TRILOGY

*In deception
lies desire...*

An
OATH TAKEN
DIANA COSBY

AN OATH TAKEN

As the new castellan, Sir Nicholas Beringar has the daunting task of rebuilding Ravenmoor Castle on the Scottish border and gaining the trust of the locals—one of whom wastes no time in trying to rob him. Instead of punishing the boy, Nicholas decides to make him his squire. Little does he know the thieving young lad is really . . . a lady.

Lady Elizabet Armstrong had donned a disguise in an attempt to free her brother from Ravenmoor's dungeons. Although intimidated by the confident Englishman with his well-honed muscles and beguiling eyes, she cannot refuse his offer.

Nicholas senses that his new squire is not what he seems. His gentle attempts to break through the boy's defenses leave Elizabet powerless to stem the desire that engulfs her. And when the truth is exposed, she'll have to trust in Nicholas's honor to help her people—and to surrender to his touch . . .

THE OATH TRILOGY

An
OATH BROKEN

DIANA COSBY

"Diana Cosby is superbly talented."
— Cathy Maxwell, *New York Times* bestselling author

AN OATH BROKEN

Lady Sarra Bellacote would sooner marry a boar than a countryman of the bloodthirsty brutes who killed her parents. And yet, despite—or perhaps because of—her valuable holdings, she is being dragged to Scotland to be wed against her will. To complicate the desperate situation, the knight hired to do the dragging is dark, wild, irresistible. And he, too, is intolerably *Scottish*.

Giric Armstrong, Earl of Terrick, takes no pleasure in escorting a feisty English lass to her betrothed. But he needs the coin to rebuild his castle, and his tenants need to eat. Yet the trip will not be the simple matter he imagined. For Lady Sarra isn't the only one determined to see her engagement fail. Men with darker motives want to stop the wedding—even if they must kill the bride in the process.

Now, in close quarters with this beautiful English heiress, Terrick must fight his mounting desire, and somehow keep Sarra alive long enough to lose her forever to another man . . .

THE
OATH
TRILOGY

An

OATH SWORN

DIANA COSBY

"Diana Cosby is superbly talented."
— Cathy Maxwell, *New York Times* bestselling author

AN OATH SWORN

The bastard daughter of the French king, Marie Alesia Serouge has just one chance at freedom when she escapes her captor in the Scottish highlands. A mere pawn in a scheme to destroy relations between France and Scotland, Marie must reach her father and reveal the Englishman's treacherous plot. But she can't abandon the wounded warrior she stumbles upon—and she can't deny that his fierce masculinity, Scottish or not, stirs something wild inside her.

Colyne MacKerran is on a mission for his king, and he's well aware that spies are lying in wait for him everywhere. Wounded *en route*, he escapes his attackers and is aided by an alluring Frenchwoman . . . whose explanation for her presence in the Highlands rings false. Even if she saved his life, he cannot trust her with his secrets. But he won't leave her to the mercy of brigands, either—and as they race for the coast, he can't help but wonder if her kiss is as passionate as she is.

With nothing in common but their honor, Colyne and Marie face a dangerous journey to safety through the untamed Scottish landscape—and their own reckless hearts . . .

Made in the USA
Middletown, DE
29 July 2017